WHAT YOU
WISH FOR

OTHER TITLES BY THE AUTHOR

Mark Edwards

WHAT YOU WISH FOR

THOMAS & MERCER

Published by Thomas & Mercer, Seattle

www.apub.com

Amazon, the Amazon logo, and Thomas & Mercer are trademarks of Amazon.com, Inc., or its affiliates.

ISBN-13: 9781477825563
ISBN-10: 1477825568

Cover design by Jennifer Vince

Library of Congress Control Number: 2014938774

Printed in the United States of America

Prologue

The house was silent.

The wind caught the door and slammed it shut behind me. I couldn't wait to tell Marie my news. She was the one who encouraged me to break out of the rut I'd been in. I was twenty-seven and my career was going nowhere until Marie came along and shook me up, told me to stop staring at the pavement and start looking at the stars. The bottle of champagne in my bag was still cold from the overpriced supermarket on our street. I was going to pop it open, raise a toast, take her to bed. Celebrate.

'Marie?' I called.

No response.

I stuck my head into the living room. No sign of her. In the kitchen I put the champagne in the fridge. I heard movement and turned, a smile ready on my face, but it was only our ancient cat thumping down the stairs.

Maybe Marie was having a bath. She spent a lot of time in there, lying back with her pale red hair stretching like tendrils around her, or sitting up with the laptop balanced on the toilet, watching one of her UFO documentaries. I ran up the stairs, past the damp patch I'd been ignoring for months. The house was Victorian, a 'fixer-upper' that I hadn't got round to fixing up.

Maybe soon I'd have the money to turn this place into the home it could be. Somewhere to be proud of, and Marie and I would live here for years and years, and . . . and I'd ask her to marry me. I grinned as I took the stairs two at a time. I could just imagine her face if I proposed. We'd only been together four months. She'd tell me not to be an idiot. But in that moment, I felt like anything was possible, that happiness – a future filled with the stuff – was hanging like ripe fruit, saying, 'Take me, have me, here – it's easy.' Optimism propelled me into the bathroom where I expected to find her, naked and smiling up at me from beneath the water.

She wasn't there.

She wasn't anywhere.

I went from room to room, my phone in my hand, trying to call her. It went straight to voicemail.

It was getting dark outside, the shadows from the trees drawing inwards, a half moon sharpening into focus. The house felt too quiet, too cold, making me rub my arms where goose bumps appeared. The cat was running back and forth across the kitchen, making strange noises. I ended up back in the hallway, staring at the front door, waiting for it to open, for her to come home, tell me she'd popped out to see one of her friends from college, why was I so worried? Why did I look so scared?

But the door didn't open.

I was not superstitious. I didn't believe . . . well, Marie complained that I didn't believe in anything. Not ghosts or horoscopes or aliens or even destiny. But standing there then, I felt a terrible, ominous sense that by being so optimistic I had tempted fate. I could feel it, the emptiness around me, the damp patch on the wall mocking me, its shape – now I really looked at it – like a face with a twisted, mocking grin. Something had happened here. I could sense it. It wasn't rational, it didn't make sense to feel this afraid.

But I knew, even before I knew, that she was gone. And life was never going to be the same.

PART ONE
CLOSE ENCOUNTER

1

FOUR MONTHS EARLIER

From *The 1066 Herald*, June 7th:

COUNTRY RANGERS SPOT LIGHTS IN SKY

Two local men spoke this week of their fear when they witnessed strange lights in the sky over the East Hill.

Barry Dane and Fraser Howard told The Herald that they had seen a cluster of red and blue lights 'dancing over the country park' where the men work as rangers.

'We were on the night patrol in the Land Rover,' said Dane, 38. 'Fraser suddenly gripped my arm and pointed upwards. I couldn't believe my eyes.'

The two men describe the lights as being in two triangular formations that circled each other repeatedly.

'The red triangle of lights was larger and moved more quickly,' said Dane. 'It was eerie. I felt all the hairs on the back of my neck stand on end.'

Howard, 57, who is currently on sick leave, declined to comment.

There were no other reported sightings that evening. Experts say that the men could merely have been seeing the lights of aeroplanes, or lights from the attractions on the seafront reflected in the night sky.

———⌣———

I never wanted to be a photographer for a local newspaper. It just kind of happened. When I left college, I foresaw a future in which I would win prizes for my photo-journalism. I imagined myself dodging bullets in far-off war zones, not snapping pet hamsters at the primary school down the road from my house, the same school I went to. I hadn't travelled a great distance in my life, professionally or geographically.

I remembered the day I had been carrying my camera home from the repair shop. It was loaded and I had planned to take a few arty shots of trees and suchlike on the way home, just to test it out, when a man came running round the corner pursued by half a dozen policemen.

As the man ran past me, I did what any self-respecting, law-abiding citizen would do – I took a photo. My advantage was that I had a DSLR rather than an iPhone.

The next day, when I was conducting my weekly hunt through the job pages, I spotted a competition in the *Herald* for amateur photographers. They wanted a dramatic action shot, with the theme of crime. I sent them my picture of the panicked thief and the puffed coppers, and the editor, Bob Milner, liked it so much he gave me a job.

Now, here I was, three years later, twenty-seven years old, on my way to take a photo of a bunch of deluded hippies who had camped out on the East Hill in Hastings, where I lived, hoping to spot a UFO. I wanted to be photographing blazing buildings, heroic deeds, distressed victims of circumstance. I wanted excitement.

UFO watchers, I thought. *Give me strength.*

'About time,' said Simon when I reached the lift.

'So nice to see your happy face,' I responded.

We paid our fare and stepped into the lift, which was in fact a funicular railway that took tourists up onto the hill during the season. Nobody who lived in the town ever used it, except for overweight journalists like Simon. I looked out at the sea as the cable car ascended the hill, a journey that took less than two minutes.

Stepping out of the lift, I was reminded why I liked my hometown, why I had never put much effort into getting out.

Old Hastings nestles between two hills. We stood on the East Hill and looked across to where its western sister rose up, the ruined castle perched atop the cliffs. Between the two hills stand the crooked Tudor houses of the Old Town, where artists and fishermen share the narrow streets. The main road cut a path of modernity between the aged, pretty dwellings, with their dark sloping roofs and oak doors and window frames. Seagulls made nests in cracked chimneys; their high-pitched cries provided an omnipresent soundtrack to the days and nights; they swooped over the houses toward the beach and the fishermen's boats and huts.

Simon noticed me surveying the vista. 'Not too shabby when the sun's out, is it?'

He pushed his glasses up onto the bridge of his nose. Simon was a few years older than me, in his early thirties, six foot two and a little overweight. He had a loud voice and the demeanour of an overgrown schoolboy. To my perpetual astonishment, he also appeared to be highly attractive to women – or at least a certain type of woman. The type who like overgrown schoolboys. This wouldn't have been an issue if he wasn't married.

'Where are these UFO nuts camped out?' I asked.

Simon pointed and we made our way across the hill before descending the steep, grassy steps at Ecclesbourne Glen. At the bottom of the glen we began the long climb to the cliff top. By the time we reached the summit, Simon was puffing like a broken-down steam train.

I looked up and saw what we had come for. A pair of blue two-man tents were pitched behind a row of blackberry bushes. I waited for Simon to catch his breath and we strolled over to where two men were examining the tents.

The first man – tall, early twenties, goatee – stuck out his hand and said, 'Good morning.'

He was American. Despite the heat he was wearing a leather jacket, which had WATCH THE SKIES spelt out in Tipp-ex on the back, below a crudely drawn picture of a UFO. 'You must be the guys from the paper.'

We introduced ourselves. Richard Thompson. Simon Ryder.

'Pete,' he said. 'Beautiful day, huh? And the forecast says we're going to have clear skies tonight. Great watching weather.'

The other man – forties, receding blond hair and wire-framed glasses, a pair of expensive binoculars around his neck – looked us over. 'I'm Andrew Jade,' he said, as if he expected us to have heard of him.

When neither of us showed recognition, Andrew Jade went on. 'I'm so glad you could find the time to come and talk to us.' He spoke slowly, as if he was choosing his words meticulously. Maybe he was just wary of the press. I guess he was used to people ridiculing his beliefs.

'Is it just the two of you?' Simon asked. His breathing had just about returned to normal.

'Oh no,' replied Andrew. 'There's Fraser. And Marie.'

As he said this there was a rustling sound and a young woman of about twenty-three pushed her way out from between two bushes. She smiled and came over.

She had long, very pale red hair and was slim and small-framed. Her eyes were concealed behind oval sunglasses, and a tiny silver stud glinted in the side of her nose. She wore a plain black T-shirt and olive combat trousers. She offered me a slim hand. It was warm.

Without speaking a word, she stepped backwards and sat down, apparently exhausted, in one of the lawn chairs.

Pete winked at Marie and I tried to tear my eyes away from her. She seemed unaware of my attention. She sat back in the chair and turned her face towards the rich blue sky. Because of her shades, I couldn't tell if her eyes were open or closed.

'Fraser's gone into town for provisions,' said Andrew. 'He should be back soon.'

Simon looked thoughtful. 'Fraser? Wasn't that the name of one of the country rangers who reported seeing the lights?'

Andrew nodded. 'That's him.'

'I thought he was meant to be off work, sick.' He scribbled something in his notebook.

'He's frightened,' said Marie. We all turned to look at her. She took off her sunglasses. She had large round eyes, the colour of blue light shone through frosted glass. She smiled. 'He's seen something he can't reconcile with what he believes.' She smiled, showing a gap in her front teeth. 'He doesn't realise there's nothing to be scared of.'

Simon rolled his eyes. Usually, I would have done the same but there was an ironic lilt in her voice – like she was aware that others might find her words ridiculous – that stopped me from sneering.

Simon looked at his watch. 'I haven't got much time, actually. Do you mind if we get on?'

Andrew shrugged. 'Go ahead.'

Simon asked them in a bored tone of voice about the lights – was this a common form of sighting? What were they hoping to achieve by camping out and keeping watch?

'Are you expecting a landing?'

Andrew shook his head. 'We don't expect this encounter to go beyond the first or second kind. We're not looking for anything other than a sign. I don't know how deeply you want to get into this, but we don't believe that the time is yet right for full contact.'

'So you're not expecting to meet any aliens tonight?' Simon smirked as he spoke.

'Of course not. All that we hope for is . . . some information. A sign.' He held his hands out, palms upward.

'I see.' Simon scribbled. 'Tell me, have any of you ever been abducted? Have you ever seen an alien?'

'No, but I know a man who has,' Pete sniggered.

Andrew ignored the young American. 'I hope you're not poking fun at us, Mr Ryder.'

'As if I would do such a thing.'

I tuned out of the rest of the exchange and turned to look at Marie. She had leant back in the chair again and put her sunglasses back on. A gentle breeze stirred her hair. She was beautiful and . . . cool. Like one of the alternative, unattainable girls I'd fancied at school, the type who had boyfriends at university and hung around with rock bands.

'—going to take some pictures? Richard? Wake up!'

I snapped back into the real world. 'Sorry, what was that?'

Simon tutted. 'I thought for a minute your brain had been abducted. I said, are you going to take some pictures?'

I looked at Marie, who appeared oblivious to this exchange. Perhaps she'd fallen asleep. I readied my camera and said, 'OK. Can you stand in front of your tents? Actually, it might be better on the edge of the cliff.'

I decided that a picture of them with the open sea behind them would be most apt and dramatic. Pete and Andrew posed by the stringy fence with its faded red DANGER sign. 'Marie?' I said.

'Leave her,' said Andrew. 'She won't have her picture taken. She doesn't believe in it.'

'Oh.' I shrugged, trying to hide my personal and professional disappointment. A picture with a pretty girl in it was a lot more likely to get a prominent slot in the paper. 'I guess it will have to be just you two handsome guys then.'

Andrew frowned. Pete gurned. I took a few shots.

'Right,' Simon said, 'I think that will do.'

I didn't want to leave. I wanted to talk to Marie some more. Or just stand and look at her.

'Are you coming?'

I was about to follow Simon when Marie spoke. Her voice seemed to come from a long way off. 'Why don't you come back tonight and help us keep a lookout?'

'I'd rather not,' said Simon.

'Why not?' I said to him, taking him aside. 'It would be great for the story.'

'This story is horse shit. I don't know why Bob thinks anyone will be interested in it. Sorry, darling,' he addressed Marie. 'Thanks for the invite but no thanks. Come on, Richard.'

I looked at Marie. She leant forward with her chin cupped in her hand, her face angled towards me, that amused smile playing across her lips. I wished I could see the expression behind her dark lenses.

'All right,' I said. 'I'll come back later. Just think, if a UFO did come swooping down and a bunch of little green men came out to say hello and I wasn't here to take their picture, I'd kick myself!'

'Cool,' said Pete, grinning.

Beside him, Andrew glowered. I guessed I shouldn't have mentioned little green men. It was an interesting group. The earnest older man, the American with puppy-dog enthusiasm and the cool, beautiful young woman.

I looked at Marie. She nodded her head almost imperceptibly and sank back into her peaceful reverie, the sun warm on her face.

I didn't give a damn about aliens and had no doubt this group would be disappointed later when the only thing they saw was the moon.

But I wanted to know more about her.

2

When I returned that evening the small group were sitting outside their tents looking at the horizon. Marie was still in the chair where I'd left her.

I said, 'Hi,' then Pete introduced me to Fraser, the country ranger. He was a tall, skeletal man in his early fifties. When he shook my hand, his palm was clammy and I surreptitiously wiped my hand on my jeans.

Fraser told me that he had worked on the East Hill as a ranger for five years. 'Part of what we do involves driving around making sure people aren't lighting fires or leaving litter or getting up to anything they shouldn't. It's a good job.' He nodded as he spoke. He made me feel nervous.

'Are we actually allowed to be up here tonight? Have you got permission?'

Fraser nodded. 'It will be fine as long as we don't damage anything. Barry knows we're here. He's on duty on his own tonight.'

He lit a cigarette which shook between his fingers.

'Have you ever seen lights in the sky or anything like that before?'

He shook his head emphatically. 'No. Not ever.'

'Couldn't it have been a plane? Surely that's the most reasonable explanation.'

'No way.' He took a hungry drag on his cigarette. 'This was no aeroplane.' He looked at me with wide, penetrating eyes.

I laughed, then, noticing his affronted expression, said, 'I'm sorry. It's just that you sound like a character in some B-movie. *That was no aeroplane . . .*'

Andrew came up and put his hand on Fraser's shoulder. 'People will always mock, Fraser. It's something you have to get used to, as a witness.'

'But there are a lot of us, aren't there?' Fraser said, eager for reassurance. 'More and more of us?'

'That's right, Fraser. One day all the doubters will have to face up to the truth.' He spoke as if addressing a dim child.

I didn't know why Andrew had taken such an instant dislike to me. Maybe he was always like this. But his attitude made me want to wind him up.

'It could have been any number of things you saw,' I said. 'Helicopters. A satellite, or a meteor shower . . .'

Andrew yawned. 'We've heard it all before. Some people will never believe the evidence in front of their own eyes.'

'What evidence?' I asked.

Pete stepped in. 'Hey, guys, let's not have a conflict, huh? Let's just watch. That's what we're here for.'

I said, 'Sounds good to me.'

'Let's eat,' said Pete. We sat on the lawn chairs and Pete passed round some pre-packed sandwiches. I made sure I got the chair next to Marie. Darkness had fallen while I was arguing with Andrew and it was hard to see her clearly. I leaned closer.

I said, 'Do you think we'll see anything tonight?'

She looked up at the moon, an alabaster disc in the starry sky. 'I'm always hopeful. I know you don't believe . . .'

'No. But I would like something to happen, if only because it would make a great picture.'

She wrapped her jacket around her and picked up a long, rubber-encased torch. She flicked it on and aimed the beam at the night sky. The others looked over at her. Was she with either Pete or Andrew? Pete had a certain goofy charm and was quite good-looking. Andrew had an air of authority about him that I know some young women go for. But there was no body language to support my fears, no touching or eye contact.

She didn't have classic good looks. Her nose was a tiny bit too narrow, there were dark smudges beneath her eyes. Her teeth were a little crooked. But she had an aura that made the air around her shimmer, and a self-assuredness that I envied.

'We should be silent now,' she said quietly. The men nodded. They stopped talking, seemed even, to stop moving, until all I could hear were the crickets and the sea.

We watched the skies.

There was a full moon and the sky was clear – the perfect conditions for seeing a UFO, apparently – but, of course, nothing happened. I heard Pete sigh a couple of times. Fraser looked more relieved with every second that passed. Andrew was stoic, unmoved, a grim expression on his face. And Marie just sat and looked upwards. I mimicked her. I didn't know what else to do. I was starting to regret being here. As the temperature dropped, I thought about my bed and how comfortable it was. I had left the house in the midst of a warm evening, without thinking that it would get cold later. Now, as the day's heat disappeared from the air, I started to shiver. I hugged myself. We weren't allowed to light a fire. We just sat holding our torches, looking at the stars, and I tried to imagine that the light contained warmth. If it hadn't been for my attraction to Marie I would have made my excuses and left.

'Have we got anything to drink?' I asked. 'Something warming?'

Fraser said, 'I've got a bottle of brandy.'

'Perfect.'

He crawled into one of the tents and brought out a litre bottle of Napoleon brandy and some paper cups. He poured a small measure into each cup and passed them round. The liquid was fiery in my throat; warmth spread through my body.

'That's better.' I had an urge to talk. All this silence was depressing me. 'I must apologise for my colleague Simon. He was very rude to you earlier.'

Andrew shrugged. 'We're used to it.'

I swirled the brandy around the bottom of my paper cup. 'I'm puzzled. Are you part of some larger organisation or group? How do you know each other?'

'We don't have an organisation,' said Andrew. He spat the last word like it tasted foul. 'It's too dangerous. It would be so easy for the government to monitor us.'

'The Government?'

'Yes, they—'

'Richard might think we're a little paranoid,' Marie interjected.

'Just because you're paranoid doesn't mean they're not out to get you.'

My joke sputtered and died in the night air.

Marie said, 'We met online.'

'That's how I know these guys,' said Pete. 'There's a huge network of believers all over the world.'

I said, 'And you came all the way from . . .'

'Portland.'

'You came all the way from Oregon for this?'

'Oh no. I was in Europe anyway, staying with other people that I'd met online, in France. There have been a couple of really interesting sightings in Normandy. When I heard about the Hastings

13

lights I thought I'd take a look and caught the Eurostar over. It's what I do. I travel all over the world. Chasing UFOs.'

'And how many have you seen?'

'Um . . . none yet.'

'*None?*

He laughed. 'People call me The Jinx. I've been everywhere – Roswell, South America, Japan, all over Europe . . . Not a single sighting. People say that if there was ever a threat of hostile alien invasion they'd just have to stand me on top of a mountain and the aliens wouldn't show.' He scratched his beard. 'Not that that would happen, of course. Hostile aliens. That's a crazy idea. But I know they're out there. One day I'm going to make contact.'

'I would have given up by now. What about you two?' I said, addressing Marie and Andrew. They looked sheepish. 'What, you've never seen a UFO either?'

'Well . . . no,' Andrew.

'But how can you believe in something you've never seen or had any experience of?'

Marie said, 'Millions of people believe in an entity they've never seen. They call it God.'

'I know, but . . .'

'You either believe or you don't,' Andrew said tersely. 'And besides, we've spoken to them. Now let's just watch, shall we?'

I drank some more brandy. I felt a little sorry for them. They were so desperate. And I could imagine how jealous they must have been of Fraser who, ironically, looked like seeing a UFO was the last thing he'd ever wanted. After downing half the bottle of brandy, Fraser had crawled into his tent and fallen asleep. I could hear him snoring.

Pete fell asleep too, sitting upright in his chair, mouth hanging open.

Marie stayed awake, looking upwards calmly, while Andrew peered intently at the sky, his jaw muscles clenched. I could sense

14

him willing the heavens to produce something inexplicable. I found myself wishing for it too, if only for his and Marie's sake.

We were disappointed.

As the sun rose, the sky turning violet then blue, we packed up. We rolled up the tents and Andrew and Pete loaded their rucksacks. I helped them carry their equipment down the hill.

'I'm sorry we didn't see anything,' Andrew said. He seemed chastened by the aliens' no-show. 'But thank you for joining us.'

'Maybe you'll have more luck next time. Are you going to try again tonight?'

Andrew shook his head. 'Fraser's going to keep a lookout while he's working. If there are any more sightings he'll let us know.'

They headed off in the opposite direction to me, along the seafront. The town was eerily quiet. No cars or people, just a few large seagulls pecking at discarded chip wrappers.

I watched them retreat along the promenade. I had wanted to ask Marie for her phone number, but I felt too awkward with the others standing there. The whole night had been like that. I'd yearned for an opportunity to talk to her on her own, but the three men stuck to her like they were her bodyguards.

When she said goodbye she had raised her hand, smiled at me and fixed me with a look that I was sure was full of meaning.

Kicking myself for being too passive, I set off up the hill. I didn't expect to see any of them again.

3

Two weeks passed. Simon's piece appeared on page seven of the *Herald*, with my photograph of Pete and Andrew (caption: Calling Occupants of Interplanetary Craft), but we had heard nothing more about UFOs or impending alien contact. We received one crank letter, scribbled in green ink, in which a man recounted in great detail a sexual encounter with 'a beautiful, golden-skinned lady alien with two mouths', which we had pinned on the notice board in the office. And a woman phoned to say she had seen what she thought were alien craft while out walking her dogs on the West Hill. She saw white globes hovering over the sea. On closer inspection they turned out to be street lamps.

That afternoon – the day when everything began to happen – had been, as Simon put it, 'shit'. We had been called out to the scene of a house fire where two primary school age girls and their dad were trapped. The fire was still blazing when we got there, two fire engines sending great arcs of water into the flames. The heat coming from the building was indescribable. Eventually, the fire crew got the better of the elements and went into the house. A little while later I watched in horror as they carried out three bodies: two small, one my size. I could smell their charred flesh.

Back home, afterwards, I couldn't get the images of the dead girls out of my head. I lay in the bath and scrubbed myself, my face, my hair. I felt unclean and irrationally guilty. I had wished for this. I had wanted excitement.

I sank beneath the water. When I surfaced the telephone was ringing. I didn't want to answer it, but the caller was insistent.

Cursing, I climbed out of the bath and wrapped a towel around me. It was Simon.

'I feel like I'm in shock,' he said. 'Even though I didn't know them. And I'm going to have to write about it. Two children died in a tragic fire in their home . . .'

'Did you phone to make me feel worse?' I asked.

'I phoned to see if you wanted to go and get pissed.'

I almost said no, but then I thought about my empty house. 'Yeah. Yeah, I do.'

———

We drank to forget. Or, at least, we tried to.

'Do you think they were already dead when the firemen carried them out of the house?' Simon asked, staring into a half-empty pint of Guinness.

'Can we not talk about it? Please? How's Susan?'

'Yeah. Fine.' He fiddled with his coaster, tearing the edges off it. I sensed he wanted to talk about something but couldn't spit the words out.

I felt the alcohol start to work, getting into my bloodstream and clouding over the memory of the fire. The world around me lost clarity. The lager tasted good. I felt good. I drained my glass. I got up to the bar to buy another.

We ended up in a club near the seafront. I felt old. There were a few other people in their late twenties, but most of the clubbers were late teens, early twenties, beautiful, skinny, fit. I hadn't been to a club for months.

Simon handed me a drink. We leaned against the bar, surveying the crowd. Simon eyed up the teenage girls in their strappy tops and little skirts. I watched the crowd. The club was packed, but still they let more people in, until we were forced away from the bar by people struggling for the attention of the staff.

Two blonde girls in mini dresses that barely covered their arses slinked by. Simon said, 'I'm off,' and followed them into the throng.

Things were definitely awry in Simon-and-Susan land. Wondering if he'd tell me more, I drained my bottle and headed for the dance floor.

And that's when I saw her: Marie.

She was talking to a couple of girls, laughing, her head thrown back, exposing her pale throat. I could only see her head and shoulders; the rest of her was obscured by the mass of people in my way. She was about ten feet away, but it might as well have been a hundred. I tried to push my way through the crowd. The moment I had seen her I had felt a jolt in my chest, a quickening of the pulse. After the night on the hill I had cursed my timidity, certain I had missed my chance to get to know her. Now, maybe, I had been given another. I looked across the river of heads between us and watched her laugh and brush her hand through her hair. I *had* to talk to her.

'Excuse me. Sorry.'

I pushed through perspiration-soaked bodies, using my shoulder, clutching my drink to my chest, and finally emerged where Marie had been standing.

She was gone. I stood on tiptoe and looked around. No sign. I swore under my breath. Maybe she was on the dance floor. I edged my way into the moving mass.

I caught a glimpse of strawberry-blonde hair on the other side of the dance floor and headed over. But it wasn't her. The hair's owner scowled at me when I touched her shoulder, and her boyfriend took a menacing step towards me. I stepped back and allowed the crowd to swallow me up.

I leant against a wall that was wet with condensation and squinted into the maelstrom of strobing lights and smoke and skin. Where was she? I started to grow angry at the crowd. Why the hell had the nightclub management let so many people in? It was crazy. God forbid if there was a fire . . .

I searched for twenty minutes, finally coming back to where I'd started. In front of me were two girls – no older than sixteen – with black circles of makeup around their eyes, lips painted purple, and I imagined the two little dead girls, their lives choked and finished that afternoon, saw them standing in front of me, looking at me with blank eyes.

I squeezed my eyelids shut. Marie had probably gone home. It was time to call it a night.

As I moved towards the exit, the door of the Ladies opened and a couple of girls ran out. They grabbed a bouncer by a thickly muscled arm. 'There's some bloke in the Ladies, puking.'

The bouncer's eyes narrowed and he and another doorman went into the Ladies. They emerged, holding Simon between them. His eyes had rolled up into his head and a smear of sick glistened on his chin. The two girls laughed as the bouncers dragged him through the exit into the fresh air. I followed and watched Simon hit the pavement. 'Don't come back,' one of the bouncers warned.

Simon pushed himself up onto his hands and knees. 'Wankers,' he slurred, then threw up in the gutter to a chorus of disgust.

'Come on, get up,' I said, pulling him to his feet. He reeked of beer and vomit.

'Richard. My mate.' His eyes were all over the place. 'I'm gonna write about this in the fucking paper. Those bastards have had it . . .'

'Yeah, yeah.'

'No one gets it,' he slurred. 'Everyone thinks I'm the bad guy. But it's just as hard for me.'

'I have no idea what you're talking about.'

I managed to get him into a taxi and watched the car pull away. I shook my head. No doubt tomorrow he would have forgotten all about it.

I was about to head home when I heard a voice say, 'Hello,' and I turned around.

It was Marie. She was wearing a short black and gold dress and strappy shoes, and was carrying a small black bag. She smiled at me, a little ironic uplift at the edge of her full Cupid's-bow lips. Two other girls stood behind her.

'Your friend was in the toilets making a fool of himself,' she said.

'Friend? I prefer colleague.'

She laughed. Her large eyes looked up at me, big and round and wide awake. It struck me how little she was, and how pretty. The grime and sweat of the nightclub didn't seem to have touched her. She looked like she'd just been for a pleasant stroll along the promenade. Whereas I must have looked terrible, with my hair all messed up, my clothes sticking to me and my eyes bleary from too much booze.

One of Marie's friends said, 'You coming?' and she shook her head. They staggered off towards the taxi rank.

Still with that little smile on her face, Marie said, 'So how are you?'

'OK. Well, actually that's a lie. I've had a shitty day. I came out to get drunk and forget about it. Except it hasn't worked, really.'

'Why don't you walk me home and tell me about it on the way? My flat's just along the seafront.'

'Cool.' I tried not to look *too* enthusiastic. I didn't want to scare her. She was just being friendly, after all.

The nightclub was a pebble's throw from the beach. We crossed the road and walked side by side along the promenade.

I told Marie about the fire. 'It was horrible. Not just because two children died, but because I was so excited by it all. When I was taking the pictures my heart was really pounding.' I thumped my chest in illustration. 'I kept thinking, this is why I'm a photographer. Not much happens in Hastings, does it? The occasional murder that everyone gets hysterical about, or the odd drugs bust. But most of it isn't stuff that you could take pictures of – not on the scene, anyway. So this fire was something different. We were actually there, capturing it. And it was aesthetic and cinematic, with the firemen running out of the house, the hysterical mother, the concerned crowd. I loved the drama of it.'

'So you feel guilty.'

'Yes. I feel cheap and nasty and dirty.'

She put her hand on my arm. 'And that's good, Richard.'

'Good?'

'Of course. What if you'd been unmoved? The fact that you feel . . . unclean shows that you're not desensitised.' She smiled at me. 'I sensed that when we first met. Beneath that cynical facade, you're a good person.'

I looked out at the sea. 'So it's good to feel bad.'

'Put that on a T-shirt and you'll make . . . well, maybe a fiver.'

We shared a laugh. I noticed her eyes slip upwards to the sky, where a half-moon hung among a gallery of stars. I followed her gaze. 'Were there any more sightings on the hill after that night?'

She shook her head. 'Andrew says that maybe they found what they were searching for the first time they came, so they didn't need to come back.'

'I see.' I took a deep breath. 'Are you and Andrew an item?'

She found this hilarious. 'Me and Andrew? What made you ask that?'

'I don't know. It's just the way you talk about him. I thought maybe . . .'

'Andrew's a great man. He's taught me a lot. But we're definitely not an item.'

'What about Pete?'

I'd gone too far.

'What is this?' she asked, irritated.

'Sorry.' I tried a disarming smile. 'When you hang out with journalists they start to rub off on you. All the questions, you know?'

'Hmm. Well, in answer to your journalistic query, Pete and I are not seeing each other either. He's gone off on his travels again, anyway, so even if I did want to fuck his brains out I wouldn't be able to.' She rolled her eyes then smiled at my sheepish expression. 'This is where I live.'

We crossed the road. She lived in a block of flats next to a gutted Victorian hotel. This whole row of hotels, B&Bs and flats needed cleaning up. In old photographs of the town this row of buildings looks so grand, but years of sea air and neglect had faded the paint and rotted the wood, and most of the old places had been converted into bedsits. Marie lived in one of them.

We stood outside her front door.

'Thank you for walking me home.'

'No, thank *you*. For telling me I'm a good person.'

'Despite the cynicism. And being so nosey.'

I longed for her to ask me inside for a coffee. I was about to miss my second chance. She looked up at me through her eyelashes while I struggled to think of something intelligent to say.

'Goodnight, then,' she said.

Before she could close the door on me, I blurted out, 'Can I see you again?'

She raised her eyebrows. 'When?'

'Tomorrow?'

She gave me a long, searching look, then nodded. 'I've got college until five. I could meet you after.'

'Six o'clock at the Coffee Bean?'

I floated all the way home.

4

I sat in the Coffee Bean, stirring damp Demerara sugar into a latte and looking out of the window. Marie was late, but only by five minutes. I sipped my coffee, feeling the caffeine add to the buzz of anticipation.

It had been a while since I'd had a serious relationship, or any relationship at all, for that matter. Three years since Mikage left me. We had lived together in the house where I still lived. It lasted for two tempestuous years. Two years in which all we ever seemed to do was fight – real screaming matches, thrown crockery, thrown punches (her fists, my body), the works. Mikage was dark and pretty and half-Japanese.

I loved her but we brought out the worst in each other, and when the passionate fights turned to snide remarks and bickering, when the fights ceased to be an intense form of foreplay, it was time to call it a day. It turned out she already had another man lined up and she moved in with him. They're married now, with a baby.

I missed the feeling I'd had when Mikage and I first got together. That pounding, heart-squeezing feeling. The way I felt now, waiting for Marie. Just this side of sickness. Not that I thought about love, not right then, not until a little later, but I think I fell in love with Marie almost as soon as we met. Love at first sight. It's easy to be cynical about such things. But sometimes, maybe once or twice in your life, if you're lucky, you meet someone and it's like planets colliding.

I looked at my watch again. She was fifteen minutes late. I had finished my coffee. I looked out of the window, trying to see if there was any sign of her. I had definitely said the Coffee Bean at six, hadn't I? What if she had just been trying to get rid of me when she had agreed to meet me? She might be laughing about me this very minute with one of her friends. In a few short seconds my paranoia grew from a tiny seed to a full bloom. I told myself to stop being so stupid. I would give her another quarter of an hour.

Fifteen minutes passed.

I slurped the sugary, cold dregs of my coffee and went out into the street. I was embarrassed and disappointed. I saw a girl with light red hair walking towards the cinema and my heart jolted, but it wasn't Marie. I considered walking along to her bedsit but decided that would be too humiliating, too much like begging.

I made my way past the cinema, past the pretty but shabby Georgian terraces of Wellington Square, and as I looked up from the dusty pavement I saw her. She was about twenty feet away, sitting on a bench outside McDonalds. She was with Andrew and they were arguing, quite animatedly. I could see both their faces: he looked angry and hurt; she wore a shocked expression. I hesitated for a moment then walked up to them.

'Fancy bumping into you here,' I said.

They looked up at me, startled. Marie got to her feet. 'Oh, Richard . . . I was on my way. Am I late?'

'Only a bit.' My annoyance evaporated at the sight of her. She looked wonderful, fresh and bright, and her freckles had come out in the sun.

Andrew gave me a look that I couldn't read. 'I'm sorry if I've made Marie late. It's entirely my fault.'

I shrugged. 'Don't worry about it.'

The tension between them crackled. They avoided looking at each other, and I noticed that Marie's fists were clenched.

'I'd better get going,' he said to Marie, who still didn't look at him, pretending to be fascinated by a one-legged pigeon pecking at a discarded chicken nugget. 'I'll see you tomorrow.' He nodded goodbye to me and walked off, holding himself straight, his hands in his trouser pockets.

'I'm really sorry,' she said again.

'Don't worry, honestly.'

I waited to see if she would say any more, tell me what the argument had been about. After a long pause I said, 'So what do you want to do? Eat, drink? Play Crazy Golf?'

She laughed. 'You really know how to spoil a girl.' She took hold of my hand and said, 'Let's just walk.'

We walked down to the beach and trod along the pebbles, still holding hands. Hers was very warm. My heart was doing all sorts of strange acrobatic things in my chest. There were still people sunbathing, even though most of the heat had gone out of the sun by this time of the day.

'What were you and Andrew arguing about?' I asked, unable to hold back any longer.

'We weren't really arguing,' she replied. 'We were having a discussion. We're going to a convention in London tomorrow and we were talking about which train to catch. Andrew wants to leave ridiculously early to get there before the doors open, but I don't see the point.'

It seemed a rather petty thing to be arguing so vehemently about, but I didn't want to push it. I asked, 'What kind of convention?'

'It's called Encounters.'

'Let me guess – it's about online dating.'

'Very amusing. It's actually a convention for people who are interested in UFOs and alien abductions. It should be really interesting. There are some visiting American researchers who are going to give some lectures, and there's this guy who used to work for the FBI . . .'

'A real-life Fox Mulder!'

'Sort of. And basically people can get together and discuss their beliefs and experiences and hopefully learn something.'

'And buy the merchandise.'

'You really are a cynic.' She stooped to pick up a pebble that had caught her eye. It was smooth and round and green. She offered it to me. 'Here, have a present.'

Her face took on a serious expression. 'Please don't mock me, Richard. If you want to be my friend, you don't have to believe too, but you do have to accept that it's what *I* believe. Do you think you can cope with that?'

She fixed her huge eyes on me and I felt myself melting.

'I'm sorry,' I said. 'I do respect your beliefs. Really.'

'OK,' she said, after a long pause. 'Though you're right to be cynical about these conventions. They do attract some real weirdos. But Andrew thinks this will be a good one.'

'I would like to know more about what you believe in,' I said.

She gestured across the road. By accident or design she had led us to her flat.

'Come in and I'll tell you.'

The hallway smelt of fried eggs and dog hair. We climbed six steep flights of stairs to reach Marie's front door. 'Welcome to paradise,' she said, pushing open the door.

She lived in a box-room with just enough space for a single bed and a wardrobe. A door to the left revealed the smallest bathroom I had ever seen: just a sink and a shower in a space the size of an airing cupboard. She had a Baby Belling cooker and a tiny fridge – more a coldbox, really. The walls were papered with pictures of extraterrestrials, stills from the Roswell autopsy among them. An ancient-looking PC gathered dust on the floor beside a litter tray. There was a cat sitting on the bed, purring and dribbling on the quilt.

Marie sat beside the cat and stroked its beige and brown fur. 'This is Calico.'

'Hello, Calico,' I said, stroking the cat, which looked pretty old. Its purr rattled like an old motorbike that needed attention.

'I've had him since I was nine,' Marie said. 'When I left my mum's house I couldn't bear to leave him behind. Not with her.'

'How old are you now?' I said.

'Twenty-three.' She kissed him between his ears.

'Isn't it unkind to keep a cat locked up in a little place like this? He can't get any exercise.'

Marie smiled. 'He does. Look, I'll show you.' She leant over and pushed up the sash window. 'Go on, Calico, go play.'

The cat stood up, blinked, stretched and jumped out through the window. A broken fire-escape stretched up to the roof. Calico ascended the twisted black metal, then leapt onto a piece of drain-pipe and finally jumped onto the roof, where he had plenty of room to run around and chase seagulls.

'Cool cat,' I said.

She nodded proudly. 'Very cool.'

'I bet your Facebook page is full of pictures of him.'

'Uh-uh. I don't use Facebook, or Twitter, or any social network-ing sites.'

I raised an eyebrow.

'They're New World Order tools. A perfect way to monitor us.'

I wasn't sure what to say to that.

She opened the mini-fridge and produced a bottle of wine. 'I only have plastic cups, I'm afraid,' she said, 'and the wine is very cheap.'

'What are you studying at college?' I asked. There was no sofa in the room so we sat on the bed, very close to each other. I won-dered if she could hear my heart beating.

'Coding.'

'I thought you seemed like a geek . . .'

'Hey!' She slapped me playfully.

'Have you got a job too or do you live off your student loan?'

'A job, kind of. Andrew and I offer a consultative service. Sounds grand, doesn't it? All it actually means is that we offer people help and advice and charge them for it.'

'What kind of help?'

'Well, say somebody's seen something that's worried them, or is having strange memories, or thinks they've been abducted – anything along those lines, really – we talk to them and either put them in touch with others who have had the same experience, or just try to make them feel better. For example, I had an email yesterday from a man in Scotland who believes his wife has been, um, tampered with by aliens. Apparently she's gone off sex, her eyes keep glazing over when he's talking to her and she spends a lot of time staring out of the window at the sky.'

'And he sees this as evidence that she's been abducted?'

'Well, it's possible! I gave him a list of other possible things to watch out for and took his credit card number.' She smiled.

'So you make a lot of money out of this?'

She exhaled a thin stream of smoke. 'Not much. Just enough to cover my rent, my broadband and phone.'

'So this is all paid for by suckers.'

Marie frowned. 'That was an extreme example. We don't rip people off. We offer genuine advice to people who are frightened or confused and need reassurance. Like Fraser. I mean, we didn't charge him but we talked to him and made him feel a lot better about what he'd seen.' Her voice rose a little in indignation.

'Hey, I'm sorry. I wasn't judging you.'

I put my cup down and reached across and lightly took hold of her wrist. She looked into my eyes and something shifted in the air between us. My breathing became deeper. Her pupils expanded.

She crushed out her cigarette on the window ledge and orange sparks fell into the open air. I shifted closer to her and put my arms

29

around her back. I kissed her cheek then her lips. She kissed me back. She tasted of wine and smoke. I could hear blood pounding in my ears. I was kissing her. This was what I'd wanted to do since that night on the hill. I felt my lips curl into a smile against hers.

I opened my eyes. Marie was looking at me. We broke off and laughed, holding each other's hands, foreheads touching. I felt exhilarated and light-headed. She kissed me again and made an 'Mmm' sound as her lips left mine. I felt hot. There was very little air in the bedsit. We had used it all up.

'I was going to tell you what I believe in,' she said.

I wanted to carry on kissing her, but she was calling the shots here. I could wait.

I couldn't take my eyes off her as she spoke. She was so animated, gesturing, drawing symbols in the air with her hands.

'OK,' she said. 'There are four recognised types of close encounters. Type one is merely a sighting of a UFO.'

'Like the sighting over the East Hill?'

'That's right. Type two is when the UFO has some sort of physical effect on its surroundings. For example, a patch of ground might be scorched or trees might be damaged.'

'This is simple so far.'

She smiled. 'Type three is the famous one, and that's when aliens are actually sighted, like in the film, though we don't really like to call them aliens because it has negative connotations. We call them visitors.'

She lit another cigarette. 'The fourth kind of encounter is one where a human is abducted.'

'Uh-huh.'

'Please, Richard . . .'

I kissed her. 'Sorry. Carry on. I'm interested, genuinely.'

'OK. So, abductions. The most common description is that somebody will be in their house and they'll be seized by a beam of light and be taken aboard a spacecraft. Or they might be in their car. The car stalls and they don't know what's going on. Very often people only remember this under hypnosis. They get home and find that their journey took two hours longer than expected. They call this "missing time". There are a lot of variations, but the basic encounter is usually the same. The people tend to find themselves lying on an examination table. That's when they see the visitors. Often the visitors will talk to them – sometimes telepathically – and usually they carry out some kind of . . . procedure.'

'Like what?'

'Well, it might be a physical examination, or sometimes they pass lights over the human, or they might simply talk to them.' She cleared her throat. 'Sometimes the encounter is sexual. There are loads of reports of women being made pregnant by extraterrestrials. Or men being asked to father half-human babies. Hybrids.'

It took all my willpower not to laugh.

'The similarity between people's experiences is incredible. It's one of the reasons why the abduction phenomenon has so much credibility now. Everyone's telling the same story.'

'But surely—' I was careful not to offend her. 'Surely that's because they've all heard it before and they're copying each other.'

She shook her head. 'I don't believe that. I can't believe that that many people would lie. Why risk all that mockery?'

'I don't know. Perhaps they're attention seekers. Maybe they're the kind of people who will do anything to get in the paper. Or they're – how can I put it? – crazy.'

'No, Richard.' She shook her head. 'These are ordinary people. And there are thousands of testimonies, books filled with interviews and stories – true stories. Some people have said it could be a mass hysteria, but I think it's the truth. Every day, people are having encounters. And the people who come forward, well, that's only the tip of the iceberg. How many are too frightened to tell anyone? And there are thousands more who have blotted out the memories because they're too traumatic. So many people have had memories of abductions brought back under hypnosis or during therapy. And they all tell the same stories.'

I wasn't convinced, but I nodded thoughtfully. I stroked her fingers as she spoke. I realise that it might seem like I was being cynical in more than one way. That I was humouring her because I wanted to get into her knickers. But it was more than that. I liked her. I liked that she believed in something. I spent my life surrounded by nihilists and irony. It was refreshing to meet someone who wasn't like that.

She went on. 'The visitors themselves are usually one of two types.' She smiled. 'They used to be described as tall and beautiful with long blond hair. This was back in the fifties and sixties. They're usually known as the Nordic type. But the Nordics have mostly been replaced now by the Greys. They have large, egg-shaped heads, big almond-shaped eyes, tiny noses and mouths, and grey skin.'

I looked around the room. Many of the cuttings on the walls showed artists' impressions of Greys – it was a familiar image and again I thought that the reason everybody described aliens as such was because they were echoing all the others who'd gone before them.

'We believe that Greys exist, as do many other types of extraterrestrials. We think the Greys come from a system that is relatively close to Earth and that the other extraterrestrials nominated the Greys as a kind of scout party, to see if we humans are worth inviting into the Chorus.'

'The what?'

'It's a community of non-humans made up of intelligent species from different planets. We call it the Chorus.'

She sounded like she was quoting directly. 'Like an alien club?' I said.

'More like a council. Or, I don't know, like the UN or something.'

I laughed. 'United Planets.'

'Yes.' She gave me her 'don't mock' look and I adopted a straight face. 'Andrew believes that the Chorus are monitoring us to see if we are worthy of joining them. This will lead to what we call a close encounter of the fifth kind. Which is where a select group of humans will be chosen as ambassadors, or emissaries, to join the Chorus in order to represent this planet. Eventually, if this group is successful in showing that we can make a positive contribution, the Chorus will reveal itself to the planet as a whole and the entire human race will be invited to join.'

I laughed again. 'It sounds like joining the European Union. Will there be a single currency? Will we be able to opt out?' Another look. 'Sorry.'

'It's all right.' She looked sad as she looked up at me. 'So now you think I'm a complete nutter and you're never going to want to see me again. I guess I don't blame you.'

I took her hand. 'Don't be silly. It doesn't bother me at all. If you were a neo-Nazi or believed that you were a vampire or something, then I would be put off, but believing in aliens . . .' I shrugged. 'I really like you, Marie. I think you're beautiful and . . . different. That's *why* I like you.'

She leaned into me and kissed me again. We lay down on her bed and I kissed her neck and face, and she put her hands inside my shirt and touched my skin. I closed my eyes and inhaled her, the sensation of a body against mine. I had forgotten how good it felt. Outside, the sun went down and the room darkened. I pushed up Marie's T-shirt and kissed her belly. She sighed, but when I moved to unbutton her jeans she said, 'Not yet.'

Warm in the fading light, I kissed her and smiled. I forgot all about aliens and UFOs and intergalactic councils. This was here, this was now, and this was real. For the first time since I could remember, I was happy.

5

'Move in with me,' I said, three weeks later.

She was naked beneath the quilt in my bedroom, warm and drowsy and beautiful, looking up at me with her hooded eyelids, her make-up smudged and hair tangled on the pillow.

'It makes sense,' I said. 'You won't have to worry about rent or being evicted. And I want you to live with me. I love you. I want you in my home. I want you in my bed every night.' I kissed her.

'I'm in it every night anyway.'

It was far too soon to ask someone to move in with you. But I didn't care. I was smitten. No, more than that. I felt *possessed*, as if some spirit had got inside me and was running around my body, bumping into my heart, spinning in my stomach, filling me up with energy. I felt half delirious. Marie, Marie, Marie. I whispered her name to myself as I walked down the street or drove my car. I breathed in and could smell her, her scent in my nostrils, like she was a perfume that I wore on my skin. I could taste her on my tongue, feel her imprint on my body. I couldn't concentrate on my work; I drove Simon mad by repeatedly breaking off in mid-sentence and smiling secretively, some memory of Marie rising up and making rational thought or conversation impossible. I must have been a nightmare to be around.

'Well?' I said to her. There was a pink flush across her collar bone. 'Will you move in with me?'

'I might . . .'

'If?'

'If you do what you just did to me again.'

I put my head under the quilt and she giggled.

———

One night, a little while after she'd moved in, I woke up and became aware that Marie was not lying beside me. I looked up. She was silhouetted against the window, holding the curtains aside and looking out at the night sky.

I pushed the quilt aside and stood up. She turned and smiled. I put my arm around her waist and said, 'What are you doing?'

'Listening,' she said. 'I'm listening for the voice.'

I gave her a quizzical look.

'Do you know what brought Andrew and me together initially? It was because I told him I could hear the stars. It's like a very high-pitched call, very faint, like a choir heard from a very great distance.'

'Does it play tunes?'

She ignored my sarcasm, which slipped out occasionally. 'It's more abstract than that. It's more like a voice than music. The voice of the Chorus. Andrew can hear it too. Of all the people we know here, we're the only two who can hear it.'

It made me uncomfortable when she spoke like this. It was like listening to somebody who has embraced religion, who talks in awed tones about their god, a god that I could not believe in. It made me feel excluded, especially when she mentioned Andrew. I accepted her beliefs, and I was happy that she felt so passionately about something. But it wasn't a faith we shared.

We stood and looked up for a few moments, her head resting on my shoulder. I ran the tip of a finger over her small, pale breasts, causing goose bumps to spring up on the surface of her skin. Her nipples hardened and I lowered my mouth to them. I wanted to distract her from the stars and their voice and make her concentrate on me. I moved my hand down her spine and pulled her against me. I led her to the bed and we fell among the rucked-up sheets and made love slowly with the starlight filling the room where she had left the curtains half-open.

I wonder if she could still hear the celestial voice as we made love. Did she listen to it as I moved inside her, as our pelvic bones pressed hard together, as she bit into my shoulder? Did the voices take on a higher pitch – did they reach a crescendo – when she came? Her eyes were closed and she wore a smile. I put that smile down to me – my body, our lovemaking – but maybe it was down to something else. Maybe she was smiling at the sound of the stars.

'They're coming closer,' Andrew said, his voice coloured with excitement.

I passed him a glass of Coke. He had just got here and was sweating; the temperature outside was rising daily. The weathermen said that we were on the brink of a record-breaking heat wave, as the mercury in our thermometers crept into the mid-thirties.

Marie sat beside him on the sofa while I sat on the floor cushion. She was almost bouncing up and down with excitement. This was one of the things I loved about her: her child-like enthusiasm.

'We're getting so many reports of UFO sightings at the moment,' Andrew continued, addressing me. 'All over Sussex and Kent. It's pretty much unprecedented in this area. This morning alone I had six reports of sightings in a forty-mile radius, including a sighting by a police officer. You can probably write half of them off as mis-sightings – where people have seen planes or balloons or natural phenomena – but not all of them. There's a real buzz in the ufology community at the moment.'

He smiled and pushed his glasses up onto the bridge of his nose. He looked at Marie, who leant forward, listening keenly. 'And it's not just UFO sightings either. We're getting a lot of reports of abductions. A man in Tunbridge Wells has contacted me. He says he was taken aboard a craft and he can remember them carrying out some medical procedure on him. He's going to see a hypnotist to try to remember the rest. Plus there have been loads of reports of crop circles, especially over towards Ashford. Do you know a village called Wye? There's a big agricultural college there. Anyway, there have been a load of crop circles appearing. Marie and I are going to go over there this weekend and check it out.'

He paused to sip his Coke. Crop circles. I hadn't heard anyone mention them for years.

I said, 'So this girl you've got coming here tonight, she's had an abduction experience?'

Andrew nodded.

Marie looked over at me with her big eyes. 'You don't mind her coming here, do you?'

'Of course not. I don't mind who you have here. It's your home too now, Marie.'

'I do appreciate this,' Andrew said.

'Like I said, it doesn't bother me.'

Marie and I had been living together for a few weeks now. During the day, while I went to work, Marie sat at home and communicated with her fellow believers. When I got home from work she would usually be a little stir crazy, and we would take a bottle of wine into the garden. As it got dark, Marie would point out the constellations, teaching me their names. She had planted an assortment of flowers in the beds that I'd completely neglected since moving in. She talked and sang to them as she watered and tended to them.

'You think I'm nuts, don't you?' she said one night as I stood watching her.

'I prefer "kooky",' I replied.

'Cuckoo?' She did a cartwheel across the lawn, singing *I'm a Cuckoo*, a song by a band she listened to all the time.

'A kooky cuckoo.' I shook my head. I knew some people might find Marie's behaviour irritating, but she was so guileless and unbothered by what people thought of her . . . I wished I could be more like her.

Now, Andrew stood up and looked out of the front window. 'She should be here any minute.'

'Do you want me to make myself scarce when she arrives?' I asked.

I was sure Andrew was about to say yes but Marie shook her head. 'Of course not. You might find it interesting.' She came and sat beside me, kissing me quickly and winking.

'I feel like an outsider when Andrew's around,' I had confessed a few days before.

'Maybe you could become more involved,' she had said. I thought about it. 'Maybe.' But how could I get involved if I didn't believe?

'She's here,' Andrew said now. He went to the front door and opened it. I took the opportunity to kiss Marie, and then Andrew led a dark-haired girl into the room.

'This is Sally,' he said.

Sally was about twenty-five, skinny with short black hair that needed a wash. Her eyes were bloodshot and puffy. She looked scared. She made me think of one of those wild children that they sometimes find in the woods in films, raised by wolves, unused to human company; or a beaten dog. She trembled and almost spilled the glass of Coke I handed her.

Marie sat beside her on the sofa. 'Hi, I'm Marie.'

Sally looked around her. She refused to make eye contact with any of us. She said, 'Will you be able to help me? Will you?'

'We'll try,' Marie said in a soothing tone.

Andrew and Marie sat either side of the woman.

Marie said, 'We want to help you understand what happened to you. We should be able to answer some of your questions. We've spoken to a lot of people who've had similar experiences.'

Sally nodded, her fringe falling into her eyes. 'It's such a relief to find somebody who believes me. Who doesn't think I'm mad.'

'Why don't you talk us through it?' Marie coaxed, her voice gentle. She seemed more mature; kind and trustworthy. *She would make a good journalist*, I thought.

Sally drained the glass of Coke in one go. I thought she was going to throw it back up. She took a few deep breaths and swallowed.

'I've been trying to get pregnant for ages. My boyfriend John and I – we really want kids, you know? I've *always* wanted kids. I had a miscarriage a couple of years ago and since then we've been trying . . . We weren't having any luck and everyone said we were trying too hard, that we should relax and let it happen. I became convinced I was infertile. I was so unhappy. But then, this Easter, I fell pregnant. At last.' A smile flitted across her face then slipped away. 'I was so happy, you know? This was what I'd always wanted, and the doctor said that as long as I was careful I'd be all right.'

She put her empty glass down.

'Go on,' Marie said gently.

Tears slid down Sally's cheeks, thin trails that made me look away, self-conscious. This woman was a stranger, opening wounds and her heart to us. It didn't feel right.

She went on quickly, before she lost her nerve. 'Then it happened. I was in bed. John was asleep. We'd had a bit of an argument. John wanted to make love. I said no because I didn't want to risk harming the baby.

'I fell asleep and then about an hour later I woke up. It was just after midnight. I closed my eyes to try to get back to sleep and then I had this weird urge to open them again. But along with the urge there was, like, something telling me *not* to open them. It sounds really weird, I know. Anyway, the urge to open my eyes was stronger, and when I did I saw small grey figures standing at the end of the bed.'

Andrew leaned forward.

'I didn't feel scared. I felt . . . calm, like I was detached from myself. I couldn't really make the figures out properly because it was dark. I wanted to see them better, so I pushed the quilt down and as I did this a beam of light came through the window. It was really bright, white but with a blue edge, and suddenly I felt scared. I nudged John, then shook him, but he wouldn't wake up. I looked at the figures and said something like, "What do you want?" but they didn't answer.'

She wiped the tears from her cheeks with the palm of her hand. 'Then I felt myself lifting up off of the bed, floating. I screamed John's name but he still wouldn't wake up. And then I started floating towards the window. I couldn't see the figures any more. I had my hands on my belly, like I was instinctively trying to protect my baby . . .'

Her words tumbled out faster and faster. 'I actually passed through the window – through the glass. It felt horrible. I can't describe it. And then I kind of blanked out and when I woke up I was lying on a table in a brightly lit room. It was a metal table, cold on my back. I'd been wearing a nightie in bed but now I was naked. I tried to sit up but I couldn't. I thought I'd been paralysed. I tried to wiggle my toes and, thank God, I could. I just couldn't get up. I tried to look around. There was a grey metal door in front of me and a load of, like, controls on the ceiling. You know, switches and stuff. Flashing lights.'

'What happened?' Andrew said. His glasses had practically steamed up with excitement. I felt angry. I wanted to leave the room, but something compelled me to stay and listen.

'The door slid open,' Sally said, 'and these little creatures came in. They were the ones who had been standing at the bottom of my bed. They had huge heads and little dwarfish bodies and great big black eyes. They were wearing what I suppose were uniforms. They scuttled around me and I tried to speak but my throat was so dry nothing would come out. They looked at me with their big eyes . . .' She started to cry again, covering her face with her hands. Marie put her arm around her and stroked her hair. She offered Sally a tissue.

'Thanks.' She blew her nose and sniffed. 'Are you all right to go on?' Marie asked. Sally nodded. 'Yes. I'm sorry, it's just . . .'

'We understand,' Marie said.

Sally blew her nose again and continued her tale. 'The creatures, the aliens, stood around me and then a larger creature came into the room. He had the same head but he was taller. His uniform was blue and he was obviously in charge. He came up and looked down at me and said something to the others. Well, I assume he did because they started to scuttle about, but I didn't actually hear him. Then he looked at me and I heard his voice in my head. It was a nice voice – soft and deep.'

Andrew nodded enthusiastically.

She took a deep breath before continuing. 'He said, "It's time to take back the gift." I didn't know what he was talking about but then I realised. He was talking about my baby.' Sally knotted her fingers together. 'I started to get panicky. I found I could talk back to him, using my mind. Like, telepathy? I said, "No, it's mine. You

41

can't take it away." The creature said, "It's only half yours. Really, it belongs to us. Thank you for lending us your body, but this baby must be taken back to our planet." I shouted, "No!" and he shook his head like he was sad, and then I blacked out.

'When I woke up I was back in my bed and there was blood all over my thighs where they hadn't cleaned me up properly. My baby was gone.'

She sobbed now, deep, anguished sobs that were distressing to listen to. Marie held her and Andrew patted her arm. I got up and left the room. I sat in the kitchen with the cat. I could hear Marie and Andrew talking to Sally, and then, about thirty minutes later, she left. Andrew drove her home.

Marie came into the kitchen, her eyes moist but with a little smile on her face.

'What are you smiling about?' I asked, unable to hide my anger.

'She's so lucky,' Marie said. 'She was chosen by a representative of the Chorus to have his child. One day they'll be reunited and then they'll be able to live together in happiness. Oh Richard, it's so exciting.'

I was horrified. 'What the fuck are you talking about? She's had a miscarriage and to deal with it she's dreamt up some fantasy about aliens stealing her baby. She needs psychiatric help. And you and Andrew do nothing but encourage her. You're going to damage her even more than she's damaged already. Can't you see that?'

Marie's eyes widened with shock. 'I should have known,' she said.

She turned and stomped through the hall and out of the front door, slamming it hard, making the glass rattle. I ran to the door and pulled it open. I looked up and down the road but couldn't see her.

I went into the living room, followed closely by Calico, who jumped onto my lap when I sat down. I regretted my outburst. I should have been calmer, shouldn't have shouted. But that didn't mean I wasn't angry. What right did Marie and Andrew have to encourage Sally's delusions? Couldn't they see how much harm they might cause? I grappled with myself – my love for Marie and my distaste for this aspect of her beliefs. All the time she was UFO-watching and surfing the internet, it was all harmless. But this was different. I would have to talk to her about it when she came home.

———

At eleven, as I sat with a sleeping Calico heavy on my lap, the front door opened and I heard Marie come in and go straight upstairs. I pushed the cat aside and jogged up the stairs. Marie sat on the bed. She smelled of alcohol and cigarettes.

'Where have you been?' I spoke softly.

'I went to see Kathy.'

Kathy was one of her college friends who lived on the other side of town. 'How is she?'

'She's fine. She was nice to me.'

I tried to take her hand but she pulled it away. 'Marie—'

'You don't understand. You think I'm a fucking lunatic.'

'I don't.' I knelt on the bed and put my arms around her and kissed the tear-tracks on her cheeks. She didn't push me away.

'We don't want to hurt Sally,' she said. 'Or anyone. I know she's had a traumatic experience. Andrew's going to help find her a counsellor to get her help, to help her to deal with what's happened to her.'

'By which you mean that aliens took her baby, not that she had a miscarriage.'

She glared at me defiantly.

'I know it's difficult for you to understand, Richard.' She paused. 'I'm going to tell you something now. Maybe it will help you understand better.'

43

I waited.

She breathed in. 'When I was fourteen my dad left home. He disappeared. He didn't leave a note. He didn't tell anyone he was going, not his friends, his boss, no one. He just vanished. Like that.' She snapped her fingers. 'My mum went out of her mind. For months she searched for him, tried everything she could think of, but she never found him. And do you know what? I was glad. It was what I'd prayed for. Night after night I'd lie in bed, eyes squeezed shut, hands clenched, praying. *Please take him away. Please. Please. Let him die. Anything. Just get him out of our lives.*'

I held her hand. I felt sick.

'My dad was scum. Sick, violent scum. He used to beat us. Mum at first. She always had bruises and marks, burns where he'd lean across while they were watching TV and casually stub a cigarette out on her arm. He threw boiling water at her. He punched her in the face, knocked her teeth out, cracked her cheekbone. He broke her arm once. And she took it. She told everyone she'd had a fall – that old fucking chestnut. She cut herself off from all her friends, out of shame. She lived in terror, frightened to say the wrong thing or cook the wrong thing or make a noise when he wanted silence. And she insisted that she loved him, even when he started beating me.'

She spoke softly, evenly, like she was telling somebody else's story. But I had no doubt that she was telling the truth. I could see it in her eyes.

'I was only five or six when he started hitting me. I think I'd drawn on one of his books. He collected books on old motorbikes. He loved them more than he loved me. Anyway, he picked this book up and looked at where I'd scrawled across it in red crayon. I grinned up at him. I didn't know I'd done anything wrong. He took the book – it was a heavy hardback book – and hit me in the face with it. I remember screaming, blood spurting from my nose, and him shouting, and my mum shouting at him, and then he dragged her into their room and I heard her crying. I thought it was my fault.'

'Oh, sweetheart . . .'

'It went on for years. And the worst thing was that between the beatings he could be so nice. He was so unpredictable. It was like you could never relax. Even when he wasn't there, we were afraid of our own actions. You never knew how he would react. Like when we got Calico. A kid at school had kittens they were trying to find homes for. I wanted one so badly I said I'd have one, without asking my parents, and I took the kitten home, feeling elated but utterly sick and scared, part of me convinced that he would throw it out, or kill it. I tried to hide the kitten but it was too noisy. My dad heard it immediately. I braced myself, but he bent and picked up the kitten and stroked it and said, "What are you going to call him?" I was so relieved.'

I stroked her hair. I tried to imagine how she had felt. There had never been any violence in my home. Quite the opposite. Ours was a placid, repressed home, hidden emotions and feelings. Still, that was infinitely preferable to brutality.

Marie looked up at me. She reached into her shirt pocket and took out a crumpled packet of cigarettes. She lit one and exhaled slowly.

'When I was twelve my mum announced that I was going to have a baby brother or sister. I was delighted. I was past that age where I'd be jealous of another child in the house and I really started to look forward to having a baby brother – I was convinced it would be a boy – to look after. The whole atmosphere in the house changed. My dad seemed to mellow; he fussed around my mum and started turning the spare room into a nursery. They asked me what names I liked.' She smiled. 'I really thought things had changed. I was wrong. I was fucking wrong.'

She took a hungry drag on her cigarette. 'Because I was twelve, they thought I was old enough to be left alone without a babysitter and one night my dad took my mum out to the pub. I sat and watched TV. I remember it really well because *Close Encounters of the Third Kind* was on. It was the first time I'd seen it. It was almost finished when the door slammed and they came in. Almost as soon as they got through the door my dad pushed my mum against the wall and started shouting at her. He kept shouting, "Is it his? You slut!" All this shit. He said she'd looked at some man in the pub like she fancied him. He yelled all these accusations at her. I tried to run over to protect her and he punched me in the face. My mum screamed and he punched her, right in the stomach. I can see it now. I tried to jump on him and he kicked me away. Then he kicked *her*. He was shouting. Whore, slut, bitch . . .'

'She lost the baby?'

Marie nodded. 'The police came and tried to get a statement out of her but she refused. I was too young to do anything. When she was lying in the hospital bed I begged her. "Please don't make us go back there. Let's leave. Please." But we went back anyway. And he was OK for a while. I guess he felt sorry. Then it went back to exactly how it was before. I just completely withdrew. This was when I first got interested in UFOs. When I came to believe. I kept praying that aliens would come and take my father away. Dump him somewhere with no atmosphere.' She laughed bitterly. 'So when he did disappear . . .'

She started to cry, the pain of telling making her convulse, pushing sharp tears out of her, like Sally just a few hours before. She looked up at me through her damp fringe. She said, 'Hold me.'

A little later she said, 'I would never take a miscarriage, other people's suffering lightly. Do you understand that?'

I nodded. I still thought she was wrong to encourage Sally in her belief that her baby had been taken by aliens. But at that moment I was more focused on Marie's pain. I resolved to talk to her about Sally another day. But I never did.

———⌣———

Life went on. The summer got hotter. My love for Marie got stronger.

Some nights we would go up onto the hill and lie on the grass, looking at the sky, Marie teaching me the names of the constellations. During the days, she accompanied Andrew on trips to visit the sites of corn circles. They visited fellow believers. I tried to distance myself from her professional life, as if it was a job I didn't have much interest in. She didn't bring any more 'abductees' home, so there were no more arguments about that. In fact, I didn't really have much idea about what she got up to during the day.

Marie urged me to do something about the dead end my career was stuck in. 'You need to pursue your dreams,' she said. 'Contact the big news sites and magazines, send them your work. Hustle. You're good enough. Too good for the *Herald*.'

Spurred on by her encouragement, I set up a new online portfolio of my work and began to send links to picture editors. The fire of my ambition was rekindled.

The only blight in my relationship with Marie, apart from the submerged disagreement about her work, was that she wouldn't let me take her photo. I tried to cajole her, asked repeatedly why. She refused to give an answer. I pointed a loaded camera at her and she put her hand up like a celebrity being pursued by the paparazzi.

'If you ever take a picture of me, I'll leave you.'

I smiled like she must be joking.

'I'm being serious, Richard. I promise you. I'll leave you.'

I lowered the camera. 'But—'

She turned and left the room.

I didn't understand it. All I wanted was one photo, just something to put in my wallet and look at when she wasn't around. Something to show other people, all the other people who kept asking about this new woman in my life.

I sighed. I was sure, in time, I could persuade her.

Then, one late autumn afternoon, everything changed.

It was a Friday. I came home from work early. I was worried about Marie. She had gone down with a virus earlier that week and had taken to her sick bed. I had tried to persuade her to go to the doctor, but she had insisted that she was all right. 'I just need to rest,' she said.

I pushed open the front door and trotted up the stairs. She wasn't in bed. Perhaps she was asleep in the living room. I ran back down the stairs.

She was sitting on the sofa with her phone clutched tightly in her hand. It emitted a high-pitched beeping. Her eyes were pink and her face was streaked with tears. Her knuckles were white where she was gripping the phone so tightly.

'Marie? What is it? What's happened?'

'It's Andrew,' she said. 'He's dead.'

6

If it hadn't been for Marie's virus she would have been with Andrew when he was killed. She would probably be dead too.

Andrew had been on one of his trips to the far side of Kent to look at more crop circles and talk to a couple of farmers. The local press were barely interested. These days, crop circles were old news; the methods of the people who made them, using ropes and planks, had been revealed years ago. Or so I thought. Andrew and Marie still believed that some crop circles were created by aliens; that they were messages from the Chorus.

Andrew was something of a self-styled expert on crop circles. He had been all over the country to study them and had even written a couple of articles, and numerous pamphlets. He had phoned Marie that afternoon and told her that he was convinced these were the real thing. He knew a manmade crop circle when he saw one. He took some photographs and headed home in his car.

In his excitement, I guess he drove too fast. Maybe he wasn't concentrating. Apparently, he was driving through some narrow country lanes, far too fast, and as he turned the corner he had swerved to avoid something – probably an animal – in the road. He went through a barbed wire fence and struck a tree. He was killed instantly.

Along with Marie's grief came a comprehension that she was lucky to be alive and she spent the few days after Andrew's death in a kind of stunned silence, contemplating her mortality, while I was filled with relief that I hadn't lost her.

'If I die,' Marie said. 'This is what I want you to do for me.'

'Please don't talk like that.'

'I'm serious, Richard. This is what I want. Which is how I know it's what Andrew would want.'

We had climbed back to the top of the East Hill, where I had first met Marie, and walked along to an area known as the Firehills. It was a beautiful spot, verdant yet rugged, with glorious views across the English Channel. On this late September evening, it was windy and chilly, and it would soon be dark.

There were five of us. Me, Marie, Fraser – who looked as queasy as the first night I'd met him – plus two young women I hadn't met before, but who were members of Marie and Andrew's little group. Melissa was a curvy brunette with trendy glasses and Katie was tall, slim and twitchy. Neither of them spoke much. They seemed as grief-stricken as Marie, and the whole group was solemn and quiet as we made our way towards the cliff edge.

Marie held a little urn in her hand. It contained Andrew's ashes.

'Perfect weather,' Marie said, standing by the cliff, the wind whipping her hair. I was worried she might blow over, go flying into the sea, but she stood firm and strong.

'Didn't Andrew have any family?' I had asked when Marie told me of this plan.

'No. His parents died years ago and he was an only child. He's going to be cremated and then we're going to hold a ceremony on the hill, to scatter his ashes to the winds, so they are carried up to the sky.'

I wasn't sure if this was quite feasible, but didn't say anything.

'Will you come?' she asked. 'Please?'

'Of course.'

So here we were. Marie unscrewed the urn and tipped ashes onto her palm. She murmured a few words which I couldn't hear well with the wind in my ears, but she said something about travelling well, and then she cast the remains of Andrew towards the cliff edge.

The others took turns to do the same. Everybody was crying, except me. I wasn't sure that Andrew would have wanted me to scatter any of his ashes, but Marie insisted. 'He respected you,' she said.

Fraser, who was the last in line, seemed particularly upset, which surprised me. I hadn't realised he'd known Andrew that well. I guessed they had formed a strong bond over Fraser's UFO experience. His hand trembled as Marie tipped ashes into his palm. I watched as he turned towards the sea, many metres below, and swung his arm, the wind catching the ashes and carrying them, swirling and eddying, towards the sunset.

'So how did it go?'

Simon wiped his brow with the grimy cuff of his white shirt. We were sitting on a bench in Alexandra Park to cover a story about dog shit. Simon and I were supposed to be talking to dog owners and finding out how many of them used the poop scoop bins. This was part of the editor's campaign against dog mess.

Simon bit into his Magnum. 'So?'

The day after the ceremony on the hill, a woman called Theresa Smith had phoned and told me she loved the portfolio I'd sent her. The *Sunday Telegram*, of which she was the picture editor, was looking to commission a number of unknown photographers to put together a series of articles on modern Britain. She wanted to meet me. By the end of the conversation I was giddy with excitement. This could be my big break.

It was now a few days after my meeting with Theresa at the *Telegram*. 'It went pretty well. She loved my pictures. But I haven't heard anything yet.'

He grunted. 'So you'll be buggering off and leaving us then.'

'It's only a commission. Even if I get it I won't be leaving this job.'

'Yeah, but it will open doors, won't it? *Then* you'll be buggering off.'

I couldn't help but smile. 'Well, that's the idea.'

After we'd interviewed and snapped an assortment of criminal dog owners, we walked back into town.

'How's that bird of yours?' Simon asked.

'Upset.' I told him about the ceremony.

He shook his head. 'Poor her. But I didn't like that bloke at all. There was something creepy about him. Sort of slimy.'

'I know what you mean. But he was Marie's business partner, so—' I turned my palms upwards.

'Yeah.' He lit a cigarette. 'Is she still into all this UFO crap?'

I leapt to Marie's defence. 'It's not crap. I mean, she believes it, and how do we know for sure that it's her who's wrong? Maybe we're wrong.'

Simon laughed. 'Fuck, it must be love.'

'Speaking of which, how are things with Susan?' We hadn't mentioned his behaviour at the nightclub since it had happened, but he had been acting shifty recently, checking his phone all the time, taking calls and wandering out of earshot. I was pretty sure he was having an affair.

'No comment,' he said.

When I got home, Marie was hunched over the PC, tapping away at the keys. As soon as I entered the room, she swung round, an alarmed expression on her face. She quickly turned back and closed the browser window she had been looking at.

'What are you doing?' I asked.

'Sorry, it's private.'

'Oh.'

She stood up and put her arms around me. 'You wouldn't be interested anyway.'

'Let me guess: visitors.'

'You got it in one. I'm sorry, Richard, but now Andrew's gone, I have to work twice as hard to keep the network and the consultancy going.'

'I know.'

'You hate it, don't you?' she said, standing up, her hands on her hips.

'No, I understand . . .'

'You don't, though, do you?'

I stared at her. 'Marie, why are you being like this? What did I do?'

She sank back into the computer chair and put her hands over her face. I realised she was crying silently. I tried to put my arm around her but she shrugged me off.

'Please. I need some space,' she said.

'Is this about Andrew?' I said. 'I know you miss him.'

She wiped her eyes. The tears had stopped as quickly as they'd started. 'I'm OK,' she said. 'I'll be OK. Just . . . let's just leave it.'

I stroked her shoulder. 'All right. If that's what you want. But if you need to talk—'

'I know.'

I turned to leave the room to make a drink and Marie said, 'Richard, there was a message for you. Theresa Smith. She wants you to call her.'

I listened to the voicemail.

'I don't believe it,' I said. 'I got the commission.'

On the sixteenth of October I had a second appointment with Theresa Smith. I had already sent her the photos and now she wanted to meet 'for a chat'. I had spent the last couple of weeks working hard, taking and editing photos every spare minute I had.

'What time will you be home?' Marie asked, kissing me goodbye. Over the past few days she had seemed a little brighter, but busy with college work along with her consultancy. She spent half her life on the computer.

'I don't know. Five or six, I expect.'

I sat on the train and tried my hardest not to feel nervous. I needn't have worried. The meeting went better than I could have hoped. Theresa wanted me to do more regular work, and we discussed a few initial assignments.

I walked back to Charing Cross with a spring in my step. I couldn't wait to get home and tell Marie. I tried to call her but there was no answer.

I tried to call her several more times from the train home. It wasn't unusual for her to let her phone die, forgetting to charge it, especially if she was coding or chatting on one of the internet forums she frequented. I wasn't too worried. With the money from the commission I decided I would take Marie away; it might help her get over Andrew's death. I browsed holiday sites on my phone.

I took a taxi home from the train station and got the driver to drop me at the little supermarket up the road from my house.

I bought a bottle of champagne and walked home, feeling buoyant.

'Marie?' I called. No response, just silence. I looked at my watch. Just after six.

I checked every room. I went back outside, that feeling that something was very wrong nibbling at my guts.

Back indoors, I tried to distract myself, flicking through a magazine, browsing holiday sites again on my phone. I was planning on taking Marie away somewhere hot and exotic, was going to surprise her. She'd been through a lot recently. She deserved a break.

The ominous feeling that something was wrong intensified, while at the same time I tried to stay rational. There was no sign in the house that anything sinister had happened. No signs of a struggle, no blood. Nothing out of place. I went upstairs and ran a bath, thinking the hot water might relax me. It was eight o'clock now and her phone was still off.

By ten I had reassured myself that she must have met one of her college friends and gone round to see them, maybe gone out to the pub, was enjoying herself, getting drunk. She deserved to let her hair down. I didn't have any of her friends' numbers, would have felt foolish contacting them anyway. I could picture them laughing about Marie's over-protective boyfriend, teasing her about having a curfew, asking if she'd turn into a pumpkin if she wasn't home on time. I needed to chill out.

I checked my phone numerous times to make sure it was working. I looked around again for a note. I poured myself a beer and drank it too quickly, then drank another. Marie's cigarettes were lying on the worktop. Surely she wouldn't have gone to the pub without them? She must have bought a fresh packet.

I had a dreadful thought: what if she had left me? I ran upstairs and looked in the wardrobe. All her clothes seemed to be there. In fact, all that was missing was her jacket and her bag. I relaxed a little. She must be at the pub. I could go looking for her but, again, I didn't want her to think I was being possessive, the kind of person who goes out to drag his girlfriend home if she's out late.

I drank another beer and the tiredness hit me. It had been a long day. Midnight passed and I lay on the sofa. Calico sat beside me and purred. I fell asleep, the cat's soft purring like a lullaby.

When I woke up on the sofa the next morning, surrounded by beer bottles, a crick in my neck, she still wasn't home.

I felt cold. I tried to call her for the hundredth time. I paced the house. I wanted to stay in, wait for her, but I had to go to work. I scrawled a note asking her to call me as soon as she got home and left it on the kitchen worktop. I hesitated by the front door, tempted to call in sick. But I thought staying in, waiting for her, would be even worse than going to the office. At least there I would be distracted.

I was on edge all morning. 'What the fuck's wrong with you?' Simon asked.

I didn't want to tell him. Not yet. I was sure when I got home she would be there and I would feel foolish for being so anxious. So I kept quiet.

I tried to phone her at every opportunity. At lunchtime I drove home to see if she was there. I ran up the front steps and unlocked the door. The mail lay on the doormat: junk mail, brown envelopes.

'Marie? Marie!'

She wasn't there.

Marie – my Marie, my beautiful Marie, the woman I loved – wasn't there. She had gone. Disappeared. Like a falling star that shoots across the sky one night and then vanishes.

She had gone.

PART TWO
STARING INTO SPACE

7

The first forty-eight hours were the worst. After the euphoria of getting the *Telegram* commission, my bubble was well and truly burst. I didn't know what to do or who to contact. I wanted her to walk through the door and say, 'Sorry, I meant to phone . . .' and the relief would have been so great I would have forgiven her. I would have forgiven her anything.

The logical first step would be to phone everyone Marie knew: friends, colleagues, parents. But I didn't know any addresses or phone numbers that would help me. The only friend of hers I knew personally was dead. I assumed all her contacts were on her phone and PC. The former had disappeared with her, though the charger was still in the kitchen. The PC was password protected. I would get to that later.

I phoned the local hospital: the Conquest, plus the hospitals in Eastbourne and Tunbridge Wells, just in case. No Marie Walker had been admitted, nor anyone fitting her description.

I asked my next-door neighbours.

I knocked on the door to the left. Mr Taylor, an elderly widower who I very rarely spoke to, opened the door and leaned out. 'Yes?'

'I don't suppose you saw my girlfriend yesterday at all?'

He squinted at me. 'The pretty girl with the red hair?'

My heart pounded. 'Yes. That's her.'

'Hmm,' he said thoughtfully. 'Yesterday . . . No. I don't think so.'

'Did you hear anything? Music, the TV, a door shutting?'

He tapped his left ear. 'I don't hear very much these days. A bit mutton, I am.' This was something my dad used to say: Mutt and Jeff, Cockney rhyming slang for *deaf*.

I thanked him and tried my other neighbours, Kevin and Sarah, a young couple who had only recently moved in.

Sarah came to the door holding their little boy, Jack. 'Hello.' She sounded quite pleased to see me. I guessed she must get bored, stuck at home all day with a toddler. Kevin worked as a telephone engineer. I didn't have much to do with them: just the odd hello over the garden fence.

I asked Sarah whether she'd seen any sign of Marie.

She thought about it. Jack gawped at me like I was causing him a terrible affront by standing on his doorstep. Sarah said, 'No, not that I can remember. Why, what's happened?'

'Probably nothing. It's just that . . . she didn't come home last night.'

She raised an eyebrow, hoisting Jack on to her hip. 'Had an argument?'

I said not. 'What about Kevin? Might he have seen her?'

'He never sees anything. Lives in a dream world. But I'll ask him when he comes home tonight.'

I didn't really want to go back into my house. It felt too empty; more so, with all her stuff everywhere – her clothes and toiletries and make-up.

My eye fell upon the landline phone in the corner. I barely used it – only had it because we needed it for the internet connection – and the handset was coated with dust. By dialling 1471 I could check if anyone had tried to call while I was out.

She hadn't, but there was a missed call from a local number that I didn't recognise. The call had come in at just after five p.m. yesterday, the day Marie disappeared. I called back immediately.

A woman who I guessed was in her fifties or early sixties answered, repeating back the phone number in the way that older people often do.

'Hello,' I said. 'I got a missed call from this number yesterday afternoon?'

She breathed heavily. 'Are you sure?'

I told her I was sure. 'My name's Richard Thompson. So you didn't try to call me? Can I ask your name?'

She paused. 'Is this a sales call? I'm not interested. My husband told me—'

I interrupted her. 'Can I ask your husband's name?'

She made a strange noise, like she was sucking in air through her teeth and groaning at the same time. Eventually, she said, 'My husband is Fraser Howard.'

The park ranger. I hadn't seen him since the ceremony on the hill.

'Can I talk to him?' I asked.

'No, you can't.'

'Mrs Howard, it's really—'

'He's not here.'

'Oh.' How frustrating. 'Can you ask him to call me when he gets home? Or does he have a mobile I can call?'

From the background I could hear a dog barking. 'I have to go,' she said suddenly. She put the phone down.

I slumped on the sofa. It wasn't unusual for Fraser to call here. He spoke to Marie regularly, although I was sure he usually called her mobile. His wife sounded very highly strung. I decided I would try to call again in a couple of hours if I didn't hear back.

Calico ran into the room, looked at me and ran out again. He had been doing this all day, running in and out of rooms, looking for Marie. He kept blinking at me accusingly, like I'd done something to her.

It was time to call the police. But they told me to wait forty-eight hours and then if she was still missing, report it in person at the station.

Next, I phoned Simon and told him what had happened.

'Has she done this before?'

'No! Not to me anyway.'

'And you've got no idea where she might be? She might have gone off E.T. hunting and you've forgotten all about it.'

'I'd remember. I'm not senile yet.'

'Even in all the excitement of this *Telegram* thing? You have been pretty wired lately. I bet that's what's happened. She's probably camped up on the East Hill again waiting for UFOs.'

I looked through my front window, up at the hill. Might she be up there? It was possible. God, anything was possible.

I dropped the receiver and left the house again. I had about an hour before it got dark. I parked and ran along the path that leads to Ecclesbourne Glen, feeling ridiculously hopeful. I made my way to the spot where I had first seen her. Nothing. I looked all around. I met a couple of people walking dogs and asked them if they had seen any tents or anyone who fitted Marie's description. They frowned and said they hadn't.

The sky darkened. I found myself standing on the spot where we had made love. I looked down. That flattened daisy – had we done that? I sat on the grass and hugged myself.

Back home, I phoned Simon again.

'She's not on the hill,' I said. 'Simon, what the fuck am I going to do?'

I couldn't wait forty-eight hours. The next day, I walked down to the police station in town. On the way, I tried to call Fraser Howard. This was my third attempt since I'd spoken to his wife. There was no reply.

PC David Ashcroft – who I had been at school with – walked into the interview room and pulled a chair out from beneath the table; it scraped across the floor. He looked at me. I must have been a mess. I hadn't shaved for three days and probably stank of stale smoke. The day I realised Marie was missing I had smoked my way through her left-behind packet of cigarettes. Then I had gone out and bought another carton.

'How are you feeling?' he asked.

'Like shit.'

He opened a notepad and asked me to describe 'the missing person'.

'Her name's Marie Walker. She's twenty-three. White, blue eyes, pale red hair, small stud in the side of her nose, about five foot three, beautiful.' I had already been asked to complete a questionnaire, giving Marie's details, which Ashcroft now picked up and scanned quickly.

He looked up. 'Have you got a photo?'

I shook my head. 'I know, it seems ridiculous. I'm a photographer and I haven't got a picture of my girlfriend.

'Right,' said Ashcroft, looking at me curiously. 'Let me get this straight. You came home two days ago and Marie wasn't there. You have no idea where she might have gone?'

I shook my head again.

'And nothing was missing?' He looked at the questionnaire. 'Just her jacket, her phone and her bag. What was in the bag?'

'I have no idea.'

'The usual woman's stuff, I suppose.' He chuckled to himself. 'Any idea what she was wearing? Apart from the jacket?'

I had thought about this and tried to work it out. I was pretty sure her black jeans were missing, but apart from that . . .

'I don't know,' I admitted.

'Does she drive?'

'No.'

'Does she have a job?'

'Not as such. She's a student.' I didn't want to get into the whole UFO consultancy thing.

'What about family and friends? Have you tried ringing them to check if anyone's seen her?'

'Her dad ran off when she was a kid and I don't know where her mum lives. In Hastings, I think, but I couldn't say where exactly. And I don't have the contact details of any of her friends either.'

He shook his head despairingly. *How* long had you been together?'

'Four months.'

'What about another boyfriend?'

I was offended. 'No!'

'Are you sure?'

'Well, of course . . .' But was I sure? How could I be? She had so much spare time during the days while I was at work, she could have been doing anything with anyone. My paranoia flared up.

'Had anything happened recently, anything that might suggest why she'd go off? Any bad news?'

'Her best friend died in a car crash.'

He drummed his fingers on the table and looked around, up at the small, grimy window that hardly let in light. He looked bored. 'Richard, I'll be totally honest with you, all right, seeing as you're an old mate.' This was an exaggeration. He had been a twat at school and we'd barely spoken. 'We don't give much priority to cases like this. She's not a juvenile or a pensioner. She's not what we class as vulnerable. She's an adult, capable of making her own decisions, able to go where she likes. It's not a crime to go missing, you know. This girl seems to have no ties – no job, no kids, just you it seems – and therefore she's free to go wherever she pleases, with whoever she wants. I know you're worried. I expect I would be in your situation. But . . .' He shrugged.

I stared at him. I couldn't think of anything to say. It was obvious he wasn't going to help. I was wasting my time. I stood up.

'Look, I'll enter her details on the MISPER database, OK? But I reckon she's just gone off somewhere to get her head together. I mean, your best friend dying, that's a pretty big deal, isn't it? She's probably just gone off to think. I'm sure she'll be in touch soon, Richard. Most missing persons reappear within two days.'

I stepped out into the fading afternoon sunlight and wondered what to do. I was certain by now that she wasn't going to suddenly reappear. I felt completely and chillingly alone.

What had happened to her? I decided there were six possibilities:

1. She had run away with another man.
2. She had run away for some other unknown reason.
3. She had been called away suddenly and for some reason that I couldn't imagine had been unable or unwilling to contact me.
4. She had been kidnapped or murdered.
5. She had had some sort of breakdown or crisis (possibly because of Andrew's death) and had gone away to sort herself out. Somehow. Somewhere.
6. She'd had an accident and was lying injured or dead in some remote place.

And there was a seventh possibility, wasn't there? The possibility that she had been taken away by aliens. I thought it was the craziest thing that had ever entered my head, but the thing was, she had talked about aliens (or visitors, as she called them) so much that I couldn't help but think of it, even if I immediately dismissed it as ridiculous. I didn't believe in aliens. I certainly didn't believe that my girlfriend had been stolen away by little grey men. No, whatever had happened to her was something grounded in reality. Something earthly.

After leaving the police station, I called Simon and asked him to meet me for a coffee. I named a little café in the Old Town. I sat outside, smoking, until Simon arrived.

He sat opposite me. 'Bob said to tell you he hopes you have a happy holiday.' Luckily, the *Herald* owed me annual leave, so the day after Marie disappeared I had phoned Bob, the editor, and asked for a couple of weeks' holiday. I didn't tell him why.

Simon looked at my smouldering cigarette, then at my face. He said, 'You look fucking terrible, mate.'

Simon and I didn't usually do emotional support. Occasionally, when very pissed, he would tell me about his marital problems and I would tut sympathetically, but that was about the extent of it. Now, wincing, Simon asked, 'How are you feeling?'

'Sick with dread. I'm so worried that something awful's happened to her. She could be lying in a ditch somewhere. And then I think, *What if she's gone off with another bloke?* I keep picturing all these terrible scenarios – her being hurt, or wandering around, lost and confused, or in hospital.' I sucked on my cigarette. 'You know when you're having a really bad dream and you wake up and you're overwhelmed with relief and you kind of laugh but feel a bit shaky? That's what I want to happen to me. I'll wake up and she'll be asleep beside me, all warm, and I'll lean over and kiss her and not want to close my eyes in case she vanishes again.'

Simon stared at me like I had lost the plot. 'Right. I want you to think hard. Did she say anything that morning, or in the few days before, that might give you a clue as to where she's gone?'

I ran a finger around the rim of my coffee cup. 'Monday morning I left really early. She was still in bed. She asked what time I'd be home and said goodbye. That was about it. And no, she didn't say goodbye wistfully or regretfully. It was just a "What time will you be home, see you later" – nothing more. I've replayed that scene so many times that it feels like a hallucination now.'

'And she gave you no other clues at all over the weekend?'

'No. We stayed in on Saturday night with a DVD. I spent Sunday preparing my photographs for Theresa Smith. Marie sat at her computer. I think she was just browsing the web.'

'So you've got no clues at all?'

'No.'

He sighed. 'For a photographer, you're not very observant, are you?'

'I didn't know I was going to be investigating her disappearance.'

'Hmm. And you've tried to contact everyone she knows?' Simon said.

'I don't have any of her friends' details.'

'Aren't they on her computer? I take it you've looked?'

'I would, but it's password protected.'

He rolled his eyes. 'You're not very good at this stuff, are you? Listen, try all the passwords you can think of. Including "password" itself. If you can't crack it we'll take it to someone who can.'

'OK.'

'If you really want to find her you're going to have to start thinking like a detective. Try to put aside your angst and grief and be logical.' He swallowed. 'If you need any help, I'll be there for you. Although I still reckon she'll turn up.' He looked thoughtful. 'Didn't she used to go to a lot of conferences on UFOs? You should find out if there have been any this week. Think, Richard, think. Stop sulking and moaning and do something.'

We left the café and I thanked him.

'Remember,' he said, 'if you need any help . . .' He barked a laugh. 'You're definitely going to need it.'

8

I sat in front of the PC. What was her password?

First, I tried vanity and typed *richard*.

No joy.

I tried again. I looked over at the windowsill, where Calico looked out at the street. I typed the cat's name.

Access denied.

I had a horrible feeling that if I failed a third time I would be locked out. I thought hard. With my heart thumping, I typed *chorus*.

I was in. I hissed, 'Yes.' I wasn't such a shit detective after all.

I started to click through the address book, which was sorted by first name. The top entry was Andrew, with his phone number, home address and email address. Well, that wouldn't be much use, would it? I moved to the next one, then flicked back and forth through the addresses.

There seemed to be the phone number of everyone she knew, as well as the addresses of various organisations, such as the Ministry of Defence, the British UFO Research Association, *UFO Magazine*, *Quest International*. One that caught my eye was 'Mum'. As far as I knew, she hadn't had any contact with her mum while we'd been together.

I exported the address book, after a lot of fiddling, onto my phone and felt my despair lift a little. Now I could make a start.

The first number I called was Marie's mum's. There was no answer. Did anyone ever answer their phone? Then I called some of the other numbers. First, I phoned Kathy, who told me she hadn't seen or heard from Marie for a few weeks. Not since she'd stormed out during our argument about Sally.

'You've got me worried now,' she said. 'I can phone around people from college if you want, see if anyone's heard from her?'

'That would be great.'

While waiting for Kathy to make her calls, I phoned the college itself to see if they'd heard from Marie. The woman on the switchboard put me through to a Pete Stapleford, the head of the computing department.

'Let me check,' he said, putting me on hold for a minute. 'No, she hasn't been to any of her lectures this week. We left her a couple of messages asking if she was sick. You've got me worried now. I'll ask around.' I asked him to call me if he found anything out.

I scanned the list of addresses again. Kathy was taking care of most of the names in the file; I tried a few other local numbers, but they were all people who hadn't seen Marie since she had left school. There were a few other private numbers, scattered around the country. My finger hovered over the phone, undecided. I sat and waited for Kathy to call back.

When she phoned, an hour later, Kathy said, 'I've spoken to Narinder, Tracey, Zoe and Amanda. None of them have heard from her since the end of August. Amanda's on the same computer course as Marie and she said she hasn't been to any classes.' She spoke breathlessly. 'I feel sick with anxiety. What if something awful's happened to her?'

I took a deep breath. All of a sudden I felt terribly cold. 'Can you think of anyone else who might have seen her?'

'No. I've been racking my brain since I spoke to you. There's no one. The thing is, Marie kept herself to herself. It's like she had two sets of friends: her friends at college and . . . everyone else. The spooky lot.'

'Spooky?'

'Yeah, you know. The "We Are Not Alone" brigade. That creepy Andrew bloke. I know you're not one of them. Marie always said you were a cynic.'

'She talked about me, then?'

'Oh yes. She told us all about you. She really liked you.'

Suddenly, I wanted to get off the phone. I didn't like the way Kathy kept referring to Marie in the past tense. Like she was dead.

'Well, thanks for your help,' I said.

Kathy exhaled loudly. 'I'm sure it will be all right, Richard. She'll come back. Just wait and see.'

But she didn't sound very confident.

The spooky lot. I wasn't the only person who wasn't a big fan of Marie's alien-obsessed friends. But it made me think. Marie was always on an internet forum called Experiencers Unite. Sometimes she sat up late into the night sharing her opinion with fellow enthusiasts. I went onto the site now and scanned the list of recent posts, skim-reading a few of them.

I shook my head. All of the posts were about abduction experiences, UFO sightings around the world, talk of the 'coming revelation', arguments about the New World Order, a long discussion about how aliens were more likely to visit pregnant women . . .

I wasn't sure what Marie's user name was so couldn't tell which posts she'd written. I searched the site for her name but got no results.

I had nothing to lose, so I registered on the site and wrote a post:

My girlfriend, Marie Walker, is a regular user of this site. I'm not sure of her user name – sorry. But she's on here all the time so I'm hoping some of you will know her by her real name.

Marie has gone missing and I'm worried sick. I came home two nights ago and she wasn't here. I can't believe she would leave without letting me know she was safe. But she has been very upset recently after her friend, Andrew Jade, was killed in an accident.

Marie, if you read this, please call me to let me know you're OK.

If anyone else knows where Marie is, please contact me.

Thank you.

I hit refresh multiple times over the next half hour. Although the number of views ticked up, there was no response for ages. Then, after fifteen minutes of growing anxiety, I saw that I had a reply. I clicked to read it.

Maybe she's been abducted. The wife of a friend of mine vanished WITHOUT TRACE a few years back. He never found out what happened to her but in the days before she went she had unexplained cuts and bruises on her body, all signs of an abduction, and he is SURE the extraterrestrials came back and took her PERMANENTLY.

I stopped reading.

I hit refresh a few more times – and then noticed my forum post had disappeared. There was a message in my inbox from a moderator.

I thumped the desk and swore at the computer. My message had been 'deleted for breaching forum guidelines around using real names'.

I shot back a reply – thinking this moderator might know Marie, or could look up her details – asking for help. Could they put an appeal on the site for information?

I waited, growing increasingly irritated, my feeling of helplessness intensifying as they didn't reply. Finally, I turned off the PC.

It was getting late. The sun was going down, dipping behind the hill. I tried to call Marie's mum again but there was still no answer. I checked the address. It was only a five-minute drive away. That surprised me. Marie's mum lived just around the corner yet Marie had never taken me to meet her. I had no time to waste so I got in my car and drove to the Walker residence.

Marie's mum lived in a new terraced house on a council estate. Rows of identical, pebble-dashed houses with off-colour lawns. I rang the bell.

There was no reply so I rang it again. Nothing. I pressed my face to the window and looked inside. There was no sign of life. I pushed open the letterbox and peered through it into the gloom. Unopened mail lay in a pile on the doormat. My stomach lurched. Had she disappeared as well?

I hung around for a few minutes, wondering what to do next. Just as I was about to get back in my car, a man with incredible sideburns came out of the next house.

'Can I help you?' he said, narrowing his eyes. I couldn't take my eyes off his sideburns. He looked like he'd been going to the same barber and tailor since 1973.

'I'm looking for Mrs Walker.'

'And you are?'

I admired his directness. 'I'm a friend of her daughter's. She sent me round with a message for her mum.'

'Marie? Christ on a bike, I haven't seen her for years.' He shook his head. 'Little Marie. Tut.'

'Maybe you could give Mrs Walker my phone number,' I said, reaching in my pocket for a pen.

'Give it to her yourself,' he said. 'She's in the Conquest.'

I hate hospitals. The smell of death and disinfectant, the ghosts that stalk the sterile corridors, the pain and suffering and germs. I have a horror of ending up in one, sometimes have nightmares in which I'm lost, wandering the maze-like corridors of a hospital like every other, in my pyjamas, searching for an exit, unable to find it.

Kate Walker was a pale, fragile-looking woman. She looked exactly how I imagined Marie would look if the next twenty-five years of her life were full of nothing but pain and misery. Kate was in a ward with seven other women, most of them lying quietly, watching TV or fiddling with their phones. Most of them had visitors, but there were no signs that Marie's mother had been visited by well-wishers. There were no flowers, no bunches of grapes or even cards.

I pulled up a chair and sat beside her. I felt nervous. Would this woman be able to tell me something that would help me? Would she be able to shed any light on the dark space her daughter had left behind?

'I'm a friend of Marie's,' I said.

She inspected me, then nodded. She didn't smile. 'Richard.'

I was taken aback. 'How did you know?'

'Marie told me she had a new boyfriend. She came to see me a couple of weeks ago, just before I came into this place. You're a bit younger than I expected. She's always gone for older men in the past.'

'I'm twenty-seven.'

'That's young for Marie.' Before I could ask more, she said, 'So what brings you here? Did Marie send you? Couldn't she come and see me herself?'

I decided to get straight to the point. 'Mrs Walker . . .'

'Call me Kate. Please.'

I paused. 'Kate. Marie went missing last Monday. That is, I went out for the day and when I came home she wasn't there. I haven't seen or heard from her since. None of her friends have seen her either. I'm going insane with worry. And I came here to find out if you've heard from her.'

Her mouth opened and she shook her head. After a moment she said, 'Just like her father. He did the same to me, when Marie was little.'

'Yes, she told me.'

'And I expect she told you all sorts of horror stories about him. About how he used to beat her and beat me.' Bitterness tainted her voice.

'Are you saying it's not true?'

She pursed her lips, revealing the puckered pout of a long-time smoker. 'Her father was a good man. Yes, he used to lose his temper sometimes, but men do. My father was always losing his temper. Marie's so intolerant and blinkered. All she sees is the bad side. She doesn't appreciate that her father always loved her. He doted on her.'

'That's not what she says.'

She tutted. 'Life's not black and white, Richard. Family life, especially.' She laughed humourlessly. 'It's funny. Marie hates her father, and now she's gone and done exactly what he did. Buggered off.'

75

No wonder Marie rarely visited her mother, if she had to listen to her defend the bastard who had made her childhood a misery. I was tempted to get up and leave, but I still had questions to ask. And something made me identify with this woman. We had both been left behind. Perhaps I was as deluded as she was.

'Would you be a good lad,' Kate said, 'and get me a cup of tea? There's a vending machine just down the corridor.'

'OK.' I stood up and made my way to the machine. I bought a tea for her and black coffee for myself.

'Thank you.' She sat up as straight as she could. 'Why are you in here?' I asked, feeling awkward.

'You mean to say Marie hasn't told you? That girl . . .' She looked me in the eye. 'I've just had a mastectomy.'

'Oh . . .' I squirmed. 'I'm sorry, I had no idea.'

'Obviously not. Marie probably didn't think it was worth mentioning.'

'She knew?'

'Oh yes.' Tears welled up in her eyes. 'Where did I go wrong?'

I couldn't believe this. I hadn't even known that Marie had been to visit her mother. I tried to work it out: it must have been just after Andrew's funeral. Why on earth hadn't she told me?

'Did she tell you about her friend Andrew?' I asked.

She nodded. 'Yes she did. She was quite upset, although she didn't really want to talk about it. We talked about me, mostly. The cancer.'

'Is it . . . are you going to be all right?'

She tried to smile. 'Oh yes. I'll be fine. Tough old bird, I am. Tough as . . .'

She trailed off and silence fell over us. I could hear birds outside the window, the distant quacking of the ducks that lived on the hospital grounds.

My mind raced. Marie knew her mother had cancer. What-ever the problems between them, surely she wouldn't vanish deliberately, leaving her mother alone? It made me shudder. It pushed me into thinking that Marie hadn't chosen to vanish. Something had happened to her. But was it an external force, or an internal one? Had the news about her mother, coming so soon after Andrew's death, torn her sanity from its hinges, pushed her over the edge?

'When she came to see you,' I asked, 'did she say anything at all to suggest whether she was planning something? Like going away?'

She touched her forehead with thin fingers and thought. Eventually, she shook her head. 'No, I'm sorry, but I can't think of a thing.' A look of desperation replaced the one of bravado. She clutched my hand, squeezing my fingers until they hurt. She started to cry, her body shaking with the attempt to hold back the tears.

'I need to see her,' she said. 'She's all I've got left. You've got to tell her to come and see me.'

'But I don't—'

She squeezed my fingers even harder. Her grip was shockingly strong. I thought my bones were going to crack.

'You have to find her and tell her to visit me. I need you to promise.'

'OK.' I tried to extricate my hands from her grip. 'Yes, yes of course.'

'Say it. Say you promise. You won't give up. People always give up, they always let you down.'

A nurse appeared and stared at me disapprovingly. Kate's body shook with fresh sobs.

'I promise,' I said. 'I'll find her.'

On the way home I listened to the news on the radio. I kept expecting them to say that the body of a young woman had been found on wasteland somewhere, or discovered by a dog walker. But the world didn't know, let alone care, that Marie was missing.

Approaching my house, I noticed that the front gate was open. As a habit, I always shut the front gate when I go out – a trait that was drilled into me by my dad when I lived at home. To him, leaving the gate open was like inviting burglars into your house. I paused. Had I left it open in my rush to visit Marie's mum? Or . . .

I rushed up to the house, scrabbled for my keys and thrust the door open, shouting Marie's name as I went in. I heard a movement and for a second I felt a pulse of joy, like that moment when you wake from a nightmare.

But it was only Calico, who had jumped down from his spot on the windowsill. I ran from room to room but, of course, she wasn't there.

So who had left the gate open?

It was probably me. Or someone delivering leaflets, or a pack of Jehovah's Witnesses. But there were no leaflets on the doormat and the Jehovahs usually came in the morning. Feeling spooked, I went out into the front garden. It was fully dark now, the stars bright in a clear black sky.

There was a window box on the sill beside the door. Marie had put it there, one of the things she'd done when she moved in, to add a splash of colour and character to the house. I made a mental note that I needed to remember to water it. But as I was about to go back inside, I noticed that the heads of a few of the flowers were broken, hanging as if in shame towards the window. There was dirt on the floor too, just visible in the poor light. It looked like someone had knocked the window box off the sill before putting it back again. Carefully, I lifted it down so I could get a better look.

This window, which looked into the living room, was one of the original features of my Victorian house: a sash window that rattled when it was windy, that let in drafts and noise. It was painted white, and a few weeks before, after Marie had pointed out how shabby it looked, I had given it a fresh coat.

There were dirty fingermarks on the paintwork now. Like someone, having knocked over the window box, had tested the window with muddy fingers to try, unsuccessfully, to open it.

Marie? But she had a key, and knew the window was always locked.

I went round to the back of the house, checking for footprints or other signs that someone had tried to break in. I spotted one immediately: the ladder, which I kept in the garden shed, was poking out of the door.

It seemed pretty clear what had happened: someone had started to pull the ladder out, but had been disturbed or frightened off, quickly making an exit.

Maybe they had been scared off by the sound of my car pulling up out front. They were probably in the back garden when I got home.

I quickly ran to each side of the garden fence, peering over. A dog two gardens away began to bark. Whoever had been here was long gone.

I went back inside and turned all the lights on, nerves jangling like I'd just watched a horror movie on my own. Someone had tried to get into my house. I knew there had been a number of break-ins in the area recently, and I should probably call the police. But I also knew, from reading the reports in *The Herald*, that the police hadn't been able to do anything for the people who had actually been burgled. It would be a waste of time.

No one had got in. Nothing was missing. I was lucky.

But I couldn't help but feel this hadn't been a burglar.

'Was it you?' I whispered. Then I laughed at myself. What was I doing? Talking to Marie like she was a ghost. I needed to do something to shake this spooked sensation. I needed a drink.

———⌣———

Sitting down with my second beer – I had guzzled the first one standing by the fridge, the radio turned up to blast away the creepy atmosphere in the house – I switched on the PC. Earlier, I had held off doing what I was about to do, because it felt like a violation, but now I thought *fuck it*. What other choice did I have? My emotions lurched between anger at her for running off and terror that something awful had happened. Whatever had happened, I felt justified looking at her emails.

She used Gmail, where the password was also 'chorus'. I knew that she would be able to easily access her email wherever she was, as long as she could get online. Would she know that I would be able to access them, that I had guessed her password? If I were her, I would assume my emails were private and would carry on sending emails freely. Within moments, I might know if she was alive and well, and where she was.

Of course it wasn't that easy.

There were dozens of unread emails in the inbox, almost all of them junk. I went back a few pages and got a shock.

I had last seen Marie on the sixteenth of October. All of the emails received before that date had been deleted.

Unless Marie habitually deleted all her emails after she read them, which seemed unlikely, this indicated that her disappearance had been planned. That she had been worried that me or somebody else – the police? – would access them. Unless someone else had done it. Someone else who had, what, forced her to give them her log-in details?

I rubbed my eyes, then opened the first of the only three messages that weren't commercial. The first, dated yesterday, read:

Hey, Cosmic Girl!

Haven't heard from you for aaaaaages! Whatcha doing with yourself? I've just got back from India. Life changed bigtime, babe. Met some Americans in Goa who are going to Roswell next summer. Gonna scale the fence. Asked me to join them. Cool, huh? Mail me and we'll chat about life, everything, nothing.

Love-vibes

Alpha centaur xx

The email address it had been sent from was alpha-c@hotmail.com, which wasn't very helpful. I opened the next email, which had been sent earlier that morning. It was from a Louise Webster:

Hello Marie

I've just heard about Andrew. I can't believe it! He was such an inspiration to me and I can't believe I missed the funeral :(

Please get in touch. Would be great to meet up.

Seeya soon

Louise xxx

The final email, also received today, read:

Hey Marie – how are you feeling, huh? I'm so bored right now I could scream. Thanks for the advice. It really helped. My head's been kinda fucked up lately, since my visitation. I keep remembering little snatches of it. Like, I remember the leader standing over me

81

and another visitor attaching this stuff to my – excuse me – balls and making me come.

I feel kinda cheap but privileged too, you know?? It hurts that they didn't ask me first, they just went ahead and did it. It's rude, I think . . . Though I don't mean any disrespect. I'm sure they know best and there's a reason for the way they do it. Still, it would have been nice to be asked. What are your thoughts on this? Will I see you at the convention on the 19th? I hope so. We can chat then, face to face. That would be a great help.

See you there then,

Buzz

Alpha Centauri. Buzz. Cosmic Girl.

I felt like I'd entered some weird alternative world, a crazy world in which aliens really did visit men in the night and attach stuff to their testicles. Buzz's email address, again unhelpfully, was buzzboy@yahoo.com.

'Will I see you at the convention on the 19th?'

That was the tantalizing line, the only one that gave me any kind of lead.

What convention? Where? Marie often went to conventions, large and small, where she would meet up with like-minded people and talk aliens. She hadn't been to any since Andrew died. But I vaguely remembered that she had some flyers advertising a convention that was coming up. If I could find out its location, maybe I could find Buzz. He might be able to help me.

Maybe Marie herself would be there.

I pulled open the desk drawers and rifled through. I found wads of internet print-outs, pages about abductions and conspiracies, Area 51 and theories about cosmic breeding programmes. I found bank statements and telephone bills, college notes and photographs of Andrew, Kate, Calico and various people that I didn't recognise. I sat and flicked through, page by page, looking hard at every piece of paper, every photo, all the train tickets and receipts that she had hoarded. None of them offered any enlightenment. Nothing jumped out at me and grabbed my attention. By the time I had finished hunting through it was growing dark outside. Dusk fell across the country like a veil of lace. It was time to eat, but I wasn't hungry. I made a pot of black coffee and smoked a cigarette.

I went back to the computer and replied to Buzz, pretending to be Marie. If she looked at her emails from wherever she was, she would see what I'd done. But I didn't care at that moment. I typed:

Hey Buzz – I think I must be going crazy! ;) What conference are you talking about?
  Love Marie

I also googled everything I could think of to try to find the convention, but nothing came up. I went back into Gmail and hit refresh a dozen times, with increasing desperation, hoping Buzz would respond. I was gripped by a kind of mania. I needed to find those flyers.

I was about to leave the desk to start my search when I remembered that I probably now knew Marie's forum name. I went on to the site and was about to enter a search for her name when I noticed that I had a private message sitting in my inbox.

It was from somebody called The Watcher and contained two simple words:

Forget her.

9

I turned the house upside down.

I hunted through every cupboard, opened every drawer. I flicked through books on the shelves, thinking a sheet of paper might fall from between the pages and flutter to the carpet. I looked behind furniture, under the sofa and in the bathroom cabinet. I came across letters and photographs I had forgotten existed. I found a screwed-up ten-pound note behind the stereo. I disturbed a sleeping spider in the cutlery drawer. By the time I had finished downstairs it looked like I really had been burgled.

I tried not to think about the message from The Watcher. I had no idea if he or she knew something or was just, as Marie would say, 'some random', a person interfering, trying to be clever or cool. I had fired back a message asking if he or she actually knew something, and if so, could they please tell me more. I had resisted the urge to tell them to fuck off.

I went into the spare bedroom, a room that contained nothing but junk and cat hair. This was where Calico slept, although right now he was back in his spot on the windowsill in the living room. The spare room yielded nothing. No bounty. No clues.

I moved into my bedroom. I looked at the unmade bed which until recently had been the scene of so much pleasure. Now it felt too big, too empty.

I missed her body so much. Not just sex, but the feel of her beside me, being able to stretch out my arm in the night and touch her. I missed the sound of her breathing in the darkness. I missed waking up and seeing her. I felt lovesick, bereaved, but the not-knowing made it even worse than that. I was tormented.

I opened the wardrobe and, one by one, pulled out all her clothes. I threw them on the floor. I searched the pockets, shook each garment, held them against my face. When every article of clothing lay scattered on the floor I knelt among them and shouted, 'Where the fuck are you?'

I crawled through the discarded innards of the wardrobe towards the bed. It was a divan bed, with doors that slide open to provide storage space. This is where I keep junk: old birthday cards, holiday souvenirs, photographs, letters, schoolbooks, old copies of the *Herald* from my early days, when seeing my name credited beneath a picture was still a thrill. Marie, too, had started to store stuff here.

I rooted through, dragging everything out onto the bedroom carpet. I sorted through the paperwork, finding Marie's birth certificate among other old documents. There was no passport, though I didn't know whether she'd ever had one.

In a folder near the back of the storage space, I found it at last: the flyer. I sat back on my heels, letting out a sigh of relief. I was exhausted, the house was trashed. But here it was at last: what I'd been looking for.

There were a few of them, slightly crumpled, though there was nothing to suggest they had been hidden on purpose. The leaflet featured a photograph of an old-fashioned flying saucer, below the words GALACTICA 99. At the bottom of the page it stated that this was the fifth annual Galactica convention, with guest speakers from across the world, many stalls, films, etc, etc. It was to take place on the nineteenth of October in Camden Town. My heart thumped. This had to be the one.

I started to pack everything back beneath the bed, not bothering to put it away neatly, just shoving it back in. My mind was elsewhere now, planning my trip to the Galactica convention. Among the junk in the bed was some old jewellery that had belonged to Mikage, my old girlfriend, cheap stuff that she had left behind. As I shoved it back in I dropped a ring and it rolled and slipped beneath the bed. There was a gap of about half an inch between the carpet and the bed, just enough for the ring to roll in on its side. I put my fingers beneath the bed to fish it out and felt something there. It felt like the corner of an envelope. I pinched it between finger and thumb and pulled it out. It was an envelope – a brown A4 manila envelope. It was sealed but nothing was written on the front.

I sat on the bed and opened it.

Inside were four black and white photographs. They were of Marie. She was naked. She looked two, maybe three, years younger than she was now. The photographs were very good quality, quite professional looking. I would have been pleased with them myself, technically.

I looked at all four in rotation, over and over. My whole body trembled. My stomach spasmed suddenly and I ran to the bathroom and threw up in the toilet. I rinsed my mouth and walked back to the bedroom, holding onto the wall for support. This couldn't be real. I must have imagined it.

But the photographs were still there, lying on the bed, and they were real. Although when I say real, I mean they existed. Because they were faked. Marie was real – she was there in the flesh, one hundred per cent real, but the pictures had been cleverly manipulated so she was not alone. In the photographs, she appeared to be having sex with an alien.

It was a Grey: the standard image, with the large head, enormous deep-black eyes, tiny mouth, slight body. At first, I couldn't work out if it was someone in a suit, but it looked too realistic. It had to be a computer image, I decided, something created on a machine. Then this image had been cleverly Photoshopped onto the image of Marie.

In the first photograph, the Grey lay on top of her; then she was astride it; the third picture showed the alien with its lipless mouth on her breasts. In the final picture Marie knelt on all fours facing the camera, her face screwed up in mock ecstasy, the alien positioned so that it appeared to enter her from behind, its long fingers stroking her back. Every inch of Marie was on display.

Marie, who would never let me take her photograph.

I shook the envelope, but there was nothing else inside. Questions raced dizzily through my head. Who had taken the photographs? For what purpose? Was this connected to her disappearance? And were there more? I would have to search her computer. Maybe, I thought, there were videos too.

I wanted to tear the pictures up, burn them, wipe them from existence. But I knew I mustn't. I put them back in the envelope. I didn't want to have to look at them. Not yet. I walked downstairs on shaky legs and opened a bottle of vodka. I drank straight from the bottle, until I passed out. My last thought was that at least now I had a photograph of Marie. A dark part of me laughed bitterly, and then consciousness slipped away.

10

I went to the Galactica 99 convention on my own. I would have liked to take a companion, but who? Certainly not Simon, because although his journalistic mind might have been useful there was no way I could let him see the pictures of Marie. I wondered whether I could involve him without showing him the photos, but it seemed too difficult. Instead, I took advantage of his offer of help by phoning him and asking if he could do some research for me. I wanted details about Andrew – biographical details, age, place of birth, schools, jobs, friends. As much as Simon could find.

'Why do you want to know all this?' Simon asked.

'I'm convinced that if I can find out more about Andrew it might help me find Marie. She was so close to him, but she hardly told me anything about him. It was because I was jealous – I didn't want to talk about him. Except for when he was right there in front of me, I tried to pretend he didn't exist.'

'But they weren't shagging, were they?'

'So she said. But what if she was just saying that to stop me getting even more jealous?' There had definitely been something between them. And if I had to take a wild guess to identify who had taken the pictures, I would say it was Andrew.

I had an idea that her disappearance had something to do with Andrew's death. Either because his death had affected her more deeply than I'd realised and had prompted her to run away or – though I hated to think about it – harm herself. Or because something that I was unaware of had happened as a consequence of his death. Had she met someone at the funeral who was involved in all this? Had Andrew and Marie been working on a secret project that she now felt compelled to continue on her own? Did she suspect that foul play had been involved in his death and was out there, searching for the truth? This last one made my head spin. Was I searching for someone who was out there looking for answers herself?

Apart from Simon, I had nobody to help me. Marie's friends were supposedly keeping their eyes peeled. Her mum was no use. And as for my friends . . . well, I had hardly been in touch with any of them since I'd started seeing Marie. I had been so besotted with her, so absorbed, that I had broken contact with the handful of friends that I had. Marie and my work had taken up all of my time and attention. Now I was paying the price.

I was walking into a world I didn't know, and I was doing it alone.

I paid my entrance fee and walked through the double doors of the former concert venue in Camden Town into the main body of the convention. In my right hand I held a slim briefcase that contained the photographs of Marie. The briefcase was locked. I had a horror of the photographs falling into somebody else's hands. But I knew I might have to show them to someone. They were the best lead I had.

I looked around at the tables piled high with merchandise: books, videos, T-shirts, badges, models . . . every piece of alien paraphernalia you could imagine. I walked up the first row of stalls, glancing at books and videos with titles like *Encounters, The Truth About Roswell, An International Conspiracy, Without Invitation.* I flicked through a couple of the books, which were packed with testimonies of people who believed they had been aboard alien spacecraft. I wandered around the hall, my head spinning.

In many ways, it was what I had expected. Get a group of like-minded people together and they will try to sell each other stuff. But I quickly realised that this was just the surface of the convention. This was where the money was. But in order to make any progress I was going to have to locate the hardcore alien obsessives. People like Marie and Andrew. And, I guessed, Buzz, who hadn't replied to the email I'd sent. The Watcher hadn't replied to my message on the forum either. In fact, the original message had been deleted.

I felt like I was dancing with phantoms.

I looked around the hall. Marie and Andrew would not have wasted their time perusing the stalls at these conventions. I knew that. But where would they have been? I had to find the inner sanctum.

I wandered around for another hour, soaking up the atmosphere, flicking through pamphlets, listening in to conversations. I was surprised by the variety of people present. It was a true cross-section of society, from the predictable computer-programmer nerds in cheap glasses to smartly dressed pensioners. There were young couples with babies in tow, suited businessmen, hippies, Goths and people who dressed like me. Ordinary people united by one thing: the belief that we are not alone in the universe. These were the masses Marie had told me about. I wondered how many of them had seen a UFO. How many of them claimed to have been abducted? How many had seen an extraterrestrial? How many wanted to? They paid their ten-pound entrance fee to spend a day among fellow believers, away from sceptics like me. They bought goodies and chatted and exchanged email addresses and Twitter names. I overheard them talking about other conventions, about trips to the States. I listened out for names. Margaret, Roy, Kevin. No Buzz or Alpha Centauri. No references to a Cosmic Girl. Again, I had the thought that this was just the surface of this world. I was going to have to stop listening and do something if I wanted to dig deeper.

An announcement came over the PA: *'Ladies, gentleman and any friends from other galaxies who might have joined us today . . .'* There was a ripple of laughter. *'The eminent UFO research scientist Dr. Jonathan Grimes, PhD, all the way from Boston, will be beginning his lecture on Patterns of Abduction, starting in the lecture hall in five minutes . . .'*

People started to shuffle out through a set of double doors into a hall filled with wooden chairs. I followed them, but remained standing. The seats filled quickly. The audience rustled and murmured until Dr Grimes appeared to a tumult of applause. Just as he was about to start the lecture, I slipped back through the double doors into the main hall, which was now much quieter.

I approached a stall near the centre of the hall. It seemed less commercial than the others. A man sat alone behind piles of photocopied pamphlets. He had long hair, greying at the temples, and thick glasses. He rolled a cigarette with yellow-edged fingers and looked towards the exit.

As I approached he looked up. I smiled and took a cigarette from my shirt pocket. I said, 'I was about to sneak out for one myself.'

He asked someone to mind his stall and accompanied me outside.

He squinted at me through a cloud of smoke. 'You're not in the business, are you? How come you're not in there listening to Dr James?'

'No seats left,' I lied.

The man snorted. Smoke puffed out of his nostrils. 'He's a bullshit merchant anyway. Most of the people here are.'

'I get the impression most of them are in it for the money.'

'Very astute, my friend. Money, money, money. Not enough truth.' He put out his hand. 'I'm Don.'

I shook his hand. 'Richard.' We looked at each other for a moment. I said, 'This is the first Galactica I've been to. I came here to meet a friend of mine, but I haven't been able to find him. His name's Buzz.'

Don shook his head slowly. 'Don't know the guy. Maybe he's upstairs?'

'Upstairs?' For a moment, I thought he meant in space, and suppressed a laugh when I realised he merely meant upstairs in the building.

'There's a gathering upstairs. For the VIPs.' He sounded bitter.

We finished our cigarettes and went back inside.

'How do I get into the VIP area?' I asked

He looked meaningfully at the pamphlets on the table. I got the message. I picked up a few and paid for them. Another ten pounds gone. Don put his hand in the air and waved at a teenage girl who was drinking tea near the exit. She came over. She was no older than sixteen, with copper hair and freckles. She looked me up and down, a slight sneer on her face.

'What is it?' she said.

'Hey, Lottie, meet Richard. Can you take him upstairs? He thinks a friend of his might be up there. Guy by the name of Buzz?'

She sighed melodramatically. 'OK. If I have to.' She walked off towards the exit at a brisk pace and I followed.

'May you find what you're looking for,' Don said behind me.

Lottie showed me a door concealed behind a curtain. She pushed the door open and led me up a narrow staircase. At the top of the stairs was another door. 'Through here,' she said. 'This is the real Galactica. Good luck.'

She trotted back down the stairs, leaving me alone. I felt nervous. My palms were clammy. I opened the door.

I found myself at the end of a narrow corridor. There was a door at the far end and another to its left. As I watched, a young woman came through the door to the left – which, I soon discovered, was the ladies' toilet – and went through the other door. I followed her.

A group of people were sitting around on rickety wooden chairs and old tables.

Some of them were smoking joints or cigarettes, blatantly breaking the law; most of them had alcoholic drinks. A few people looked up at me and then went back to their conversations. The first thing I did was scan the room for Marie, but of course she wasn't there. I wasn't sure what I should do next. While I thought about it, the woman I had followed through the door turned around and said, 'Hello.'

'Do I know you?' she asked, smiling. She was very thin, on the verge of anorexia by the looks of her. To add to this impression she was wearing a Karen Carpenter T-shirt.

'I'm a friend of Buzz's,' I said, trying to sound confident, like I fitted in.

She frowned. 'I don't think I know him.'

'What about Marie Walker? You must know Marie.'

She chewed her lower lip. 'It rings a bell, but I can't place her.' She spoke slowly, dreamily, as if she was on something. Stoned, I guessed.

'Do you come to a lot of these conventions?' I asked.

'A few.' She smiled and suddenly took my hand. 'What's your name?'

I told her.

A look of sheer horror came over her face. 'I'm sorry, but I can't talk to you.'

'What?' Before I could get any sense out of her, she had retreated across the room, where she hid behind a large group of people.

I stood there with my mouth open. These people were weird. *Very* weird. Maybe I should go. But then a man sidled up to me and nodded over to where the anorexic girl had gone. 'Don't worry about her,' he said. 'She's one of the Karens.'

'Pardon?'

He laughed. He was about my age, tall and thin, hair receding a little. 'There's a group of them. They believe that Karen Carpenter was an extraterrestrial who was sent to Earth to teach us how to love each other and heal the world's ills through the power of song. They say that her 'brother' Richard is also from another planet, but that he was sent to sabotage her aims. They've built up quite a complex mythology around it. Your name doesn't happen to be Richard, does it?'

I nodded.

'I thought so. The Karens think that anyone called Richard is evil and is going to want to harm them.'

'That's crazy.'

'Exactly. The kind of people who give us a bad name.' He stuck out his hand and I shook it. 'I'm Oliver. I haven't seen you around before. Are you with somebody?'

For some reason, I instinctively trusted this stranger. I needed to trust someone. 'Actually, I'm looking for someone – my girlfriend. Her name's Marie Walker.' I looked at him expectantly. 'She comes to a lot of these conventions.'

He stroked his chin and frowned. 'No, I don't know the name.' He looked at me curiously.

'She's gone missing,' I said, deciding to be open. I told him the story.

'Have you got a photo?' he asked.

I hesitated. I didn't want to have to show the pictures, but what else could I do? I realised I should have photocopied the pictures and cut out a section just showing Marie's face. Another mistake.

'Is there somewhere private we can go? I've got pictures, but they're rather, um, well. I'd prefer not to show them in public. You'll see why in a minute.'

'How intriguing.' He led me through the crowded room to another door. I felt eyes on my back as we went through the door, but when I turned, nobody was looking my way.

Oliver led me into an empty room that contained nothing but a woodworm-eaten desk and a couple of dusty armchairs. A small window offered a view of the neighbouring buildings.

'Here we are,' Oliver said. 'Why the need for this secrecy?'

I unlocked the briefcase and clicked it open. I took out the photos and handed them to him. He looked through them without changing his amused expression. Then he laid them on the table between us.

It hurt me to look at the photographs. To see Marie's image like that . . . It tainted my memory of her, the times when we had made love, starlight brightening the room, words of love on our lips. The pictures were grotesque and upsetting. And not just that. They bewildered me. Why had they been taken in the first place? Oliver was about to answer some of my questions.

'Alien porn,' he said. 'This is a pretty sophisticated example, although I have seen some that were even better – where you would swear the scenes are real. You can see the joins in these, but only if you look closely.' He nodded. 'I'm impressed. Did you create them yourself?'

'No!'

'But this is your girlfriend? This is Marie Walker?'

'Yes, but I didn't take them. I didn't know they existed until the other day.' I explained how I had found them.

'Shit.' He looked at me carefully, then back at the photographs. He tapped them with an index finger. 'You know, I *do* recognise her. I've seen her around, definitely. Thing is, though, you see so many people at these conventions, and you don't get to know everybody.

95

But yeah, I definitely recognise her. She's very attractive. Shame about her friend.'

I didn't laugh. I said, 'So this alien porn, as you call it . . .' I gestured for him to tell me more.

Leaning closer, he said, 'You know what I was saying about the Karens, that they give us a bad name? There are a lot more people like that. Most of us believe in UFOs and everything that surrounds them for what I would call "pure" reasons. We simply believe that they exist and that they are contacting humankind for reasons that nobody is sure about. There are a lot of theories, and everybody has their favourites . . .'

I interrupted. 'Marie believes that aliens are going to land and take a group of people away as ambassadors for this planet, before revealing themselves to the world and inviting us to join them.'

'That's a common one. A utopian theory – the idea that beyond Earth there is this wonderful society of planets and species where life is perfect. It's the idea of Heaven, basically. There are a lot of religious ideas within ufology. Some people think aliens actually are gods. And to many, this is their religion. They base their whole lives around it. Coming to one of these conventions is like going to church. Going to Roswell or a site where UFOs have supposedly landed or been seen is akin to a pilgrimage. For them, it's like going to see the Turin Shroud.'

I nodded, remembering Pete from the hill, who travelled the world trying to get a glimpse of the thing he so fervently believed in.

Oliver went on. 'The unfortunate thing is that as more and more people have become interested in this whole alien thing, or at least since the internet has made it easier to communicate, the more we've seen way-out and sick beliefs creep in. This alien sex thing is the perfect example. You must know that a lot of people think that the aliens are using us in a vast breeding programme.'

'Yeah.'

'And there have been loads of abductees who have spoken of sexual encounters with extraterrestrials – mostly men, unsurprisingly. They always talk about finding themselves being seduced by some beautiful lady aliens. There's nothing to say that some of them aren't telling the truth, but some people have taken the testimonies of these people and decided to make some money out of it. The internet caters to every conceivable taste. There's even a series of ebooks that have done very well about a well-endowed alien who seduces a young college student and introduces her to his red planet of pain. It's called *Fifty Shades of Greys*.'

I laughed, then looked at the pictures again.

'To some people,' Oliver said, 'this is the height of erotica. Seeing young women being fucked by aliens. There are tons of videos too. Of course, they're even more popular but they are harder to get right than still photos.'

'So you think these pictures are on a website somewhere?'

'If they aren't I'll eat my commemorative "I've been to Roswell" cap.' He stroked his chin. 'There's actually somebody here who knows a lot more about this stuff than I do. Do you mind if I go and get him?'

Oliver left the room. I was bombarded with images of alien-loving perverts sitting in front of their computer screens, ogling pictures of Marie, masturbating over these images of her. Anger rose up in me. I wanted to wire them up to their precious PCs, electrocute the bastards.

And who had taken the photographs? Who had made her do it? Because I had no doubt that somebody must have coerced her. I dug my jagged, heavily bitten fingernails into my palms. The prime suspect was a man who was already dead.

Oliver came back into the room with a guy for whom the term 'pizza face' could have been coined.

'This is Kevin,' Oliver said.

Kevin grinned at me and picked up the pictures. 'Very nice,' he said. 'Your girlfriend, huh? You're a lucky man.'

'Except she's disappeared,' said Oliver.

'Really?' Kevin looked at him, then at me. 'That's really odd.'

'What do you mean?' I said.

He looked at the picture again. 'I recognise this girl. I'm, well, I'm a bit of a connoisseur of this stuff.' He said this like it was something to be proud of. 'I've got loads of stuff at home that I've downloaded over the last couple of years. I know most of the girls that they use in these pictures. Not personally – just to look at. And I know a lot of the people who are in the business. Most of them are in America.'

He went on. 'The weird thing is that one of the English girls who's in a whole load of the pictures – she's one of the top girls – went missing recently as well. Her name's Cherry Nova. That's not her real name, obviously. A call went out on the Net a couple of weeks ago – has anyone seen Cherry? She's vanished from the face of the Earth.'

We all looked at each other.

Kevin picked up the photographs again. 'There's something really familiar about these pictures. Maybe I've got copies of them at home. We can get the Tube there now if you want. I can show you my collection. I might have some more pictures of your girl-friend.' He traced Marie's naked, black-and-white outline with a dirty finger. He was foul, but I needed every bit of help I could get.

He said, 'You know, she really is gorgeous.'

He licked his cracked lips and I snatched the photographs back. I dropped them into the briefcase and snapped it shut. I took a deep breath and counted to ten. Then I said, 'Let's go.'

11

Kevin lived in a flat above a newsagent in a street that was hidden away between Trafalgar Square and Covent Garden. The rent must have been astronomically high. As he showed me up the stairs into the flat I asked him what he did in the way of work.

'I'm a programmer,' he replied.

I should have guessed.

The flat was a disgrace. MDF bookshelves were stacked with DVDs, many of the discs separate from their boxes, dribble-streaked mugs nestled among them. More DVDs were scattered around the floor, along with computer and girlie magazines, mould-lined takeaway cartons, dirty glasses and dozens of cables, like an exploded snake's nest. A large brown stain took pride of place on the rug – it looked like he had dropped a whole curry and not bothered to clean it up. The room smelled of cream cheese and dust.

'Right,' said Kevin. He booted up the PC and invited me to pull up a chair beside him. While he waited for the menu to appear he squeezed a whitehead that throbbed on his chin and wiped it on his jeans.

'How long have you been into . . . all of this?' I asked.

'Since I was six or seven. That's when I was first abducted by visitors.' He paused as if he was waiting for me to express disbelief.

When I didn't respond, he went on: 'They came while I was in bed. I remember seeing these funny little men – that's how I thought of them at that age – standing around my bed, and then they took me aboard their ship. They took my pyjamas off and poked and prodded me. They had long fingers like in *E.T.*, and I remember one of the funny men putting his finger in my anus.'

Oh God. Another story of personal pain. I didn't want to hear it.

'Afterwards, they returned me to my bed as if nothing had happened. This went on until I was about twelve or thirteen. They'd come every few months. I looked forward to it. They told me I was special, that I'd been chosen. They hypnotised me so I couldn't remember most of what happened, but I know that afterwards – after they'd returned me to my bed – I would always feel happy. I guess they made me feel wanted. Then they stopped coming for a while and I was mortified. I thought I'd never see them again.'

As he spoke his fingers flickered over the keyboard, clicking into different screens, typing in passwords.

'Then they came back and I was so happy.' He smiled, displaying his crooked teeth. 'I was fourteen by then so I was sexually mature. They told me they wanted my seminal fluid. They said it was a valuable commodity where they came from, and that mine was really good quality. They collected it during sex . . .'

I interrupted. 'What did you say?'

'I said they collected it during sex.'

I drew back. 'You're claiming that you've had sex with aliens?'

'Yes.'

'Female aliens?' I asked.

He looked at me like I was an idiot. 'They were polysexual.' He giggled. 'It was amazing. Completely out-of-this-world. After you've had sex with visitors, sex with people just doesn't compare. Once you've had Grey, faithful you'll stay.'

I gawped at him.

'The visitors would come every month, regularly. They were the happiest days of my life. Because after my sixteenth birthday they didn't come any more. I looked out for them, waited for them every night, but they never came back. That was eleven years ago now.'

I felt horribly sorry for him. It seemed obvious that something awful had happened to him when he was young – sexual abuse, at the hands of his father or stepfather or older brother? – which he dealt with using these bizarre fantasies. But what was I supposed to do? Suggest he go to see a therapist? Try to uncover the real memories? This fantasy was probably the only way he could cope.

Kevin nodded at the screen. 'Here we go.' The words THE SHOCKING EVIDENCE flashed across the screen in red. I read:

Here is the incredible EVIDENCE that They didn't want you to see. On the following pages you will see the startling PROOF that ALIENS from other galaxies are visiting Earth and forcing YOUNG WOMEN and GIRLS to take part in UNNATURAL ACTS! These poor women are hypnotized and sometimes even taken to other planets where they are used to BREED human-alien HYBRIDS for who knows what purposes?!

'There are about twenty of these sites,' Kevin said, flicking through. 'I subscribe to most of them. It's all rubbish. I mean, the aliens don't force women to shag them. They enjoy it. It's a privilege.'

The images were similar to the pictures of Marie, although some appeared more professional, and many were in colour. The aliens were usually Greys, with a few Nordic types thrown in for good measure. There were loads of videos too, which appeared to feature small men dressed up as Greys. Their penises looked human, except they were wearing grey condoms. I rubbed my eyes.

'Beautiful images, aren't they?' said Kevin. 'Especially the ones that are real.'

I barely had the mental energy to respond.

He tapped the screen. 'Didn't I tell you? There are real pictures among these. Most of them are fake, but some of these are of actual visitors having sex with humans. That's why I study them so closely, why I collect them. I keep hoping that one day I'll see a picture of the visitors that seduced me.' He sighed. 'You see, Richard, we're actually quite alike, you and me. We're both searching for our lost love.'

I was speechless.

'Ah,' he said, pointing at the monitor. 'That's Cherry Nova.'

The picture displayed was of a large-breasted woman with pillar-box-red hair straddling a Grey. 'She's my favourite human,' Kevin said.

'Who actually runs these sites?' I asked.

'Lots of different people. Some of the pictures come from America or Europe, some from Japan. This site is British, though. Cherry's one of the top English girls. Or she was, anyway.' He pointed to the corner of the screen. The logo read *Planet Flesh*. 'They're based in Brighton. That's just along the coast from you in Hastings, isn't it?'

I nodded.

Kevin accessed more sites. I was sure I would be confronted by a picture of Marie at any moment, but there were none.

'That's really strange,' he said. 'I was sure I recognised her.' He drummed his fingers on the desk beside the mouse. 'Maybe I've got hard copies of the pictures. I keep a box of my favourites under my bed. Wait here and I'll go and have a look.'

He went off to his bedroom. I dreaded to think what it smelled like in there. Precious seminal fluid, probably. I smoked a cigarette while I waited. A few minutes later Kevin burst through his bedroom door clutching a sheet of paper which he waved at me. 'I found it!'

He handed it to me and sat back down. It was the picture in which the alien was behind Marie. The one I hated the most.

There was a date in the corner – the image had appeared online two years ago. 'Look,' said Kevin, 'these appeared on the Planet Flesh page. The same page that Cherry Nova always appeared on. Shit! Are you thinking what I'm thinking? This is really exciting!'

I stood up and pushed him off his chair. He landed on his back on the filthy carpet. In a flash I was astride him, and I put my hands around his throat and started to squeeze.

'Exciting? *Exciting?*' I yelled. 'This is my life! My fucking life!' All of my pent-up fury and frustration surged through me. Kevin gasped for air, his eyes nearly popping out of his head. He made a horrible choking sound and grabbed my wrists. He dug his finger-nails into my flesh. The pain broke the spell I was under and I let go.

He stared at me, rubbing his throat. 'Get out,' he croaked.

'I'm sorry . . .'

'Get out!' he cried. 'You're a maniac.'

I picked up my briefcase and walked backwards away from him, repeating my apologies. He started to sob. I opened the front door and made my exit.

Outside, I flattened myself against a wall, gasping for breath, afraid.

Afraid of what I might have done to him. But more than that: terrified of what this search for Marie was doing to me.

———〜———

On the train home, my mobile rang. It was Simon.

'I've got that information you wanted about Andrew. Shall I pick you up at the station? What time's your train due in?'

Simon was waiting in his car outside Hastings station, the radio turned up so loud I could hear the thump of the bass as I approached. I opened the door and climbed in. The interior of the car smelled of gherkins and fries. It had been raining on and off all day; raindrops drummed on the windscreen; the wipers squeaked back and forth.

Simon turned the radio down and pulled a sheet of paper out of his pocket. 'OK,' he said. 'Andrew Jade.' He paused and looked at me. 'Are you all right? You look like shit, mate.'

'I'm OK,' I said.

He nodded, impatient to share his news.

'I found out some good stuff, but I don't know how much any of it is going to help.' He rustled the paper. 'He was born in Eastbourne on March seventeenth 1967. He seems to have lived in Eastbourne all his life. Went to the local comprehensive. Left at eighteen with three A-levels and went to Sussex University where he read geography . . . He was an only child, it seems. There's no record that he was ever married. In fact, his name hasn't appeared in the paper since he graduated.'

'Apart from our piece.'

'That's right. I got a friend at the DSS to check his benefits history. He signed on for a couple of years after university, then got a job.' He smiled. 'You'll like this. He worked in a camera shop for years. Seems he was something of a camera buff.'

'But he never mentioned that. Surely he would have?'

Simon pulled a face. 'I'd have thought so too. I went over to the camera shop this morning. It's still there, in the back streets near the Arndale Centre. An old bloke called Saul runs it. I asked him if he remembered Andrew Jade and he nearly threw me out of his shop. I could tell that Andrew wasn't exactly well-liked by this bloke so I pretended I was a debt collector trying to find him. That worked a treat.'

He turned the windscreen wipers off.

'Andrew worked for Saul for ten years. Apparently he was really good. Although, get this, Saul said he had some weird ideas. He said Andrew used to go on about flying saucers and space invaders and all that. It gave him the creeps. According to Saul, Andrew was always being visited by these "nutters" who would bring in photos of UFOs and want them developed immediately. Saul didn't mind, he said, because it was extra business.'

I said, 'So he was interested in UFOs at least twelve or thirteen years ago.'

'Yeah. And that's not all he was interested in. One night Saul left Andrew working late on his own. Saul had to go to a council meeting or something. He did go on about it at great length, but I didn't really listen. Anyway, after the meeting, he remembered that he'd left that day's takings at the shop so he had to go back and collect them. That's when he caught Andrew.' He smirked. 'Remember, this was in the days before digital photography went mainstream. According to Saul, Andrew was in the darkroom, developing a load of "mucky pictures".'

'My God!'

'Yeah, that's what I thought. Although I always thought Andrew looked like a creep.'

'What . . . what kind of pictures were they?'

'Well, I don't know what Saul's idea of mucky is, but it sounded like the pictures weren't just of naked women. It wasn't like the stuff you see in *Playboy*. From what I could gather they were of people fucking. Saul sacked Andrew on the spot and told him to take his filth with him. And that was the last time he saw him. Although he did see our story in the *Herald* this summer, and he says he remembers thinking that Andrew hadn't changed: that he was still a weirdo.'

Had the pictures been of alien porn? It wasn't a subject I could raise with Simon. I didn't want him to know about Marie being in such pictures. I wouldn't tell him unless it was absolutely necessary. Later that evening I would tell him everything else, just leaving out the bit about the world of alien pornography and my encounter with Kevin.

'After that, I can't find any trace of what Andrew did for a living. He didn't go back on the dole. If he had another job then I don't know what it was. Maybe he made a living from his consultancy thing. Did Marie ever say how she and Andrew met?'

'They met through their interest in UFOs. But I don't know exactly how or when.'

Simon looked thoughtful for a moment. 'You know, I reckon you're right. Andrew's death and Marie's disappearance have got to be linked. Even if it's just that she's done a runner because she's so grief-stricken. Are you sure they were never, you know, shagging?'

I sighed. 'No. No, I'm not sure. I'm not sure about anything anymore.'

There was a brief pause during which all I could hear was the rain on the windscreen. 'That was all I could find out, anyway. I checked the electoral register for his address, but he wasn't on it. I could try and check his Council Tax records, but that's pretty difficult.' He laughed. 'Fucking Data Protection Act. I'm going to have to get some more contacts like my one at the DSS. You know, I'm enjoying this. Investigative journalism. It's what I've always wanted to do. Like you and your flash photos for the *Telegram*.'

He saw the way I was looking at him and put his hands up.

'Hey, I'm just saying, that's all. I know you're not enjoying any of this. Neither would I. Although I wouldn't mind if Susan vanished into thin air right now. Talking of which, I've got a favour to ask.' He coughed.

'What is it?'

He nodded at the back seat. A grey leather suitcase lay there.

'I've been kicked out,' he said. 'Can I come and stay with you? Just for a few nights, until I find myself a flat? I figure you owe me a favour.'

The thought of Simon staying in my house was horrifying. He was such a slob. But he had helped me, and maybe I could use the company . . .

'What have you been up to?' I asked. 'You've been having an affair, haven't you?'

He coughed. 'Well, yeah, I've been seeing this girl. Cassandra. Works on the media sales team . . .'

'You idiot. Can't you stay with her?'

'Uh-uh.'

'Why not?'

'Her boyfriend wouldn't like it.'

I laughed, even though I knew it wasn't really funny.

'And it's over now, anyway. The ironic thing is that Susan found out the same day Cassandra dumped me.'

'How unfortunate.' I sighed. 'OK. You can stay. But just for a few nights.'

'Nice one.' He grinned. 'You're a true mate.'

After we got back to my house, and while Simon made himself comfortable (unpacking his suitcase, grumbling about having to sleep on a futon, inspecting the contents of the fridge), I made a few phone calls.

I phoned the Conquest hospital and asked after Kate Walker. 'She's had her operation and she's doing well,' said the nurse. I hung up before she could ask me any questions.

Next I called Kathy. 'Any news?' I asked.

'Oh God, no, nothing. I'm so sorry . . .'

Finally, I phoned the lecturer I had spoken to; the man who headed Marie's computer course. He hadn't heard anything either.

I went upstairs and took a bath. Calico sat on the rug beside me and miaowed. He was probably asking me why I was letting a strange man stay with us.

'Don't worry,' I said. 'He won't eat your cat food. At least, I hope not.'

I went into the bedroom and dried myself. I looked at myself in the mirror. I had lost weight. You could see my ribs. I hadn't been this skinny since I left school. My cheekbones had become more prominent, the circles around my eyes deeper. I looked like a junkie.

I got dressed and went into the spare room, which doubled as my office.

My cameras were lined up on the table. Examples of my work were tacked to every surface. Portraits and seascapes and nature shots and news shots. The photograph that had first attracted Bob Milner's attention took pride of place – the red-faced policemen chasing the crook. And there were prints of my *Telegram* pictures. They were due to be published very soon. It should have been a momentous occasion, something to be proud of, preceded by a sleepless night. But it held no excitement for me now. I was unable to gather an ounce of enthusiasm.

I crossed the room to the cupboard that was set into the far wall. In a cardboard folder beneath piles of dusty exposures, I found what I was looking for. I took the pictures out and studied them, nodding to myself. They were just as I remembered.

I put the folder back and went downstairs. Simon was eating pizza. 'Want some?' he asked, offering me a slice.

I poured myself a vodka and Coke and lit a cigarette. Then I made one final call, to Bob Milner, the *Herald*'s editor.

'Yes?' he answered in his gruff voice.

'Bob, it's Richard. I'm just phoning to let you know: I quit.' I dropped the receiver back into place and took in a lungful of smoke.

Simon looked up at me, his mouth open. I could see the half-chewed pizza on his tongue.

12

I couldn't sleep that night. My head was too full of questions and images: those pornographic photos, the fight with Kevin, the way the strange 'Karen' had stared at me at the conference. All this, mixed up with anxiety over whether I'd done the right thing quitting my job. I hadn't put much thought into it. I only knew I needed all my time to search for Marie. I told myself that, when all this was over, the lack of a steady pay cheque would prompt me to pursue my dreams, to make sure the *Telegram* commission wasn't a one-off. When money started to run out, I would be forced to find work.

I opened one eye to check the time on the bedside clock. Three a.m. I had a vague memory of Marie telling me this was the most common time for alien visitations. And at the exact moment that I thought this, I heard a noise downstairs. A thump and click, like someone closing the front door.

I jumped out of bed and quickly pulled on my jeans and a T-shirt. At the top of the stairs, I called down, 'Simon?'

I could hear someone moving about in the kitchen, opening drawers, shutting cupboard doors. I jogged down the stairs tentatively, calling Simon's name again. But as I neared the bottom step I heard faint snoring coming from the living room. Simon's snoring.

I froze. Did I have a weapon upstairs? I scanned each room in my mind. There was a heavy vase in the spare room, a small pair of scissors in the bathroom. I couldn't think of anything else, though. I was so panicked that my brain couldn't focus. I was trapped between fight and flight, my reptilian brain letting me down at this crucial moment.

Before I could decide what to do, a man came out of the kitchen. He was dressed in dark green, with heavy boots. He had a balaclava over his head.

He turned and saw me.

'Simon!' I shouted, as loud as I could. The intruder looked towards the living room door, then back at me, hesitated – then ran towards the front door, yanking it open and escaping before I could catch him.

I ran into the living room, shaking the still-snoring Simon and yelling his name.

'What? What is it?'

'Get up! There was someone in the house. He's just run out the front door. I need to catch him.'

Simon sprang into action, pulling on his trousers and shoes, and the two of us ran out into the street. The man in the balaclava was just visible on the corner of the street.

'Come on!' I shouted, and Simon and I sprinted after the man. Adrenaline flooded my body, overcoming the burning in my lungs. Who was the intruder? What was he looking for? Could he lead us to Marie?

We reached the corner and looked around. The man was now at the end of this street, which led to the West Hill, an expanse of green with the ruined castle at one end and a path down to the Old Town at the other. Steps led down to the seafront. Just before the castle there was also a rugged cliff-face, with rocks that formed a kind of natural climbing frame down to sea level. The intruder would have several options and plenty of places to hide. We needed to reach him while he was still in the open.

Panting, with Simon lagging behind me, we reached the end of the street.

'I'm going to puke,' Simon said.

I ignored this. 'Can you see him?'

I ran across the road. There was no one around, no cars. Here in the dead of night, no one stirred.

'Where the hell has he gone?' I asked the cold air.

A pair of seagulls took flight over to the right, near the rocks. Had they been disturbed? 'This way,' I said to Simon, who followed me at a jog as I ran towards the cliff.

There was a flat-roofed café on the level below me and I thought the intruder might be hiding in its shadows, so asked Simon to check. While he walked towards the building I carried on to the rocks.

I peered over the edge. There were plenty of nooks and crannies below. Places to hide. The sandstone glowed eerily in the moonlight.

'I know you're there,' I called, forcing myself to sound confident. 'You can't get away. We've called the police. They're on their way.'

I heard a scuffling sound below. At that moment, Simon arrived. 'No one by the café.'

I put my finger to my lips and pointed downwards.

'He's down there,' I mouthed.

Simon nodded to show he understood.

'He's not here,' I said loudly. 'Let's go home.'

We waited.

About thirty seconds later, I heard scuffling again, and the man emerged from the crevice he'd been hiding in, onto a narrow ledge. He was still wearing the balaclava. From where we stood we could see him but, because of the overhang above him, I was sure he wouldn't be able to see us.

'One of us should go down to the bottom,' I whispered. 'If you go down the steps by the café, you'll be at the bottom before him, if he climbs down.'

'Why me?' he asked.

'You're bigger than me. More likely to be able to restrain him.'

'True.'

He jogged away and I considered my next move. As a kid, I had spent many weekends and holidays climbing up and down these rocks. Although it was dark and I hadn't set foot here for years, I felt sure that my body would remember which way to go, where to place my feet. Besides, the moon cast enough light to be able to see.

I clambered down onto the next ledge, then moved to the right, clinging to the smooth rock where generations of teenagers had carved their initials. Mine would be here somewhere. I was still above the man who had broken into my house. He hadn't moved.

I edged closer, slipping down another rock, my feet finding purchase in dents in the rock-face. I hung on and glanced to my left.

He had seen me.

'Stay there,' I shouted.

He looked left and right, trying to work out which way to go. The easiest route was towards me. In the other direction, the drop was sheer; he would need to be a skilled climber to traverse it without equipment.

Worried he was going to do something stupid, I called out, 'I just want to talk to you.'

This didn't work. After jerking his head left and right again, he chose the difficult exit. He hefted his body over the lip of the rock, holding himself up with his forearms.

And then he fell.

'No!' I shouted.

But there was nothing I could do. I watched with horror as he tumbled down the rock-face, his arms flailing at first, desperately trying to grab on to something, to find purchase.

A second later I heard a sickening crack. Skull striking rock. He hit the ground at the bottom and lay still.

Simon reached him before me, sprinting up to him and kneeling on the ground beside him, grabbing his wrist and feeling for a pulse.

'He's alive!' he yelled.

I descended the cliff as quickly as I could, choosing the safest route, heart lurching a couple of times when my feet slipped. It took me around five minutes to reach the ground. Much of the time I couldn't see Simon and the injured man.

But then I was on the ground, running over to Simon and the prone intruder.

Simon looked up at me. 'He stopped breathing,' he said. 'I tried to give him mouth to mouth but . . .' He hung his head. 'If I'd had my mobile with me . . .'

'There's no way an ambulance would have got here in time.' I heard my own voice but felt like I'd split in two, half of me talking to Simon, the other half stunned by what and who I was looking at.

Simon had pulled the balaclava off. The dead man – the man with the back of his head smashed like a dropped egg – was Fraser Howard. The country ranger.

'Did he say anything?' I asked. 'Before he died, did he say anything?'

Simon looked at me and nodded. 'He said, "She promised me."'

Simon and I left the police station together, blinking in the morning light.

After Simon had told me what Fraser said, I had walked to a phone box on the seafront and dialled 999. The police and an ambulance arrived within ten minutes, taking Fraser's body away while we explained what had happened. Then they took us to the station to answer lots of questions.

It took me a little while to realise that we might be under suspicion of pushing Fraser Howard to his death.

'Why didn't you call us?' they kept asking, until it eventually seemed to sink in that we had left my house at speed, not stopping to pick up our phones. Mine had been charging in the kitchen; Simon's was on the floor by the sofa.

After two hours, at which point I was wondering if I needed to get a lawyer, they told us we could go. Of course, we had been questioned separately and the fact that our stories matched helped us. Simon being a journalist didn't hurt either.

'I'm going to have to call Bob,' Simon said as we waited for a cab to take us back to mine. 'He's going to want me to write this up.'

I shook my head.

'If you hadn't already quit he'd be shouting at you for not getting any photos.'

'What did he mean, "She promised me"?'

Simon shrugged. 'Fuck knows. But he must have been talking about Marie, don't you think?'

'That's the only thing that makes sense. But promised him what?'

13

An October wind whipped through Brighton's North Laines. I walked against it, eyes narrowed to guard against the fine sand that blew in from the beach.

I took the printed Google map out of my pocket and refreshed my memory. I had twenty minutes.

The North Laines is where Brighton's alternative culture peddles its wares. Juggling shops and bead shops; places that sold second-hand books and comics, drug paraphernalia, old clothes and bric-a-brac. Everything but sticks of Brighton rock. I had arranged to meet a man called Gary Kennedy in a pub in the middle of these Laines. I was nervous. But also determined.

I was on a mission.

You're not going to lose Marie. That's what I kept telling myself. I was going to find her. Wherever she was.

Fraser Howard's mysterious last words had made me even more determined. What had Marie promised him? What was he looking for in my house? I needed to talk to his wife – now his widow, I realised with sadness – again. But I had decided to leave it till after the funeral, which was today. In the meantime,

I had this other lead, however weak it might turn out to be, to pursue.

As soon as I had got home from the police station, after showering to wake myself up and remove the grime and sweat from my skin, I had sat at the PC and visited the Planet Flesh site. I sent them a message:

I'm a photographer seeking work. I'm experienced, discreet, and can provide examples of previous work.
I think you will like what I have to offer.

I thought the word *discreet* might help sell me. I needed to enter their world. If my email didn't work I was going to have to go to Brighton and find them physically.

Luckily, that wasn't necessary.

An email came back hours later, asking for an example of my work. I scanned one of the pictures I had taken from the cupboard in the office into the system, then emailed it to the guy who had replied, Gary Kennedy. A couple of hours later I received the message:

Not bad. Let's meet. Bring more samples with you.

I was given the name, the time and the place. I had to wait a couple of days, but now here I was, sitting down opposite Gary. I had told Simon I was going to Brighton to visit the university, which was in nearby Falmer, to see if I could find out any more information about Andrew from people who might have known him there. I wasn't lying: I did plan to do this later. But I couldn't tell Simon about my other engagement, and therefore nobody knew where I was.

'Richard Thompson,' I said, offering my hand. Gary took it and shook it firmly.

He was in his early forties, broad-shouldered with cropped hair. He had a deep suntan and a faint scar below his left eye. He looked like a hard man, but when he spoke he was eloquent and articulate with a private-school accent. This accent only added to the sense of menace that emanated from him. If a shark could assume human form and put on a suit, Gary Kennedy would be the result.

'Mr Thompson,' he said. 'Why do you want to work for us?'

I leant forward, going into interview mode. 'Because I love the material on your website. The quality is so much better than other sites in your space. Some of them are so amateurish. But yours is top stuff. I want to be part of it.'

He laced his fingers together and cocked his head to one side. 'Tell me about yourself.'

'OK. I've done a bit of work for my local paper in Hastings, but I'm bored with it. I've always been interested in the more glamorous side of photography. I like to take pictures of beauty. Beautiful women. Like the example I sent you.'

He licked his lips. 'And you've got more examples to show me?'

'Oh yes.' I lifted my briefcase onto my lap and unlocked it. I looked around. The pub was empty except for the barman and a few elderly drunks. I had scanned and transferred the photos to my iPad, which I handed to Gary.

He swiped through them slowly. I watched his eyes roam across them, a faint smile on his lips. He said, 'I love them.'

'You do?'

'Definitely. They're tasteful. But still sexy. Exactly the kind of thing I'm looking for.'

'Great.'

He handed the iPad back to me. 'I want to take the site upmarket. Less porn, more erotica. Stuff that appeals to women and couples. You know Planet Flesh is just one of our sites and we're expanding all the time so need talent.' He sneered. 'The web is awash with amateur shit but there's still a big market for quality erotica if you do it properly.'

'Sounds exciting.'

I felt a hot flush of guilt as I slipped the iPad back into my briefcase - because the pictures were of Mikage.

I had taken the photographs shortly after we moved in together. It was actually her idea. She wanted pictures of herself that she could look back at when she was older. 'I want to be able to look back and say, "Wasn't I something?" And it will be something that we can share,' she said. Mikage never lacked confidence.

I didn't argue. I took the photographs in our bedroom. They were beautiful photographs. Mikage had a fantastic body, toned and waif-like, a little taller than most Japanese women. They were black-and-white, very arty, erotic and explicit. She lay naked on the futon, a fuck-me stare aimed at the camera; or she stood in a demure and innocent pose by the window. I remembered that we had both been very turned on during the shoot, that we'd had the best sex we'd ever had afterwards. Mikage could have been a model. The lighting was perfect, the focus just right. I was very proud of them.

When we split up, Mikage had taken the photographs with her and deleted the files. But, unknown to her, and to my shame, I had had a set printed, which I kept. I had actually forgotten they existed. They sat in the cupboard, gathering dust. I would have destroyed them after meeting Marie, but the thought never entered my mind. I was glad now that I hadn't. Though if Mikage ever found out I was showing them to other people, that I was using them to find work with a pornographer, she would kill me. Actually, she would torture me, and then kill me. And I would deserve it. I was only able to do this because I knew I would never let Gary or anyone else publish the pictures. After this, I would destroy them and delete them from my iPad.

Gary finished his pint.

'You're very lucky actually,' he said. 'Until very recently we had a regular photographer who did all our work. But he's no longer on the scene.'

'What happened to him?'

'He died.'

'What was his name?' I asked casually. At least, I hoped I sounded casual.

'Jade,' he replied. 'Andrew Jade.'

I had to put my drink down because I was afraid Gary might see that my hand was shaking.

'And to make matters worse,' he said, 'our best model has disappeared.'

'Cherry Nova?'

'That's right.' He looked at me suspiciously.

'I saw the appeal on the site, asking for information,' I explained. 'I'm a big fan of hers.'

'Oh yeah, of course. Aren't we all. She's a lovely girl. I discovered her myself, actually. As soon as I saw her I knew she'd look great on our website. And I've got to hand it to him, Jade did wonders with her.'

'And you've no idea what's happened to her? The thing is, I'd really like to work with her myself.'

Gary shook his head. 'I haven't seen her since the middle of October.'

My pulse accelerated. Marie had vanished on sixteenth October.

'I was extra gutted because she had an appointment with me.' He winked. 'If you know what I mean.'

I smiled my best fake smile. 'I'm with you. Perk of the job, right?'

He stood up and gestured for me to follow him. Into the Gents. He stood in front of a urinal and unzipped. I looked the other way.

'Are you free on Friday?'

'I think so.'

'Good. I'd like you to meet a couple of the models. If you come over to my office on Friday I'll introduce you to them and we'll discuss schedules, money, etcetera.'

He zipped up and stuck out his hand. I shook it, forcing myself not to hesitate.

'I think we're going to enjoy working together, Richard. We're on the same wavelength.'

He gave me the address of his office – it was actually in his house – and I left the pub, my briefcase under my arm.

I felt a little shaky, queasy. I couldn't believe my meeting with Gary Kennedy had gone so well. It had been almost too easy. But I also felt dirty, and not just because of what I'd done with Mikage's photos. I had just been hired by a pornographer. I was getting deeper into this world. This alien world.

I went straight to a public toilet and washed my hands.

———

I walked back uphill to the train station. It was just two stops to Falmer and the campus of Sussex University.

It was near the beginning of the new term. All around me were wide-eyed freshers, eighteen years old, away from the protective arms of their parents for the first time, three years of freedom ahead of them: three years of late nights, cheap beer, drugs, casual sex and the occasional lecture. God, I envied them.

I had become almost as obsessed with Andrew as I was with Marie. I was convinced their fates were intertwined, that any clues I could find about his past would help me understand Marie better. I had become convinced that he had some kind of hold over her. If I could understand him, really get to 'know' him, then maybe I could understand more of what made Marie tick. And what made her vanish.

First, I went to the library. I wanted to see if they had a copy of Andrew's dissertation, but the librarian told me they only kept a select few and, after consulting her computer, confirmed that Andrew's wasn't among them.

'I know that name, though,' she said. She was in her late fifties, I guessed. 'Andrew Jade. Hmmm . . .' She gave me a suspicious look and I made my excuses and left.

I asked a passing fresher for directions to the geography department. She consulted a friend and together they managed to point me in the right direction. I found it without too much difficulty.

At the end of the corridor was a door marked 'Head of Department – Ronald Richardson' which stood ajar. I hesitated for a heartbeat, then knocked. A gruff voice called, 'Enter.'

The room's occupant was in his mid-fifties. He was wearing an expensive-looking suit and appeared more like a City businessman than my bearded, elbow-patched mental stereotype of a geography lecturer.

The screen saver on his PC showed an array of tropical fish drifting languorously from left to right. The window gave an impressive view of the campus, and the atmosphere was tranquil and academic. I could imagine relaxed seminars and discussions taking place in this room, the benevolent lecturer guiding his young undergraduates towards wisdom. I looked around at the bookshelves: they were crammed, sagging in the centre, dust gathered on the highest volumes. Not for the first time, I felt a pang for the life I had missed out on, the years I'd never had. I liked it here, and immediately warmed to Ronald Richardson.

It made me feel guilty that I was going to have to lie to him.

He waved a hand in the air and peered at me, waiting for me to introduce myself. I told him I was a first year and could see that he was trying to place me. No doubt he had addressed the new crop of geography freshers, but I was banking on him not knowing them individually. Hopefully, he wouldn't have a list of names to hand. I worried for a moment, but then he said, 'Ah, one of our mature students. Always a valuable asset to the course. How are you settling in?'

'Fine. Really enjoying it, in fact.'

'Good, good.' He gestured for me to get to the point.

'Um . . . You might think this is a weird one but I recently met this guy . . . this chap who used to study here. He told me I should look up his dissertation, that I'd find it helpful.'

He raised an eyebrow and waited for me to continue.

'The library doesn't have a copy. And, well, I know it's a long shot but thought I'd ask if there are any records . . .' I trailed off. I knew my story sounded pretty unlikely.

'What was this student's name?'

'Andrew Jade.'

He took off his designer reading glasses and stared at me. 'Andrew Jade. Why are you *really* asking about him?'

From his tone it was clear that Richardson was not a fan of Andrew's. I decided to change tack.

'OK. I apologise. I'm not really a student here. I'm actually a private detective. I've been hired to look into Andrew Jade's past.'

His eyebrows lifted. 'Really?'

I gambled that the professor wouldn't know about Andrew's recent death. 'Yes. My client's daughter is engaged to Jade and her father, who is very well off, wants to know about his past. Make sure he's not a criminal or a gold-digger.'

'Goodness.' He paused, then barked out a laugh. 'I ought to throw you out. And normally I would. But Andrew Jade . . . well, let's just say I feel sympathy for your client.'

I waited.

'Will Jade know I spoke to you?'

'No, sir. I operate with absolute discretion.'

He settled back in his chair, a smile on his face like someone who had waited a long time to settle scores.

'Hmm. I remember Andrew Jade well. I wasn't the head of department then, just a mere tutor, but if I had been head there's no way I would have allowed the sort of thing he got up to.' He lowered his voice conspiratorially. 'We had a few trendies here in the eighties – I'm sure you can imagine the sort – and all sorts of garbage was tolerated.' He shook his head.

'So Jade was a bit of a maverick, was he?'

'Yes. There were a few of them. Andrew Jade was one of a small number of students who saw university as a place not to study but to take drugs and develop bizarre belief systems.'

'Surely that's not rare?'

'No. But he was part of a group that I can only describe as fanatical. They had their own society which operated outside the Student Union and university guidelines. They wanted to impose their beliefs on everybody else.'

He paused, like I wasn't going to believe what he had to say.

'Don't tell me,' I said. 'Aliens.'

He breathed with relief. 'Is he still into all that nonsense?'

I nodded. I was quite enjoying playing the part of a private detective.

'In that case, your client definitely needs to know about Jade's past. Goodness me. He and his cronies got up to some *very* strange things, like campaigning for the abolition of negative images of extraterrestrials. They wanted the English department to get rid of all its copies of *War of the Worlds*. They went into Brighton and marched up and down outside a cinema that was showing some silly film in which aliens invaded earth. At first we treated it as a bit of a joke. But then they started to cause trouble on the course.'

'In what way?'

'They said that the geography degree was – how did they put it? *Terracentric*.'

'You mean *Earth*-centric?'

He nodded. 'Remember, this was back in the days when political correctness was at its most rampant. The days of *Baa Baa Green Sheep*. He and this girlfriend of his, Samantha something, started to accuse the lecturers and tutors of teaching falsehood, denying the impact of aliens on Earth's geography. For example, they said the Grand Canyon was created by a spacecraft crashing in to the Earth. A great tragedy, they called it. They told us that most of our theories about the formation of the continents were wrong.'

I was immediately reminded of reports I'd read about Christian groups who denied Darwin's theory of evolution.

Richardson went on. 'They picked on other students, told them they were blind puppets, caused a lot of bad feeling. A lot of the students really hated them. Jade got beaten up once, got a couple of ribs cracked. I can't say I felt much sympathy for him. Most of us, staff and students, wanted him and his girlfriend off the course. But the Union got involved, along with all the do-gooders and free speech merchants, and we had to let them stay.'

'And what happened after that?'

He shrugged. 'Nothing of note. Jade carried on being a nuisance, continued his studies, left us with a third, I believe. That was the last I heard of him. And thankfully, that was the last we heard of terracentrism.'

I thanked him, reassuring him again that this wouldn't get back to Andrew, and left. Before I went, he remembered the name of Andrew's girlfriend. Samantha O'Connell. I wondered where she was now. Was she worth tracking down? The thing was, I vaguely recognised her name, but couldn't remember where from.

When I got home, Simon was slumped on the sofa drinking a can of lager.

'What's up?' I asked.

'Oh. Nothing. Just been getting grief from Susan. Plus I can't get Fraser Howard's face out of my head. The way his head was smashed—'

I held up a hand. 'Please.'

'It's weird. Being the person who heard his last words. I just sort of gawped at him. My face was the last thing he ever saw.'

I shook my head. 'Poor bastard.'

I noticed that Simon had cleaned up. He had even tidied the bookshelves and cleared a space for Marie's ufology books, which had previously been piled up beneath the desk. As I glanced along the spines a name jumped out at me.

Samantha O'Connell.

So that was where I knew Andrew's ex-girlfriend's name from.

I took one from the shelf and looked at the picture on the dust jacket. Platinum-blonde hair, gold-framed glasses, a striking face.

I held the book and wondered. While I was thinking, Simon said, 'Guess who else I spoke to today.'

I waited.

'Mrs Howard.'

'Fraser's widow? What about?'

'Well, I wanted to offer my condolences, of course. And ask if she wanted to be interviewed for the paper.'

'You're unbelievable.'

'Whoa, hold up. I wasn't doing it for me. You want to talk to her, don't you? Well, the interview's all set up. You're going to pretend to be me.'

14

I dreamt that the phone was ringing.

I turned onto my front and hugged the top that Marie used to wear around the house, held it tightly, buried my face in its softness, imagined it was her flesh. I opened my mouth and imagined I was kissing her. I saw myself above her, saw the smile on her lips as her thighs parted and I embraced her, entered her.

And the phone rang.

I woke up with an erection and a sense of loss. I reached out and switched on the bedside lamp, screwing my eyes shut against the sudden brightness. When I opened them I saw a long strand of pale red hair beneath my fingers.

It was all I had left of her.

I sat up in bed and looked at my watch. Three a.m. Again. I was wide awake and knew I wouldn't be able to get back to sleep so I lit a cigarette. My no-smoking-in-the-bedroom rule had been broken a week ago, and now cigarette butts were piled high in an ashtray beside the lamp.

A flash of dream came back to me, making me suck hard on my cigarette.

I put on my dressing gown and padded downstairs into the hall, picked up the phone and dialled 1471.

'*You were called today at oh-two-fifty-eight hours. The caller withheld their number.*'

I dropped the receiver like it was hot. It hadn't been a dream. The phone really had been ringing.

Was Marie somewhere out there, sitting by another phone, fingers hovering over the numbers, wanting to contact me? I sat and waited, staring at the phone like a lovesick teenager. I was convinced it had been Marie. Who else would ring at that time, withholding their number? Marie had wanted to talk to me, but after one attempt she had given up. Why? Had she changed her mind?

Had someone stopped her?

I woke up lying on the hall carpet, Calico dabbing my twitching eye.

The Howards' house was in a village just outside Hastings called Pett Level, the kind of place one can pass through without noticing its existence: a pub, a general store, a smattering of houses and cottages, a field full of donkeys and a beach.

The house was in an unmade road. I parked my car beside a shallow stream and pushed open a gate that creaked alarmingly and no doubt served as an early warning system.

Gloria Howard opened the door before I had a chance to ring the bell.

'Who are you?' she wanted to know.

'Mrs Howard. I'm . . . Simon? From the *Herald*?'

She was about fifty-eight, a large woman with the ruined skin of a lifelong smoker. She held on to the door handle as if she was afraid that if she let go she would float away into space. She narrowed her eyes. 'How do I know you're not lying? That you're not one of that lot? One of *his* lot? Have you got ID?'

Great. I was going to have to revert to plan B.

'Who do you mean by "his lot"?' I asked softly.

'Andrew Jade. That little . . . He ruined our lives.'

I looked her in the eye. 'Gloria. I'm not really Simon from the *Herald*, although he did send me.' I spoke quickly before she could slam the door. 'Andrew Jade might have ruined my life too. I need to talk to you about him.'

She stared at me.

'Please. Or we could talk out here?'

Maybe she decided there was something trustworthy about me. Or perhaps she was desperate for someone to talk to. She said, 'All right. You can come in. For five minutes.'

A large golden retriever greeted me in the living room, pressing its wet nose into the palm of my hand. I sat on the sofa and looked around while Gloria made tea in the kitchen. An enormous television dominated one corner of the room; pictures of children and grandchildren lined every surface.

'Everything started going wrong that night Fraser saw the flying saucer,' she said, lighting a cigarette and coughing.

'Was he always interested in that kind of stuff?' I asked.

'No! Fraser never believed in anything he hadn't seen with his own eyes. He always used to say that – show me and *then* I'll believe it. He never believed in God, or UFOs or ghosts or anything like that. We used to have great arguments about it because I'm a Christian. I always tried to get Fraser to come to church with me, especially when we were first married, but he refused. He's a rationalist; puts his faith in science. He said that there was no scientific proof that God existed. And he applied that rule to everything. That's why seeing the UFO shook him so badly.'

'Do you mind if I ask something? Had he been drinking that night?'

She shook her head. 'That was the first thing I asked him. After all, he does like a drink, but he and Barry would never drink on duty. It was afterwards, after they'd seen the lights, that they had a drink, to calm their nerves.'

'I understand.'

Her dog rested its head on her knees and she petted it. 'He had to take time off work because he was so shocked. He kept saying to me, "I saw it, I actually saw it," over and over.' She took a puff on her cigarette. 'It really shook him, to think that there are things that can't be easily explained. He didn't accept that it was a plane or reflected lights or anything except a UFO.'

I nodded. 'He said the same to me, when I met him.'

'He said that he knew he was seeing something beyond scientific knowledge. It frightened him. But then, I'm pretty certain he would have dealt with it, that it would have all blown over if Andrew Jade hadn't contacted him and stirred things up.'

'Jade got to him and filled his head with ideas,' Gloria continued. 'Convinced him that what he had seen was a spacecraft from another galaxy, from some sort of space coalition. I forget what they called it . . .'

'The Chorus?'

'That's it. He told him that the Earth was visited every day by extraterrestrials who were preparing to make contact with humanity. He started coming round here a lot,' she said. 'He brought Fraser books and videos. He wanted Fraser to join this special group he said he was putting together.'

'A group?'

'Yes. Actually, I think he called it a cell.'

She reached for her cigarettes. I gave her one of mine.

'It frightened me,' she said, lighting up. 'I've had friends who have been converted by the Jehovah's Witnesses. It changed them. You see this light come on in their eyes. You remember those maniacs who murdered that soldier in London? Fanatics. They had that look. The same thing happened to Fraser. He talked about aliens and spaceships and all this mumbo-jumbo all the time. And the way he spoke about Andrew Jade? It was like he was some kind of guru. A messiah. Andrew this, Andrew that, he knows the truth. Then it got really nutty.'

I shifted to the edge of my seat.

'Andrew told my husband that when the glorious day came, he would be allowed to join them. It was like listening to one of my former friends talking about the Rapture. Fraser said that if I believed too then maybe I would also be one of the chosen. Otherwise I'd be left behind.'

'Chosen by the Chorus?'

She sighed. 'I don't know. It was all nonsense to me. Annoying nonsense. I didn't even try to understand it.'

Just like me with Marie.

'It felt to me like Fraser was being used. I don't know in what way. Maybe they wanted him as a lookout. They knew that if he saw any more lights in the sky he would go straight to them. I don't know. And then a young woman phoned us and gave us the news that Andrew Jade had been killed!'

'What did she sound like?' I asked eagerly.

'I can't remember. A young woman, that's all I recall. She asked for Fraser so I passed the phone over. All the colour drained from his face and he walked out of the room into the garden. I followed him and when the call ended he was crying. It was the first time I had seen him cry in years. Years.'

She went on.

'After that, he changed. It was as if something came unhinged inside him. I know he tried to get hold of some of the other members of Andrew's crazy group, but he couldn't even find out when the funeral was taking place. It was horrible, Richard. He kept bursting into tears. It was like he had lost his son. I was so worried. I got the doctor out to see him and he said Fraser was suffering from grief-induced shock. He asked me how well Fraser had known Andrew. He implied that they had been lovers. Homosexuals!'

She was crying now, tears running down cracked cheeks.

'I told him to get out of my house. No way was my husband gay. I'd know, wouldn't I? But in a way it would have been easier – at least then I could understand it. But aliens . . . He sat around the house all day reading his UFO books. He barely spoke to me. He started going out at night, to the pub, I thought. The night he died – I thought he must have gone to the pub and hooked up with some floozy.'

She threw her arms around her dog's neck and wept. I didn't know what to do. I put a hand on her shoulder.

And I thought about Andrew, about the portrait of him that was building up. How could I have been so wrong about him? My first impression of him was that he was a nut, but a harmless one. I was jealous of his closeness to Marie, but not wildly so. I was angered by the way he had spoken to the woman who had visited my house – the woman who'd had a miscarriage.

But I had not realised the truth. The picture I had of him now was of someone with power. Gloria said he was charismatic and persuasive. He had sold pornographic images to an internet 'entrepreneur'. He had formed a group at university whose sole purpose was to cause trouble. He was able to convert people to his belief system. And his death had sent shock waves through people's lives: Marie's, Cherry Nova's, Fraser's, Gloria's. Mine. And who else? Were there others out there that I hadn't come across yet, others who were in Andrew's thrall? There must be.

But how could I find them? And would they lead me to Marie? *She promised me.*

Marie must have made some kind of promise to Fraser after telling him about Andrew's death. But what was that promise? Why had it led him to break into my house?

It was clear Gloria Howard didn't know anything else. I sat with her for a while, consoling her. Then I left her in her empty house. I hadn't told her that I was partly responsible for her husband's death, that I had chased him to the rocks. I couldn't bear to think about it. I would deal with the guilt later.

The house was empty when I got home, except for Calico, who was still glued to the windowsill, pining for his lost mistress.

I had to wait a couple of days before my second meeting with Gary Kennedy. I only had one other possible lead to follow: Samantha O'Connell. The author.

I picked up Marie's copy of *The Masterplan* and checked the acknowledgements page. I wondered if there might be a mention of Andrew, a sign that they'd stayed in touch since leaving university, but there were just a number of names that I didn't recognise.

The book did, however, give me her website address and her Twitter name. Both told me she was doing a book signing at Nelson's Books in Charing Cross. It was the next day.

TODAY: BOOK SIGNING BY UFO EXPERT AND BESTSELLING AUTHOR SAMANTHA O'CONNELL

I glanced at the sign as I approached the book shop – and found myself face-to-face with Kevin.

His eyes widened with fear. The last time I saw him he had been lying on the floor of his flat, my thumbprints on his windpipe. I opened my mouth to apologise, to try to make peace, but he turned tail and ran off down the street, splashing through a deep puddle, ignoring my call of 'Wait!'

Shrugging, I went inside. A girl with long pink hair smiled at me from behind a counter where expensive greetings cards stood on a rack beside the till. The shop specialised in 'mind, body and spirit' titles, as well as books about the paranormal, drug culture, vegetarian cookery and left-of-centre politics. I wasn't sure exactly how ufology fitted in with all this. Did believing in UFOs go along with an interest in macrobiotic food and the Alexander technique? I doubted it, but the people who frequented this bookshop all had one thing in common: they were looking for answers, and didn't believe they would find those answers in mainstream culture.

Samantha O'Connell sat behind a table at the back of the shop, a pile of books beside her, a queue of five people in front, each of whom was granted a quick chat, a word of encouragement and a personal inscription to go with their purchase of her latest book.

She wasn't as attractive in real life as she was on her dust jacket, but she had a presence born of confidence. There was a profound intelligence in her eyes, and when she spoke she was animated, her whole face moving to accentuate her words: eyebrows arching, smile broadening, eyes widening. She entranced people, and her fans didn't want to leave their place at the table after she'd signed their copy of her book.

I took my place in the queue and awaited my turn. I wondered what Kevin had been doing here. Probably just a fan.

Samantha looked up at me. She had eyes like Marie: frosted blue. Hypnotic. She opened the copy of the book I'd just bought and asked who to make it out to.

'Can you sign it to a friend of mine? It's a present.'

'Of course. What's his name?' she asked.

I leaned a little closer. 'Andrew. Andrew Jade.'

Her pen skidded across the paper.

She looked up at me, shock and suspicion written all over her face. 'Andrew Jade's dead,' she said finally.

I leant across the table. 'I know. But I want to ask you some questions about him.'

Her voice rose an octave. 'Who are you?'

'My name's Richard. My girlfriend Marie was close to Andrew Jade and now she's disappeared. I'm trying to find her and I think I can only do that through Andrew. Because . . .'

I didn't get a chance to finish.

Samantha stood up and shouted to the girl with pink hair. 'Nicky, get security. This man's bothering me.'

I protested. 'But I just want to ask you some questions . . .'

Samantha waved her arms. 'Help! Help!'

A man emerged from a door behind the counter and rushed over at me. He grabbed my upper arm.

'I was just . . .'

Samantha was wailing, her hands covering her face. What an actress. I tried to pull away from the security man, but his grip was too strong. He dragged me to the door and pushed me out into the rain, giving me a shove. I skidded on the wet pavement and fell onto my side. The man shouted at me then slammed the shop door shut.

I got up, went back over to the window and looked through. Samantha was talking to the girl with pink hair and the security guard, acting like she'd just been through a terrible torment. I wanted to go back inside but what was the point?

I was certain she knew something important.

I could wait till she came out, follow her . . . But then the security guard came back outside.

'If you don't fuck off we're calling the police.'

'All right.' I had no choice. I walked away. I would have to find some other way of getting to Samantha O'Connell.

15

Gary Kennedy lived in a large, detached house in Hove. Ivy crept up stone walls; *koi* swam in an ornate pool beside the drive. I parked and checked the address. Surely this couldn't be the right place?

Gary saw the look of astonishment on my face as I locked my car. 'Welcome to my crib.' He grinned.

I followed him into the front hall. The walls were lined with framed photographs of naked girls, most of them signed: *To Gary, you taught me so much, Love Lynda; To Gary, my body was made for you, Tanya xxx.*

'You've made all this money from online porn?' I asked.

'Erotica, you mean. No, I'm a serial entrepreneur. Started out making DVDs, even dabbled with a magazine at one point. It's all online now, though. I've got twenty-one adult subscription sites and Planet Flesh is actually one of the smallest. It's so niche.' He laughed. 'But we're able to charge a premium because the punters' tastes are so specialist. Same with one of our other sites, Fists of Fury.' He led me up a twisting staircase while I tried not to think about what was on Fists of Fury.

He showed me into his office. I sat at the near side of the desk and he took a seat opposite. On the wall to the left was a poster-sized picture of a naked Cherry Nova, a coy expression on her over-made-up face.

Gary saw me looking at the picture. 'Stunning,' he said.

I nodded.

'It broke my heart when she disappeared.'

'I'm sure.'

The way he was looking at me made me feel nervous. He stared at me for a few seconds more and then leaned back, hands behind his head.

'The talent will be here in a minute. I want you to spend the day with them, get to know them. That way you'll work better together. These are girls I've been using for a while. They're experienced. Professional.'

'Right.'

'Today's just, like, a meet and greet. I've booked a studio for you next week so you can do the first shoot. We'll be making a couple of new movies too.'

If someone had told me twelve months ago that I would be having this conversation I would have wondered what cocktail of drugs they had ingested. For a fleeting moment I considered standing up, walking out, giving in. But I knew I wouldn't be able to rest until I had found her, would never stop wondering about her. Then there was the promise I'd made to her mum. I had to go through with this.

'I take it you've had no word from Cherry?' I said.

He gave me a look that was rather too piercing to be comfortable.

'If only,' he said. 'I was going to make that girl rich. She had real superstar quality, Cherry. You know every now and then a girl from the business crosses over, becomes properly famous? That could have been Cherry.'

His eyes misted over, no doubt at the thought of all the money he was going to miss out on.

'How did you meet Cherry?' I asked. 'You told me you'd discovered her yourself.'

He nodded proudly. 'I met her in a nightclub. Digital – do you know it? Used to be the Zap.'

I said yes.

'This was a couple of summers ago. Maybe three. She was with this other girl, dancing, really going for it. I thought they were dykes at first but they were just doing that thing girls do . . . putting on a show. I watched her all night.'

He stared into space, the image of Cherry dancing with this other girl making him lick his lips.

'Funny thing,' he said. 'That was the night I met Andrew Jade. I was doing a bit of dealing at that time. E, acid, a bit of coke – and this nervous-looking bloke came up and scored a couple of tabs of E. We got talking and he told me he was a photographer. He saw me looking at Cherry and her friend on the dance floor. "I'd love to photograph them," he said. He said he specialised in erotic photographs so of course we got talking.'

The more I found out about Andrew, the more I loathed him.

'Weird bloke,' Gary said. 'A bit older than me, not exactly a silver fox, but he'd managed to persuade a lot of young chicks to take their clothes off for him. When he first told me about aliens I thought he was nuts. But he gave the impression it was like some new religion. And he showed me the earnings potential of this niche. So Jade did me a favour.'

He sighed and looked at Cherry's picture.

I followed his gaze. 'Do you think he had something to do with Cherry's disappearance?'

It was an indiscreet question, a connection that I could only make if I knew more than I was letting on. I instantly regretted it.

Gary narrowed his eyes. 'Why do you say that?'

'I don't know. It's just that you don't seem to have liked him very much.'

He stared at me, and was about to answer when the doorbell rang. 'Ah,' he said, relaxing. 'The girls are here.'

He directed another piercing look in my direction, then got up and went downstairs. I sat at his desk and waited. I felt uncomfortable, sweaty. I lit a cigarette and looked at the bottle of scotch. Maybe I should have accepted.

I smoked the cigarette all the way down before Gary returned. There were two women with him. The first was a bottle blonde of about twenty-one. She had eyes the colour of Granny Smith apples and pale, translucent skin. The other woman was Asian, with cropped black hair and large, sleepy eyes. She looked about nineteen.

'Freya and Safire,' Gary said, indicating the blonde first then the Asian woman. 'Girls, this is Richard.'

I felt as awkward as a virgin visiting a brothel. From the way Freya smiled at me I could tell she could sense my discomfort. But Gary was too busy banging around making drinks and talking about how he was going to turn the two girls into stars to notice.

Had these women known Marie? I still didn't know if the pictures I had found were a one-off, or whether Marie's role as a star of alien porn was an ongoing one. Was that what she was doing now? Had she got sucked into the porn universe? Was she with Cherry?

Gary handed Freya and Safire their drinks and stood up.

'I've got to see a man about an alien,' he announced, roaring at his own joke. 'I'll leave you three to get better acquainted.'

Safire came over to the desk and sat opposite me. She took a ready-rolled spliff out of her inner pocket and lit up, blowing smoke in my direction. She offered me some and, after hesitating for a moment, I thought *fuck it*. I took a deep drag and felt a head rush immediately. It was strong stuff.

'How long have you worked for Gary?' I asked, trying not to cough.

Safire shrugged. 'A few months. We don't work *for* him though. I'm a free agent. I've got a lot of other stuff going on. A lot of other stuff . . .' She trailed off and took a drag on the spliff.

'What kind of stuff?' I asked.

'Like, I'm going to star in a film. This guy I know is going to introduce me to Steve McQueen. You know, the director?'

Freya laughed. 'Safire's one of these deluded wannabe-starlets,' she said to me. 'She thinks porn's a step on the ladder. She hasn't sussed out that it's a dead end yet.'

Safire tutted loudly then closed her eyes, leaned back and continued to smoke, acting like she was alone in the room.

Freya stood up. 'Let's get on with it, shall we?'

She opened a door on the other side of the room and beckoned for me to follow her.

'Is this Gary's bedroom?' I asked.

The room contained a water bed, a couple of lava lamps, a furry rug and mirrors on the walls and ceiling. It was like stepping into a seventies porno.

'This is where Gary films his amateur dramatics,' Freya said. 'See, there's a camera up there. He tapes himself with all of his girls. Calls it a screen test.'

She sat on the water bed and patted the space beside her. 'Come and sit down.'

'That's OK.'

She reached down and unzipped her boots, kicking them across the room. She pulled her top up over her head, revealing a red lace bra.

'What are you doing?'

She tilted her head. 'Are you gay?'

'No. But . . .'

'So what's the problem?'

She held out her hands towards me.

'Is that what Gary told you to do?'

She made a 'duh' face. 'He wanted me to get close to you.'

'I'm sorry. I'm . . . er . . . you're very attractive but . . .'

She found this hilarious and flopped back on the bed, the surface rippling, which made her laugh even more.

'Is it because you're being faithful to Cherry?'

I was so surprised I didn't know what to say.

Freya hauled herself up and laughed.

'What are you talking about?' I said.

'Come on, you can tell me. Gary thinks you're trying to find Cherry. Hey, don't look so shocked. You must have known he'd see through your act. You're not a photographer. You're a private detective, aren't you? You're trying to find Cherry.'

'I think I'd better go,' I said.

I moved to leave but Freya bounced up off the bed and dodged round me, so she was barring my way out.

'If you're trying to con Gary, you're in deep shit. He's dangerous. He won't hesitate to hurt you. He threatened to kill Andrew on more than one occasion. And if you have got something to do with Cherry, then you're dead. He's obsessed with her. Totally in love with the silly bitch.'

I imagined Gary coming after me. There were probably guns here. Or maybe he would use his fists. He'd probably enjoy that more.

'I think we'd better talk,' I said.

She sat back on the water bed. I stood on the fake-fur rug.

'I'm not a private detective,' I said, 'and I'm not interested in finding Cherry, although she is linked, possibly . . .'

She blinked at me. 'I don't understand.'

'I'm trying to find my girlfriend. Her name's Marie Walker and she went missing last month. After she went I found photographs of her and aliens, pictures that have appeared on the Planet Flesh site. That's why I'm here.' I explained to her about Andrew, and about the trail I had been following.

'Not Cherry?'

'No. I have no interest in her.'

She scrutinized me. Finally, she said, 'All right. I believe you, I guess.'

I shifted from foot to foot. 'What did you mean when you said that Gary threatened to kill Andrew?'

'Just that. When Gary found out that Cherry and Andrew were an item . . .'

'Hang on – Cherry and *Andrew?*'

'That's what I said. Gary went mental. He hit her, threatened to do some fucking awful things to her, and to Andrew. I was here when it happened. Cherry was talking about it with me and Safire. She was saying how inspirational Andrew was, how he had shown her the light, all this bullshit. She was besotted. She said it had been going on before she met Gary, but Andrew had told her not to tell anyone. That first night in the club, it was a set-up. Andrew arranged for Cherry to go home with Gary. He wanted Gary to use Cherry as a model. I don't suppose he realised Gary would become so besotted with her.'

I tried to get my head round this. 'How did Cherry feel about doing the alien erotica?'

'She loved it. She was always going on about aliens and flying saucers and conspiracies. Some intergalactic choir that was going to save us all.'

'The Chorus.'

'Yeah. Some such bullshit. One day, Gary overheard Cherry telling us that she was also fucking Andrew and he came storming in, really angry. He hit Cherry and then grabbed a fucking shotgun and drove off.'

'To get Andrew?'

'Yeah. Except he couldn't find him. He drove to Eastbourne to Andrew's flat and he wasn't there. I think he drove around for a while, looking for him, but with no luck. He came back here to find Cherry, to get her to tell him where Andrew had gone, but she'd pissed off as soon as Gary had left the house. She didn't come back either. We assumed that she'd gone off with Andrew. That they'd run away together.'

I was confused. 'When was this?'

She thought. 'It must have been the start of last summer.'

'What? But I thought Gary said he last saw her in October.'

'Yeah, that's right. She came back recently. She had a suitcase with her and she was in tears. We were all sitting round the pool out the back. Gary was in a bit of a mood. Then in walked Cherry, tears leaking out from behind her shades. Giving it the old boo-hoo. She walked straight into Gary's arms, told us that Andrew had been killed in a car crash and that she was back to beg for forgiveness. Gary took her upstairs. To comfort her.'

'And he did forgive her?'

'Oh yes. He was blissful for weeks. He even asked her to marry him. But then a few weeks later she disappeared again, just after they got engaged.' She shook her head. 'Fuck knows what he sees in her. It's not like he's short of opportunities to get laid. But he calls her his muse, the stupid twat. He'll do anything to find her. And he thinks that you might be able to lead him to her. He asked me to try and find out who hired you. What you were up to.'

'And now you know.'

She retrieved her boots and slipped her feet back into them.

'But maybe your girlfriend and Cherry are together. Have you got any pictures? You never know, I might recognise her.'

The only pictures I had, of course, were those of her with the fake alien. I had a photocopy in my pocket, which I unfolded and showed her.

'Oh,' she said immediately. 'It's Candy.'

'What?'

'Yeah, I know her. She's a friend of Cherry's.'

'You said Candy?'

'Yeah, that's what Cherry called her. Cherry's real name is Charlotte. Looks like your girlfriend has a pseudonym as well.'

I stared at the photographs, that familiar churning sensation returning, spinning in my stomach.

'Where did you meet her?' I whispered.

'At a photo-shoot. We went down to Andrew's flat – me and Cherry and Candy . . .'

'Marie.'

'Yeah, Marie . . . she was there, with Andrew.'

I swallowed. 'What, having her picture taken?'

'No, just hanging out, watching. I remember Cherry was ecstatic about seeing her. They kept hugging and giggling. It was quite irritating. At the end of the day, Cherry stayed behind with Andrew and Marie, and I came back on my own.'

'Can you remember when this was?'

'You're very demanding, aren't you? Is that why Marie left you?' When I didn't laugh she said, 'I suppose it was last spring. April or May.'

Before I had met her.

'Can you remember where Andrew's studio was?' I asked.

'Of course. It was actually his flat. It's in Eastbourne.'

'Can you show me?'

'What, now?'

'Yes. Please, Freya. This is really important. I'll pay you.'

She rolled her eyes. 'OK. Let me go and tell Safire. If Gary comes back and wants to know where we've gone, she'll have to tell him I've taken you back to mine to shag some information out of you. I'll say you were too shy to do it with another person in the house. Then Gary will definitely think you're weird.' She laughed.

We left the seventies-themed room and I watched Freya murmur something in Safire's ear. She told me she needed the bathroom and re-emerged a few minutes later. Enough time to phone Gary and tell him the truth. But something told me I could trust her.

After all, I had to be able to trust somebody.

'It's just down here,' Freya said, directing me into a back street behind Eastbourne's seafront. I parked the car and we got out. It was freezing. She had goose bumps on her bare arms. A sea breeze stirred her split ends.

We looked up at a detached Victorian house, painted mint green, the front garden full of litter.

We walked up the path and Freya tried the front door. It swung open.

She pulled a surprised face.

I could hear the buzz of a radio coming from the ground floor flat. We climbed the stairs to the top floor.

'This is it,' Freya said. 'Where Andrew used to photograph us.'

I sighed. 'I don't even know why we came here,' I said. 'We're not going to be able to get in.'

'Have you got a knife?'

'There's a penknife in my car, I think.'

She flapped a hand. 'Go and get it.'

I trotted down the stairs and returned a minute later with the small penknife I kept in my glove compartment. 'Are you going to pick the lock?'

'Uh-huh.'

Thirty seconds later the door stood open. I was impressed. I daren't ask where she had learned to do it. Instead, I silently followed her into the flat.

It was empty. Every room had been stripped bare. There was no furniture: no beds or chairs or tables. The kitchen was gutted, spaces left in the lino where the fridge and cooker had stood. Even the light bulbs had been taken.

Only the dim afternoon light illuminated the flat. In the gloom, I began to picture ghosts: is this where Andrew took the naked pictures of Marie? Did they have sex here? He would have slept with Cherry in these rooms. Maybe even Samantha O'Connell. What else had gone on here, in this now-vacant flat?

I felt a chill pass through me. I hugged myself.

Looking around, I noticed a pile of envelopes. They had been tossed into the corner by the disused phone point. The landlord must have thrown them there when emptying the flat and forgotten them. Andrew's uncollected post; letters that came after his death.

I crouched down and looked through the pile, Freya standing behind me. Most of it was junk mail: credit card offers, charity circulars and magazine subscription offers. There were a few magazines which Andrew must have subscribed to: *Photography Today* and *Bizarre*. At the bottom of the pile, I found a handwritten envelope, addressed to Mr Andrew Jade. It was postmarked Oregon, USA. I turned it over – there was no return address.

'What's that?' asked Freya.

'Let's see.' I ripped it open. It contained a single sheet of white A5 paper. It was a flyer.

THE TIME IS NEAR.
JOIN THE CHOSEN ONES:
COME MEET US
103 SW 30TH AVENUE, PORTLAND, OR.

Behind the text was a symbol that I recognised from my time with Marie: the symbol they used to represent the Chorus, a circle of planets with interconnecting lines.

'Let me see.'

I handed it to Freya.

As she scrutinised it I felt a bubble of excitement rise up in me. Portland, Oregon. It took me a few seconds to remember: Pete, the American who had been on the hill with Andrew and Marie that first night. He came from Portland. I had never even considered that Marie might have gone that far, and she hadn't mentioned Pete at all since that night on the hill. He had slipped from my memory. But now I started to wonder.

Had she gone to America? There was no passport in the house, which meant that she might have gone abroad, although I didn't know if she had had a passport in the first place. What if Pete – and I could only assume it must be Pete – had sent Marie a flyer as well? She had received it and decided, in a moment of madness, her world still upside-down since Andrew's death, to go.

I checked the postmark on the envelope. October fifteenth. The day before she vanished.

'Fucking hell.'

Freya looked confused. 'I don't get it.'

I was almost panting with excitement. 'I've got to go,' I said. 'I need to get home.'

'What is it?'

'I think I might know where Marie's gone.'

She looked back at the flyer. 'There? In Portland? Where is that anyway?'

'West coast of America. I need to contact this address.'

'Do you think Cherry's there too?'

'I don't know. There must be a good chance.'

I started towards the door. For the second time that day, Freya blocked my exit.

'What are you going to tell Gary?' she demanded.

'Why? What does it matter?'

'You can't just disappear. He'll be furious.'

'Who gives a shit?' My heart was thumping, my head felt light.

'Richard, I told you – he's dangerous. If he thinks you could lead him to Cherry, he'll be after you. He's ruthless. He's going to ask me what we did this afternoon, and whether I got any information out of you.'

I paused. 'Can't you tell him I don't know anything about Cherry? That you believe I'm a genuine photographer? Tell him I'll call him to sort out the photo session. That should give me a few days' grace. I'll be able to get to Portland, and if I do find Cherry I'll send her home and Gary will be happy.'

Freya didn't look convinced. She pouted. But eventually she sighed and said, 'You're lucky I like you. As long as you appreciate I'm putting myself at risk.'

'Maybe you should get away for a few days too,' I said. The last thing I wanted was for her to get hurt. 'Until I find out what's in Portland. If I do find Cherry, Gary will be so ecstatic that he won't care what happened today.'

She stroked her chin. 'I might just do that. I could use a break anyway.'

I gave her a lift to the station and gave her my number, which she tapped into her iPhone.

Before getting out she said, 'I hope you find your girlfriend, Richard. And I hope she's worth it.'

'She is.'

'I hope so, and I hope she realises how lucky she is. If I disappeared, nobody would give a damn.'

She leant forward and kissed me on the cheek.

'Be careful,' she said, and I watched her walk into the station, a few heads turning as she swung her hips.

I drove home too fast, shedding images of Freya as I went, gripping the steering wheel tightly, wishing I could make my car fly. I would fly all the way to Portland. Could she really be there, at the address I had in my pocket? I imagined myself pulling up outside a large American house with a white picket fence, and Marie would come out and smile when she saw me and run into my arms. I would cover her face in kisses and tears, and she would invite me to join her in her new life and I would say yes, yes, yes.

We would never be apart again.

I broke the speed limit but didn't care. I arrived home thirty minutes later and ran into my house.

I stopped dead.

Simon was lying on the floor in the living room, unconscious. His face was purple and grey, his left eye swollen and closed, cuts on both cheekbones, dried blood beneath his nose, his lips split and puffy. His glasses lay beside him; they had been stamped on. One arm was twisted at an unnatural angle.

In the corner, Calico crouched in the darkness, two yellow eyes peering fearfully at me.

16

Simon regained consciousness while we were waiting for the ambulance. He could barely talk because he was in so much pain. He had also bitten his tongue so what he did say came out in a barely coherent mumble.

'Dey were ooking for Terry.'

'Cherry? They wanted Cherry?'

He nodded.

A shudder went through me. Gary. He had come to my house, looking for Cherry, while I was out of the way.

I tried to get more out of Simon but he drifted back into unconsciousness. Then the ambulance arrived.

I rode with him in the back. I leaned in close, under the watchful eye of the paramedic, and whispered, 'I'm so sorry.'

He rolled his good eye towards me.

I had quickly looked around the house while waiting for the ambulance. My home had been ransacked – drawers tipped out, cupboards emptied. The computer lay on the floor, but still worked. I guessed they had tried to access it but couldn't get past the password. I was surprised they hadn't taken it with them.

Simon licked his battered lips and I leaned closer to him. He spoke in a rasp, using as few words as possible.

'There were two . . . Kept asking about Cherry . . . Where was she..? One called Gary . . . Other guy big . . . a gorilla . . .' He winced with every other word.

'Cherry's a friend of Marie's,' I said, thinking he was owed some kind of explanation. 'She vanished at the same time. Gary's her boyfriend.' I decided now was not the right time to tell him about the whole online porn thing.

Simon raised a hand weakly and pointed it at me. 'He said . . . he'll kill you.'

Then he closed his eyes.

At the hospital, Simon was checked over and treated while I paced around the waiting room. A nurse came out and told me he had a broken nose, three broken ribs and concussion. She wanted to know what had happened. 'Was it a fight?'

I shook my head. 'I don't know. I just came home and there he was.'

She didn't believe me but she didn't press for any more details. Susan, who I had called from my house, arrived just as the nurse said to me, 'He's going to be OK, but we'll keep him in for a few days for observation. The police will be here later. They'll want to talk to you.'

I had no doubt that, if he still thought I knew something about Cherry, Gary would happily torture me to get the information. I was lucky that he hadn't done that already. I guess he thought his other approach – of getting Freya to pump me for information while he searched my house – was more likely to work. But now . . .

I should tell the police about him. But I was scared that if I spoke to them they would forbid me from leaving the country while they investigated. And I had to get to Portland as soon as possible. I really couldn't risk getting held up by the police. There was only one solution I could think of.

Susan glared at me like she knew it was my fault. I turned my head away and looked at Simon. He was asleep now, his body full of pills that dulled the pain – pain that had been inflicted because of me. He looked uncomfortable even in sleep. The nurses had cleaned up his wounds so his face looked a little better, but he still had a black eye and bruises that made his face look like a Halloween mask.

I felt Susan's stare and looked up at her.

'When I found out about his affair, I had fantasies about something like this happening to him. But now . . . Do you know who it was?'

I didn't reply.

She stepped around the foot of the bed and whispered in a harsh tone, 'Who was it? What did they want? Is this anything to do with that girlfriend of yours?'

I took Susan for a coffee in the hospital café and told her everything I knew about Gary and Cherry, giving Susan Gary's address so she could pass it on to the police.

'You'll be here when the police come, won't you?' Susan asked.

'I can't.'

She looked confused and angry. 'Why not?'

'I can't explain. I'm sorry, but I have to find Marie. This could be my only chance.' I didn't want to tell her I was going to head to America. I stood up to go and she tried to grab my arm. 'Please, Susan. I have to do this. I'll explain everything properly when I get back. I promise.'

'Back from where?'

'Can you feed the cat? Simon's got keys.'

'Richard . . .'

But I was gone.

I went outside and waited for a taxi. I smoked one cigarette and immediately wanted another. Someone had dumped a fresh bunch of flowers in a bin. The sweet scent drifted up, reminding me of Marie, of nights on the hill, the smell of flowers filling the night air.

At home I quickly packed a bag. Calico watched me. He had ventured out from the corner and now crouched beneath the bedside table.

'I'm going to bring her home to you,' I said. 'I promise.'

I phoned a travel agent. The first available flight, the operator said, was at four a.m.

Before leaving the house I booted up Marie's PC and looked in her contacts. There was nothing listed for Pete, or for anyone in the States. I saw this as a good sign – if she was going to the US she would surely have deleted the address to make it harder for me. Of course that hurt, but my twisted logic told me she had done it out of love: she was trying to protect me from something. Or maybe it was because she knew I wouldn't understand, would try to dissuade her from going. Whoever had made the flyer – Pete or some other group in Portland – clearly seemed to be preparing to make contact with the Chorus. They expected it to happen soon. Marie would have known that I would tell her this was crazy. My refusal to believe had driven her away from me.

We reached the motorway and I looked up at the sky from the back of the taxi. There were no stars out.

There were things that didn't add up. Why had Pete sent the flyer to Andrew? Was it meant to act as an invitation? And would Andrew have gone if he hadn't been killed? Was Pete connected to the alien porn industry too? There were so many questions.

I was sure I was going to find the answers in America.

After checking in I had an hour to kill, so I made my way up to Gatwick Village. I went into a newsagent and bought a couple of thrillers to sustain me on my flight. On the way to the till I saw a stack of that day's *Sunday Telegram*. On the strip across the top of the front page was one of my photographs of Hastings' ruined pier.

I grabbed the paper and pulled out the magazine. There were six more of my photographs inside. They looked fantastic. For one second I forgot all my other problems and woes. The thrill of realised ambition coursed through me. I wanted to grab a passerby and say, 'Look! I took these! That's my name!'

I bought the paper and sat outside the shop and leafed back and forth through the magazine. I wanted someone to share this with. I wanted Marie beside me so we could look at the pictures together. She would be so proud of me. After all, she had pushed me to approach the paper in the first place.

I put the magazine in my holdall. I would show it to Marie as soon as I found her. Then I leafed through the main section of the paper. On page nine, a small piece in the bottom corner of the page grabbed my attention:

BESTSELLING AUTHOR VANISHES

Writer Samantha O'Connell, who has published several books on the alien abduction phenomenon, has gone missing. Worried friends reported O'Connell, 48, missing to police last night. She was last seen at a signing in a bookshop in Charing Cross Road, London, last Tuesday. Her agent, Michael Auster, said that she was expected at another signing the following day but she had not turned up. 'This is not like her at all,' he said. Police have asked anyone with any information to come forward.

17

We're standing by the automatic ticket barriers at London Bridge Underground station and Marie starts to tremble. Her Travelcard slips from her fingers and floats leaf-like to the grubby floor.

'Are you OK?'

She nods, but she looks like a child on her first day of school, staring at the escalators ahead as they sink beneath the ground.

'I think my blood sugar's a bit low. Having a crash.' She smiles at me, but it's a nervous smile.

'Do you want to get something to eat now? Or wait till we get to the other end?'

We're on a day trip to London, something I suggested: a little shopping, a ride on the London Eye, which Marie is excited about, a wander around a couple of museums.

She bends to pick up her ticket. 'No, let's go now.'

The Tube is packed; there is no air, just second-hand breath and heat. We just manage to squeeze on, Marie hesitating until the final beep. The doors shut a few inches behind our heads. I hold her hand and pull a face, trying to make it seem funny. She doesn't smile back.

As soon as the train pulls out of the station, Marie starts to hyper-ventilate. Her face turns the colour of old books. She clings to me, digging her fingernails into my skin, terrified like a cat suspended over water.

The train goes one stop, the doors open and she flings herself off, onto the platform, staggering and almost hitting the deck. I jump off after her and grab hold of her.

'Get me out of here, please, Richard.' She's sobbing. 'I can't stand it down here. Please . . .'

I take her up onto the street and, slowly, her breathing returns to normal.

As we walk to find a bus stop, she says, 'I'm sorry, I should have told you, but I didn't want you to think I was pathetic. I just . . . I can't stand being underground. It makes me feel panicky and trapped.' She grips my hand. 'I hate . . . I hate being so far from the sky.'

'This your first visit to the States?' asked the cab driver. I nodded and told him that it was. Under different circumstances I'd have been bouncing in my seat, gawping at the landscape, so familiar from a lifetime of American movies and TV shows. But all I could think about was Marie. I kept remembering the time when she freaked out on the Tube. *I hate being so far from the sky.* Such a Marie-like statement. And it made me wonder: did I make her feel like that – trapped, claustrophobic, far from the sky? Did my failure to believe in the same things as her make her feel that I was clipping her wings, bringing her down? Is that why she fled?

I needed to find her, to ask her. I had to make her understand that the last thing I wanted was for her to feel trapped by me. But I also asked myself: is it possible to be with someone and allow them to be free at the same time? How can you ensure the person you love can spread their wings without flying away from you?

We crossed a bridge that gave a fantastic view of the city, pink and black office blocks rising against a backdrop of green where pine trees lined the distant horizon.

'Portland's a great city,' the driver said. 'Real pretty. On a clear day you can see Mount Hood right over there.'

I sat back and forced myself to admire the view: straight roads, pick-up trucks, traffic lights suspended from wires stretched across the road. We headed downtown.

Inside the hotel, I took a shower and went to bed. I lay down and closed my eyes, Marie's face swimming into my mind's eye. She was here. I could feel it.

The roar of traffic awoke me. Slats of light pierced the blinds and lay across the bed in fat, hazy lines. I uncurled my body and went over to the window. The sky was blue and I felt my spirits rise – today might be the day. I was excited and impatient, but I also wanted to savour the anticipation, to hang back and appreciate what today might bring.

Plus I was starving. I needed breakfast.

It was bright but chilly outside. I walked past a huge fountain, water running over connected rock cubes. Businessmen strolled between the tower blocks, and an equal number of people dressed casually in colourful outdoor gear.

I found a diner, went inside and was shown to a table. I was immediately brought a jug of water and a mug of coffee. I searched in my pockets to find the dollars I'd withdrawn at the airport and my cigarettes fell onto the table. I looked at them. When the waitress came to take my order – pancakes and scrambled egg – I handed the cigarettes to her.

'Can you take these and throw them away? I won't be needing them anymore. I've quit.'

She raised an eyebrow and said, 'Sure.'

I ate my breakfast slowly. My coffee cup was refilled three times. By the time I'd finished I felt quite dizzy, on a caffeine and cholesterol high. I could see my reflection in a mirror across the diner. Skinny, unshaven and panda-eyed. I should have gone back to the hotel and smartened myself up. But a part of me that I wasn't proud of wanted Marie to see what she had done to me.

'Can you tell me how to get to this address?' I asked the waitress when she brought my bill. She wiped her hands on the front of her pale blue uniform and took the flyer from me.

'Southwest Thirtieth. Uh-huh, that's in Multnomah County. My folks live pretty close to there. You visiting friends?'

'My girlfriend,' I said. 'I haven't seen her for months, not since she came out here.'

'Cool. That why you quit smoking? Because she doesn't like it?'

'Something like that.' I had an urge to tell this friendly stranger the whole, strange story. But I resisted.

'You got a car?' she asked.

I shook my head.

'In that case you'll need to get a bus. Go to Fifth and look for a stop with a yellow rose on it. Get a number one or five. That'll get you there.'

A little later I was on the bus. It had started to drizzle, but the city was beautiful: apartments stacked on the slopes of hills, framed by grand, plush pine trees; long, straight roads stretching towards the mountains and the ocean. The people sitting around me were quiet, staring at the rain or reading.

I had asked the driver to give me a shout when I reached my stop. He did now. 'Second left past the church there,' he said as I got off.

I walked on and turned into an unmade road. Detached houses stood several metres apart from one another. An unlikely place, it seemed, to find an alien-loving cult. But what would be an appropriate setting? Some tower perched on a hilltop, surrounded by high fences, a landing pad in the garden?

I walked up the road, squinting at the numbers on the fronts of the houses. There was nobody around, just a couple of crows and some thick-tailed cats.

I found the place I was looking for. It was one of the smaller houses on the street, a single-storey, white timber house. There was a red sports car parked out front, beside a neat little lawn.

I stood on the path and gathered myself. I had my story worked out – had thought about little else on the plane. I walked up the path and knocked on the door.

My heart felt like it was made of lead I looked through the screen door at a tidy living room: blue sofa, pamphlets piled on coffee tables, a scattering of floor cushions. A girl came out of a back room and opened the door.

She had long, pale red hair. She was small and pretty. For a split second – the briefest flicker of time – I thought she was Marie, and my heart jolted.

'Can I help you?'

I realised I was staring and mumbled an apology. I showed her the now-crumpled flyer that I'd taken from Andrew's flat. She looked at it and beamed in recognition.

'I've come to join,' I said.

Half an hour later I was sitting on the sofa, sipping a chamomile and honey tea, which I pretended to find refreshing. The girl, whose name was Zara, knelt on a floor cushion at my feet. She looked so much like Marie, it was eerie. Only her eyes were different. They were dark grey, almost charcoal, and she stared intensely, never breaking eye contact.

Her voice was a semi-stoned drawl. 'I'm so happy you came, Richard. All the way from England! That's awesome.'

I gulped tea. 'Is there no one else from England among you?'

She chewed her lip and thought about it. She had an attractive gap between her two front teeth. Again, like Marie. 'Hmm, one or two, I think. I find it hard to keep track. There are a ton of us now. Like, thirty at the Oregon Embassy alone.'

This house, it transpired, served as a 'gateway' for people who wanted to join the group. They called themselves the Loved Ones. Zara lived here and vetted people who wanted to join, to make sure they were genuine and 'worthy'.

'How can you tell?' I asked.

'It's, like, a gift I have,' she replied, smiling proudly.

The other Loved Ones – or this chapter, anyway – were based in a large house on the Oregon coast.

'It's the coolest place,' Zara told me. 'And we'll be heading out there soon.' She looked towards the window and I couldn't help but follow her gaze. 'The time's so close now, Richard. They'll be coming for us. It's going to be beautiful.' Her voice dropped. 'So much love.'

I nodded. 'I can't wait. You know, this is all I've ever wanted. Since my first contact.'

She stared and listened as I spun her a tale about a teenage abduction, stringing together bits of stories I had heard from Marie. Zara gasped and cooed, playing with a locket that hung on a silver chain around her neck.

'And did you feel it?' she asked. 'The love, radiating from them?'

'Oh yes.' If my intent wasn't so serious, I would have found it impossible to keep a straight face. 'That's what I want to feel again. The love.'

I was disappointed that Marie was not here in this house, but she had to be at the house or coast. Maybe Cherry was there too, and Samantha. Zara, it seemed, was already convinced I was genuine so we would soon be on our way. I was desperate to get going.

'What about you?' I asked, trying to stay cool. 'Have you made contact?'

She nodded solemnly then spoke like she was reciting a passage she'd memorised. 'They come to me at night when I'm in bed. I feel a great warmth enveloping me, like breath on my skin, like I'm being wrapped in a blanket of soft air. The feeling goes right through me, starts at my toes, up through my middle, across my breasts and neck, and ends on my lips. I see them around me, shimmering figures. I feel them caressing my soul. It's so beautiful, Richard. The best feeling.'

She looked directly into my eyes. 'Like the most blissful orgasm you've ever had, times one thousand.'

'Oh.' I swallowed.

'We're going to feel that ecstasy forever,' Zara said, 'when they come for us.'

She started to sway, her eyes closed, legs crossed, her hands resting lightly on her knees. A sigh came from her throat. I stared at her, wondering what she'd been smoking before I arrived.

'Zara, when . . .'

A key scratched in the door and it banged open. I jumped to my feet.

A tall, bearded guy in a white T-shirt with the words THEY LOVE US on it entered the house, carrying a brown paper bag full of groceries. He looked at me quizzically and blinked behind thick glasses. 'Hello?' he said.

Zara stopped sighing and jumped up, bounding across the room. 'Rick,' she said, 'this is Richard. Hey, Rick and Richard, that's funny . . .'

Rick nodded at me, frowning.

'Richard's come from England. Isn't that extreme?'

'Very,' said Rick. He stuck out his hand. I shook it. 'I'm Rick. From Seattle.'

'Rick joined us last week,' Zara said. 'He's coming out to the Embassy with me too, so we can all go together. Isn't that cool?'

'Very,' said Rick.

He stalked off to the back of the house, taking his bag of groceries with him.

Zara said, 'Rick's not the most talkative guy in the world. But he makes the best soup.'

That evening, Rick proved his culinary skills, producing an incredible meal from the cramped kitchen: lentil soup, crusty bread, a vegetarian chili that burned my mouth but tasted sublime. Suddenly, food made sense to me again. We ate the chili with beer and lots of water. Zara moaned and groaned with pleasure and then, as I held my swollen belly, she told me more about the group. I couldn't ask too many questions because I had to act like I knew a lot about them already. While Zara spoke, Rick sat and munched tortilla chips, staring at the table.

'We've grown so much since the beginning,' Zara said. 'Since Lisa and Jay and I first met, which was, like, seven years ago now, we've spread the news all over the world. Jay's at the Embassy on the East Coast now, with about fifty pilgrims, down in Florida. That's the biggest at the moment, though the one in San Diego's pretty big too. That's where Lisa's based. She was the first to come into contact with the visitors, back when we were in high school.'

'Did you grow up around here?'

'Uh-huh. Lisa's amazing. One of the most amazing people I've ever met. I guess you could say she's a kind of guru to me. To all of us.'

'Is she your leader?' I asked. I imagined a bunch of E.T.s landing and saying, 'Take us to your leader.' I tried to suppress a giggle.

'We don't have a leader, but she guides us. I can't wait for you guys to meet her. She's, well, she's just a unique and beautiful person.'

'I'm worried,' I said. 'What if she doesn't like me? What if she thinks I'm not worthy?'

Zara laughed and touched my arm. 'Hey, don't worry. If I say you're OK, Lisa will like you too. And Richard, we're *all* worthy. It's just a matter of pushing yourself forward, of being brave enough to make that leap. We're going to be undertaking a great journey. We're the Earth's ambassadors, setting out to discover a new world. We're like the Pilgrims, setting sail on the Mayflower.'

I played with a stray piece of rice that had stuck to the table. 'And you say there are other English people at the house on the coast?'

'Yes. I wish I could remember their names.'

'Male or female?' I asked, trying to hide my eagerness to know. I was sure Rick was looking at me suspiciously. Did he suspect that I wasn't genuine?

Zara rocked her head from side to side, as if the motion might free her thoughts.

'Female, I think. Maybe one guy, one girl.'

It had to be Marie. It had to be. I wanted to go to the coast now. I could feel all the seconds and minutes and hours we'd been apart weighing down on me, and suddenly they were too heavy to hold. I wanted to end the separation now. I suppose that's how Zara and her fellow Loved Ones felt about the aliens. They felt lovesick. They wanted to be reunited with the object of their affection, the beings that made them glow, that brought happiness and pleasure to their lives. They wanted to be held and caressed and soothed, shown new things, feel that rush of love and life that only that connection can bring. I found myself empathising with them. For the first time, I think I understood how they felt.

I looked around me, at the expensive house, filled with tasteful furniture, the sports car parked in the drive. 'What do you do for a living?' I asked.

'I'm a psychic therapist,' Zara said. 'People pay me to look into their minds, to ease their pain.'

'And it pays well?'

'I make a good living, yes.'

'What about the people who join you? Do I need to pay you?'

She squeezed my hand. 'It's your choice, Richard. Many of the pilgrims who join us make donations. Some of them are very generous, signing over their property. But none of us will need money after we make contact with the Chorus.'

'But should . . .?'

'Let's stop. It's not cool to talk about money.'

I sat back. 'Sorry.'

'Hey, don't worry.' Her smile returned, warm and flirtatious. 'I'll forgive you. If—'

Rick suddenly announced, 'I'm going to bed.' He hurried through the kitchen into his bedroom like something had frightened him.

Zara shifted her chair closer to mine and put her hand on my knee. She leaned into me. Her breath smelled of chili and beer. 'I can read your thoughts,' she said.

I was quite drunk and, even though I fought it, she was turning me on. I was enjoying the flirtation.

I said, 'And what am I thinking?'

165

Her eyes were piercing. Her hand crept up my thigh. 'You're thinking I remind you of someone. Someone you love. Someone you've lost.'

I stood up sharply, banging my head on the low-hanging light fixture. I swore and rubbed my crown. It was the way she said it – *someone you've lost*. What was I doing, allowing this woman to come on to me?

Zara was looking at me with concern. 'Have I said something? Richard, I can sense your pain. Like a small animal . . .'

'I'm going to bed,' I said.

Before I could move, Zara took me by the shoulders and pulled my face towards hers, her cheek lightly against mine. It felt very soft. She whispered, 'I can be the balm that soothes you, sweet Richard.'

'I need to go to bed. To sleep,' I added quickly.

She held my face in her hands. It felt like her fingers were drawing tears from my eyes; the tears slid warmly down my cheeks. There was such tenderness in her eyes, and she looked so much like Marie, the temptation to give in, to let her take me to bed, was almost overwhelming. But I couldn't do it. I was so close to finding Marie now. How could I be unfaithful to her?

'Sleep,' I said again, and Zara paused, then nodded. She led me to a bedroom and I lay down on a soft mattress on the floor. She kissed the tears on my cheek and left the room, leaving me to sleep, to spend my second night under an American sky.

18

Briefly, a gap opened in the clouds, allowing sunlight to squeeze through; then the clouds closed again, and down came the rain.

Zara turned the key in the ignition and waved goodbye to her little house. This might be the last time she saw it, she said, if everything went according to plan. Consequently, a melancholy note resounded in the air, floating between the fine raindrops, a note of farewell. Zara had spent her life in this city, and although she had spent most of that life longing to be somewhere else – namely outer space – it was still hard for her to say goodbye.

Whereas I was impatient to get moving.

'Goodbye, house,' Zara whispered as she reversed the red MX-5 out of the drive. In the tiny back seat, Rick had folded his lanky body into an uncomfortable zigzag and closed his eyes. He had been up all night meditating, he said. *More like masturbating*, I almost said, but held my tongue. I had seen the way he looked at Zara. *He* definitely wouldn't have turned her down.

'How long will it take to reach the Embassy?' I asked.

'About three hours,' she said in a sad tone.

She gave me a moist-eyed smile, and then off we went.

In a way, Zara's personal sadness was a relief. Since I had shed tears on my first night in the house, all I had got from her were little sympathetic smiles, which were starting to irritate me. I kept asking when we were going to set out, and she would shrug vaguely. Then last night, over another of Rick's marvellous meals, Zara announced that tomorrow would be the day we headed out to the coast, to the Embassy.

'Lisa contacted me earlier,' she said.

'What, telepathically?'

She looked taken aback. 'By phone, silly.'

'Oh.'

I hadn't seen much of Portland. During my few days at the house I slept a lot. I thought about Marie. One day I went out and walked along the highway and took some pictures with my phone, wishing I'd brought my camera. Crows flapping around outside Starbucks; a rain-soaked Stars and Stripes on a pole outside a diner; a blue jay perched on a mailbox. In parts, Oregon looked just like England. Then you would turn around and it would look completely alien. Maybe Marie and I could spend some time exploring after I found her. A holiday in which to rediscover each other. We certainly needed some time together. Time to heal.

'Is there no way you can find out the names of the people at the Embassy?' I had asked Zara.

'Why do you want to know?'

'It's just . . . a friend of mine told me she might come out here. I'm hoping she's there.'

'A girlfriend?' I could tell from her face that she now believed she knew why I hadn't jumped into her bed.

'A friend,' I said. 'Someone else who loves the visitors.'

'And they love us,' Zara said, reaching out and stroking my cheek.

Now, the open road led to the sea. Windscreen wipers swept back and forth through the somnolent rhythm of the rain. I watched the passing country: Taco Bell, McDonalds, Plaid Pantry, Costco. Zara and Rick were silent. Soft rock played on the radio. My mouth felt dry and I kept looking at my watch. In just under three hours I would see Marie. I had so many questions, but I made a silent vow not to start grilling her immediately. By this point, I was simply desperate to know she was safe. I just wanted to see her. To put my arms around her.

What if she doesn't want to see you? What if she turns away from you, tells you to go home? Paranoid voices whispered in my inner ear. I tuned them out.

'Do you want to stop for lunch?' Zara asked.

'I've got to go to the restroom,' Rick said. I went with him while Zara ordered the food. Standing at the urinal, Rick turned to me and said, 'You're not a believer.'

'What?' I said.

He zipped up and faced me. I felt vulnerable with my penis hanging out so I zipped up too, even though I hadn't been yet. Rick said, 'I don't trust you. I want to know who you are really. A reporter?'

I tried to look shocked and indignant. 'No I am fucking not! I came here from England because I want to be one of the chosen ones. I want to be . . . reunited with the visitors.'

A trucker came out of the cubicle behind us, chuckling quietly.

'I don't believe you,' said Rick. 'I've seen how your eyes glaze over when Zara talks about them.'

'No they don't. And Zara knows I'm genuine.'

He snorted. 'Zara's a dumb hippy. Plus she's got the hots for you and can barely see past your pants.'

'Hey, listen here . . .'

'No, *you* listen, asshole.' He leaned towards me, something stale and rank on his breath. 'I looked your name up online. You work for a British paper.'

Oh shit.

'Rick, I can explain . . .'

But he wouldn't let me finish. 'This is *my* fucking story. I don't want any British reporter muscling in, trying to steal it from me. I've heard all about your British tabloids.'

Realisation hit me and I laughed with surprise. '*You're* a journalist?'

Jesus, I couldn't get away from them. I decided to lie, to play along with him. I mock-sighed. 'OK, you've sussed me. But I'm not going to steal your story. I'll just take it back to England and sell it there. It won't affect you at all. I'm a photographer, anyway. Maybe we can team up.'

'Humph.' He folded his arms.

'Look, if you're going to give me grief I'll have to tell Zara you're a fraud.'

'And I'll tell her about you.'

'And we'll both lose out. And I think this story's rather more important to you than it is to me. The ball's in your court, buddy.'

He exhaled loudly. 'OK. I'll tolerate you. But if you get in my way . . .'

'Chill out, Rick. I won't. I promise.'

He glared at me. 'OK.' As we left the bathroom he added, 'I can't believe you turned Zara down. I'd give my left nut for an hour with her.'

I decided it wouldn't do any harm to attempt a spot of male bonding. 'Hey, you've heard her alien orgasm stories. There's no way either of us could measure up to that.'

'Speak for yourself,' he replied.

We returned to the car where Zara was waiting with our subs. I felt sorry for her. Both Rick and I had completely fooled her. Her psychic powers obviously weren't working very well this week.

———〜———

We drove down roads that twisted like the tails of serpents, coiled around rocks in the mist. All around us forests clung to the land; intermittently, patches of blankness stood out where swathes of pines had been felled, and the occasional timber truck passed us on the road, heading to the paper mill.

In the back, Rick closed his eyes. This landscape held no novelty for him. He was probably dreaming of journalistic fame, of his big story. Or getting into Zara's knickers.

Zara kept her eyes on the road. Only occasionally would she glance over at me.

Once she touched my knee. I moved it away.

The road wound on until, without warning, the Pacific Ocean loomed into view. I opened my mouth to gasp but no sound came out. We crossed a suspension bridge across the mouth of a gaping river. I didn't ask its name. I just stared in awe.

'Nearly there,' said Zara, and then we were driving along the coast, and I leaned forward in my seat and felt my heart elevate into my mouth. I thought, *This is it.*

This is it.

———〜———

We turned off a few miles north of a town called Yachats – pronounced 'yah-hearts'. Zara swung the car right and we drove up a sand-strewn road between some high dunes. As we emerged through the dunes I saw the house. It was set high above the beach, surrounded by sharp grasses, and even larger than I had expected. Constructed from timber, it was painted white, like Zara's house but on a much larger scale. At the front of the house was what I can only describe as a spire, near the peak of which was a large, round window. Above the window somebody had painted a gold heart.

Zara switched off the engine.

'Welcome to the Embassy,' she said.

The ocean was just fifty yards from the house. The sand was pale and damp; pebbles and sand dollars were scattered around. Along the coast were other houses and chalets, but the beach was deserted. It felt like the edge of the Earth. I tried to imagine how the first Europeans to stand here must have felt, after their long trek across the continent. They must have thought they had finally mapped the whole world. And now, hundreds of years later, their descendants stood here, unhappy with the world that was, looking and hoping for other planets. New territories to map; territories beyond the stars.

I broke into a run.

'Hey, wait, Richard . . .' Zara called, but I didn't listen. I ran to the door of the Embassy and pushed past the man who stood there. He tried to grab my arm but I shook him off. I ran into a large room with white walls. Half a dozen pairs of eyes looked at me. I scanned the faces. No Marie. I ran out of the room and down a hall. I pushed open doors: a cupboard, a kitchen, bedrooms, an office. No Marie.

Panting, I flew up a flight of stairs. More doors. Shocked faces stared out at me. A man came out and said, 'Can I help you?' and I froze.

'Marie,' I gasped, 'where is she?'

'What?' He looked at me with suspicion and confusion.

'Marie. Where's Marie?'

'There's no Marie here, man. Is she a friend?'

'Or Candy. Maybe that's what she's calling herself.'

He gave me a curious look. 'There ain't no Candy here,' he said, and laughed.

I stopped listening and ran back down the stairs, straight into Zara, Rick and a bunch of others. Zara said, 'Richard, what's the matter? What are you doing?' Rick was glaring at me with horror.

'I . . . I . . .'

That was all I could say before I collapsed.

I woke up in a strange bed and jerked upright.

'Hey, cool it!' A young man with a wispy beard stood over me. He laid his hand on my arm and restrained me from jumping out of the bed. 'Calm down, man. Take deep breaths.'

I obeyed. It slowed my pulse a little. 'Is it true?' I asked. 'Is Marie not here?'

'I don't know what you're talking about,' the man said. 'There's nobody at the Embassy called Marie. Or Candy.'

'But . . .'

Zara came into the room. Her eyes burned into me. 'Richard, please tell me you're OK. They're having a discussion downstairs, asking questions about what kind of person I've brought with me.'

The walls of the room were pure white, like the interior of a hospital ward. The man with the wispy beard was dressed all in white too – loose white shirt over white jeans – and Zara too had changed into a long white dress. Both she and the man (whose name, it turned out, was Carl) had gold heart shapes sewn above their real hearts.

'Richard, talk to me!' Zara raised her voice for the first time since I'd met her.

I gathered my thoughts as quickly as I could. I didn't want to be chucked out of here. Even if Marie wasn't here – and the disappointment almost choked me – there might still be people who could help me. Pete, for example. Marie might be in one of the other embassies. Or she might be on her way. Somebody here had to know something.

I coughed. 'Marie . . . Marie's the name of my visitor friend. It's the name she gives herself when we're together. I guess I was so overwhelmed about being here and about . . . about what's going to happen that I got carried away and flipped out for a minute. I expected to see her here. I'm sorry.'

'Marie, huh?' said Carl, not a hundred per cent convinced. 'Weird name for a visitor.'

'Oh no,' said Zara. 'I've heard of it before. Some visitors give themselves human names to make the contactees feel more secure.'

'That's what Marie said,' I lied.

'Hmm,' said Carl.

'Would you like to rest?' Zara asked.

'No, I'd like to meet everyone. If that's all right.'

Zara kissed my cheek. 'Of course it is.'

I went to get out of bed and realised I was naked. I wondered who had undressed me. Zara? Carl? Embarrassment tinged my cheeks. 'Um, where are my clothes?'

Carl handed me a pair of white jeans and a shirt just like his. 'Here.'

I hesitated.

'Don't be shy, dude. We have no secrets here. And clothes won't be necessary after contact.'

Zara laughed at my look of consternation. 'Poor Richard's shy. Sweet thing. Come on, Carl.'

Carl rolled his eyes but followed Zara from the room. The ivory glare of everything around me was giving me a headache. I ran my fingers over the gold heart pinned to my shirt. I had a feeling I'd made an awful mistake coming here.

Zara took me downstairs and into what she called the open room. This was the room I had first entered, where a number of white-clad Loved Ones sat around drinking, chatting and watching videos on a widescreen TV. An episode of *Third Rock from the Sun* was on, the sound turned down. Rick sat in front of it, trying his best not to look out of place. Curtains were drawn across a large bay window that would otherwise have given a perfect view of the beach.

'Everyone, this is Richard,' Zara announced, and I squirmed awkwardly as a dozen heads turned my way.

'Welcome, Richard,' they said.

I knew from my dealings with believers so far that the people here would seem ordinary and normal on the surface. And so they were. There was one woman in her sixties, a couple of middle-aged men. They were all as white as their clothes, with the exception of one black man, who must have been almost seven feet tall, with a perfectly bald head. A woman with bad teeth smiled gruesomely at me. Next to her stood a hugely fat man, who held the hand of a skinny girl with raven-black hair. The only people who made me feel uneasy were a pair of bulky, muscular guys who lurked at the edge of the room, watching everything.

A group of six or seven people moved towards Zara and me.

'Richard's from England,' Zara said.

The woman with bad teeth said, in a strong Mancunian accent, 'Which part?'

'Hastings,' I whispered.

'Oh.' She looked disappointed.

'Why were you running around the house when you came in?' a man with a gold sleeper in his nose asked.

I looked to Zara for help. She said, 'Richard was so stoked to be here he couldn't control himself.'

There were nods of understanding. Rick looked over at me and sneered, though nobody else seemed to notice. They were all staring at me.

'I'm so glad . . . to be among you,' I said.

The fat man and his skinny girlfriend came over and wrapped me in a three-way embrace. 'It's good to have you, Richard. I'm Denny, and this is Laura.'

'And I'm Cory.'

'Emma.'

'Merlin.'

They each came up and introduced themselves. The tall black man, who was called Jake, said, 'A lot of the guys are in their rooms. But they'll all be delighted to meet you. You and Rick. We rejoice every time somebody new joins our family.'

'Thank you,' I said. I was amazed that nobody had mentioned aliens. Maybe it was so taken for granted here, that that was what bound them together, that there was little need to talk about it. I soon learnt that they were waiting. Trying to be patient, superstitiously afraid that too much talk would postpone the momentous event.

I sat down on a floor cushion with Zara. She put her hands on my shoulders and gently massaged the tension out of them. It felt good. 'Is there somebody here called Pete?' I asked. 'He's the guy I got the flyer from in England. I expected him to be here.'

Jake overheard. 'You talking about the Jinx?'

That was what Pete had called himself the night I met him on the East Hill. 'Yes,' I said, unable to keep the excitement out of my voice. 'That's him.'

'He's off on his travels,' Jake said. 'He's been gone a while. All over the world, visiting the other embassies. Last I heard he was in Italy. I must admit I'm kind of hoping he doesn't come back. Nothing ever seems to happen when he's around.' His laugh was deep and velvety, but there was something in the way he looked at me, like he was sizing me up, that made me uneasy.

'But he is due back?'

'Oh yeah. Pretty soon, I think. Lisa would know.'

I spoke to Zara. 'Is that the friend that you told me about?'

'Yes. But you can't see her at the moment. She's communicating in her room.'

'Communicating?'

'With the Chorus. Listening to the *vox celeste*. She says the voices are getting louder, which means they're coming closer. But she can't be disturbed. Although I'm sure you'll meet her soon.' Her voice brightened. 'Hey, are you hungry?'

I was.

Zara led me into the kitchen, another room that I had run wildly into earlier. I must have looked crazy. I was so certain that Marie would be here, but I had come all this way and I was still no closer to finding her. What if I was wasting my time? I remembered watching a TV documentary once about a woman who spent twenty years searching for her daughter who had disappeared after attending a party. The woman scoured the world, devoted her life to the hunt, lost everything in her obsessive search: her husband, her money, her sanity almost. In the end, the deathbed confession of a man who had been at the party revealed that the girl had died on the very night she vanished. She had been murdered and thrown to the crocodiles in a Florida swamp. The twenty-year search had been a waste of time.

Was I wasting my time, looking for Marie? My search had veered into its current direction because I had become increasingly convinced she had run away. If that *was* the case, then the longer my hunt remained fruitless, the more my frustration grew. She knew I loved her; she'd said she loved me. But could she really love me if she had deliberately left me? Doubts whispered in my ear: was she really worth searching for? But as this thought popped into my head, more questions crowded in. If she had run away, was she of sound mind? Had she been coerced? Was she scared of something or someone?

And if she hadn't run away, what had happened to her? Had she, like the woman who had been fed to crocodiles, been murdered on the day she'd gone missing? Was her body in Hastings somewhere? Had she been abducted? Was she, now, being kept prisoner somewhere, hoping desperately that I would keep looking for her?

I groaned and Zara looked at me, probably thinking I was regretting my earlier foolish behaviour. If I fully believed that Marie had run away, had deliberately and calculatingly left me in the lurch, then I might have decided at that moment to move on – or at least take the first step towards moving on. I might have given up.

But the possibility that she had been murdered, or abducted, or hurt . . . I couldn't give up. Even though I was exhausted.

'What do you want to eat?' Zara asked.

We found some pasta in a cupboard and I stirred the sauce while Zara buzzed around the kitchen, setting out plates and breaking bread. There was a bottle of Californian pinot in the fridge, which Zara opened. We ate and drank and talked.

Zara asked me about my life back home, and I told her an edited version of the truth.

In turn, Zara shared her background: high school, college, dead end jobs in restaurants . . .

'And then I discovered my gift. I was waitressing, and I found that I often knew what customers wanted before I asked. I spoke to Lisa about it and she encouraged me to develop my talent, to exercise it. I spent hours flexing my mental processes. It was tougher than any gym.' She laughed and gulped wine. 'Lisa says she knew it would be useful for the group, a way of seeing if people were genuine. We attract a lot of frauds. A lot of kooks.'

'I bet.'

'Yeah. It sucks. I mean people think *we're* kooks. Group hysteria, they call it. Lost people with nothing else to believe in. But they're the deluded ones. The last laugh will be ours, Richard.'

It was so much like talking to Marie. But with Marie I might have argued back, if I was in the mood, while with Zara I had no choice but to nod and agree.

She asked suddenly, 'Why are you in so much pain?'

Why did she have to ask questions like that? I faked a smile. 'I think I feel a little better now I'm here.'

She liked that. She reached across the table and touched my hand. I felt the spark, the *frisson* of lust, and I tried to fight it. I stood up and said, 'Shall we join the others?'

We took our glasses of wine into the open room. There were about twenty-five people, glowing in their all-white clothes, sitting or standing around, drinking, passing around spliffs, laughing, chatting. Somebody had put a Calvin Harris CD on and a couple of girls were dancing together in the corner; every couple of minutes they would beam and hug each other.

'They're on E,' said Jake, coming up and saying hello. 'I don't touch that shit myself. I don't need artificial joy. I've felt the real thing.'

I asked him what he did before joining the Loved Ones.

'I was a teacher in LA. Same hood where I grew up. Kind of place where the kids have to walk through a metal detector on the way in. I left a couple of years ago and travelled all over the States. I was looking for the truth. This is where I found it.'

The others told a similar story. They had all had encounters. Seen UFOs close up, been abducted, or had visitations during the night. Rick loitered behind me, making mental notes for his story, while I talked to a group of Loved Ones. They were all so friendly and welcoming, it was instantly apparent to me how someone could get sucked in to one of these groups – a cult, if that's what you wanted to call it. They made you feel special and worthwhile. They were beautiful and happy and seemed to be having so much fun. And they had found something to believe in. Each of them had experienced an epiphany; now they were awaiting the rapture.

Denny had been a self-professed bum in Wisconsin. 'I sat in front of a TV all day, watching adverts and eating junk. I didn't even know I was looking for anything until I came across Lisa's website one day. It hit me right here.' He tapped the flesh that padded his heart. 'I went to see a hypnotist and he retrieved all these memories from when I was a kid, every night being taken from my bed by visitors. They wiped my memories. But they were still there, buried deep, waiting to be retrieved.'

Laura was a farmer's daughter from the Deep South. 'We were plagued by crop circles. One would appear practically every week. And the cows . . . mutilated, poor things. My daddy went crazy; it damn near killed him. But I knew the reason. I'd seen the ships.'

Merlin ran a bookstore in San Francisco. 'I was driving across the Golden Gate Bridge at night and I saw these lights above me. I stopped my car and got out. There were flashes of silver in the sky, like, y'know, quicksilver. All the other drivers were tooting their horns. I think they thought I was going to jump. When I got home and told my partner he told me I must have imagined it. I left him.'

They must have told these stories so many times, but they weren't bored with repeating themselves. This was the core of their existence. It drove them, influenced everything they did. Most of them had given up everything, signed over their property and possessions to the group. Only those with children had not done this, like Joan, who was sixty-two, whose sons wrote to her every week, begging her to leave this crazy life and return to normality.

'Once they tried to take me home by force,' she said.

'I remember,' nodded Jake.

'They came in their van and tried to snatch me. Said they were going to take me back home, where I belonged. I had to tell them this is where I belong. This is my family now. Why would I want to return to that world of drugs and violence and dirt and hatred? Jake and some of the others had to scare them off and tell them to never come back.'

Her eyes were wide, and burned like the eyes of a zealot. But it was the fire of passion. What did I have to be passionate about in my life? I drifted along like a raft on a placid lake, never really going anywhere. I'd had a job that bored me, and I didn't even have that any more. I earned money and used it to pay bills and buy clothes, books, DVDs, furniture. I acquired stuff. I watched TV. I got drunk and had hangovers. I worried about my health. I phoned my parents when I had to. I slept. I looked forward to weekends so I could lie in bed late.

That was my life.

And then when Marie had come along she changed things. She gave my life, and heart, a new beat. She made me happy to get out of bed in the morning, to come home at night. She gave me ambition. I spent money on presents for her. We drank together to have a good time; blurred memories. We made love and slept in each other's arms. I looked forward to weekends so I could spend more time with her.

She was my passion; she was what I believed in. And again I thought that if she didn't come back, if I didn't find her, I would have nothing.

I looked around me at the radiant faces. Did it matter if they were deluded, if one day they would be disappointed? These people had something to believe in, a dream to follow, a creed to defend. All I had was my need . . . my search.

'Have you ever heard of someone called Candy?' I asked Denny and Laura quietly, using Marie's alias.

'It sounds familiar.'

'She was on some alien porn sites,' I said.

He looked embarrassed. 'Well, no, I wouldn't know her then . . .'

'We're not into that kind of thing,' said Laura, giving me a hostile look.

I held my hands up. 'Well, neither am I. She was just, um, a girl I knew.' Their reaction had been one of horror. But there was also something defensive about it, like it was something they didn't want to talk about. All of a sudden, I wanted to get away from them. From the whole group.

I turned to Zara and fabricated a yawn.

'Do you want me to show you to your room?' she said, and I nodded.

I followed her up and along the corridor. She was carrying a half-full bottle of wine. We stopped outside the door of her bedroom, which was just along from mine. When I stopped walking I realised how drunk I was.

'Do you want to come in and help me finish this off?' she said, holding up the bottle.

'Yes,' tumbled from my mouth before I could stop myself.

She had a room to herself. I sat beside her on the bed. She drank straight from the bottle and then passed it to me. Before I had a chance to put it to my lips she leaned over and kissed me.

The disappointment of not finding Marie had knocked me off-balance, and here I was, crying out, desperate for love. I needed comfort, warmth, the basic healing power of another body.

Zara wrapped her slender arms around me. I wanted her, and it would be so easy, would feel so good, to give in, to undress her and slip beneath the sheets with her, to feel the warmth of another body against mine . . .

'No, I can't.'

She pulled back as I stood up, moving across the room. I was aroused; my body wanted to do this, but I couldn't.

'I'm sorry, it's—'

'Hey, don't worry,' she said rapidly. 'Just please don't say "It's not you, it's me" or I'll kill you.'

'I really want to,' I said. 'But there's somebody—'

She raised a hand. 'OK. I think you'd better go.'

'I'm sorry.'

'If you say that *one* more time, Richard.'

I went back to my room and grabbed my phone from my bag. The phone was usually attached to me all the time, in case Marie tried to contact me, but since meeting Zara I'd been keeping it hidden and checking it sporadically, worried that my urge to check it every other minute might make people suspicious.

As I left my room, a group of people came up the stairs. I concealed the phone behind my back and trotted down the stairs. I managed to make it out the front door without bumping into anyone else. I walked down onto the beach and sat on a rock a good distance from the Embassy. I looked up at the spire – the window was lit and I thought I could see a figure moving around. Behind the spire the sky was starless, though a segment of moon appeared through the clouds. Behind me I could hear the sea as it kissed the shore.

I turned the phone on and waited for it to connect to a network. It immediately chimed to let me know I had a text from Simon asking me to call him. It was eleven p.m. here so would be seven a.m. in the UK. I called him. The phone rang a dozen times before he picked up.

'Richard?'

'Sorry, did I wake you up?'

He grunted. 'Have you found her?'

There was a slight time delay which made the conversation feel stilted.

'No. She's not here.'

'Oh shit. Sorry, mate. There's no news at this end either.'

'How are you feeling?' I asked.

'How do I feel? I feel like someone owes me a huge fucking favour.'

'I know, I know. I feel terrible.'

'But,' he coughed, 'I suppose you have let me stay at yours. And Sue doesn't appear to hate me so much now she's seen me with my head kicked in. We're having crisis talks. I'm staying at yours till she agrees to take me back.'

I told him I was going to stay here for a short while and see what else I could find out. I had no other leads.

'Did you tell the police about Gary Kennedy?' I asked.

'Susan told them what you told her. But I haven't heard anything since.'

I thought I heard someone on the beach.

'I'd better go,' I said. 'I'll call you if anything happens. Take care, all right? Don't forget to feed Calico.'

'That bloody cat . . .' he started, but I hung up.

I looked up the beach but couldn't see anyone. My skin prickled. I was sure I was being watched. But all I could see were the rocks and sand; all I could hear was the rhythmic lapping of the waves. I headed back to the house.

19

Zara shook me awake. I lifted my head from the pillow and moaned. It felt like there was a cannonball attached to my neck.

'Hey, sleepyhead,' she said. 'I made you coffee.'

She set it down on the bedside table and perched on the edge of the bed. She smelled of soap and looked pretty and fresh in the morning light. Again, I was struck by how much she looked like Marie. The difference was that Zara was *here*, next to me. Last night she had tried to kiss me and I had rejected her. Part of me wanted to pull back the quilt, invite her into my bed. But I couldn't.

A frown darkened Zara's features. 'I heard that,' she said softly. 'What?'

'That thought. It was loud and clear.' She turned away sadly. 'There's somebody else. You should have told me, Richard. I hate . . . awkwardness.'

Surely she couldn't really read minds? I prayed not.

I sat up. 'Zara . . .'

Her eyes shone with moisture. 'You don't need to say anything. I get it. Men are always in love with somebody else. Who is she?'

I put my head in my hands. How much wine had I drunk the night before? My tongue felt like I could use it to sand wood.

I didn't see any harm in telling her now. Maybe she would have some information.

'Her name's Marie.'

She furrowed her brow. 'Isn't that—?'

'I kind of . . . lied about that. Marie isn't really an alien. She's a woman. A flesh and blood woman. One who walked out on me, vanished into thin air. I'm sorry I wasn't honest about that . . . I didn't want people to think I only came here looking for her.'

'But you thought she might be here?'

I nodded. 'Marie is really into the whole alien thing.'

Zara tipped her head.

'As well,' I added hastily. 'We, er, talked about coming here together. I thought maybe she'd beaten me to it. That's why I ran into the house looking for her. I was a little over-excited.'

The secret of lying convincingly, I had discovered, was to make yourself believe what you were saying at the moment you were saying it.

Zara scrutinised me, apparently trying to work out if everything I was saying was bullshit. But what she said next surprised me.

'This girl broke your heart.'

I sighed.

'Are your motives pure, Richard?'

I blinked at her. 'What do you mean?'

'I mean, your reasons for wanting to join the Chorus. Are you doing it for Marie? Or because you are running away from your heartbreak? You need to make a decision now – do you really want to come with us, or do you want to stay behind and try to fix the love that's broken?'

I wanted to fix what was broken. I said, 'I want to come with you.'

She rubbed her eyes. 'You're sure? Because your reasons need to be true and pure.'

'Yes, yes . . . This is what I've always wanted. To join the Chorus. It's my destiny.'

Last night, when I went to bed, I had decided I would stay here for forty-eight hours, talk to everyone, see if anyone knew anything about Marie or any of the other missing Brits. Then I would do my own vanishing act. Until then, though I hated deceiving kind, trusting Zara, she and the others had to continue to believe I was a genuine believer.

I held my breath, waiting to see if Zara trusted me, trying to think about random nonsense – just in case she actually could read minds.

Zara looked right into my eyes, and I was sure she was going to tell me to get out.

'I believe you,' she said. 'Now, you'd better get up and get dressed. It's Trance Time.'

I showered and put on my white underwear, white jeans and white shirt. Zara led me downstairs.

All of the other Loved Ones were in the open room – I counted just over thirty. They sat cross-legged on cushions, in rows of six or seven, facing the window. Their eyes were closed and they were silent and still.

At the front of the congregation, sitting beneath the window, across which the curtains were drawn, sat one of the most beautiful women I had ever seen. She had crow-black hair cut in a bob that fell like silk drapes to her shoulders. Her face was the image of tranquillity: her heavy eyelids were closed; her skin was smooth and tanned and free of any blemishes. She wore white like everyone else, and her slim, lightly tanned arms lay on her crossed legs. She opened her eyes – the pupils were the colour of rich coffee – and looked over at Zara and me. She nodded and, after Zara and I had sat down beside Jake and Joan, she said, 'Let the Trance take hold.'

I could see Rick across the room. He had one eye open and he peered around surreptitiously. He saw me, also with one eye open, and we were both forced to suppress a laugh. All of the others had closed their eyes now and had placed their hands on the people beside or in front of them, palms resting on shoulders, some holding hands, so everyone in the room was connected. The only sound was that of our communal breathing. A thin stream of light pushed through the gap in the curtains; dust swirled in the shine. Not wanting to be caught out, I closed my eyes too.

Lisa began to speak in a deep, husky drawl: 'I hear the first bars of the symphony. I hear the beating of drums. I hear chords swell and boom. I hear the music of the stars. I hear the *vox celeste*.

'The love is building, rising, travelling like light between suns and planets. The love is directed at us. We absorb the love, soak it into our skins. It gives us strength. The love comes closer, the distance diminishes every day. The love is in the song, in the music, in the voice. They want to show us the way to the stars. They have so much to teach us.' She let out a long, whispered sigh. 'Oh, the love . . . it's here in this room, it's here for us. Can you feel it?'

All around me people began to sigh like Lisa had done. I joined in. Although I felt foolish, I couldn't help but be affected by the vibes around me. Sex hung in the air like clouds of steam in a sauna. Beside me, Jake breathed heavily; Joan let out little gasps of pleasure; Zara groaned as I imagined she would in bed. Everyone in the room was in a high state of arousal. Surely this wasn't going to turn into an orgy? It was only nine in the morning.

Lisa continued to speak. I badly wanted to look at her but forced myself to keep my eyes shut.

The excitement in her voice grew. 'The music moves up an octave. Strings and horns and bass . . . Oh, listen! Hear the words!

Listen to them say they love us. Listen to them tell us we're special, we're chosen. We can see the truth. We do not doubt, for we can hear the voice. Oh, the voice, the love, the love . . .'

Marie would have loved this. I recalled the night she had stared at the stars from our bedroom window and told me about the voice, about how only she and Andrew could hear it.

The moaning and sighing grew louder. I braced myself. But nobody made a move towards anyone else. They were locked inside their minds, in a trance. What were they picturing? Images like those I had seen on the internet? Or was I the only one here thinking about sex? Apart from Rick I was the only one in the room who didn't believe.

'Listen! Listen!' Lisa was saying, and the sighing swelled and people began to pant and emit little squeaks and low groans that grew louder and louder until Lisa made a sound like she was climaxing and everyone else made the sound too, an orchestra of orgasms, and then there was silence.

Seconds passed.

I opened my eyes. The people around me were damp with sweat, a beatific expression on each of their faces. Gradually, they too opened their eyes and exchanged looks, like lovers after great sex. They smiled, touched each other tenderly, their eyes moist, skin glistening with perspiration.

I glanced at my watch. An hour had gone by since I'd entered the room. The gathered Loved Ones began to rise to their feet and were about to file out when Lisa said, 'Please wait. I want to speak to all of you.'

All eyes focused on her, eyes full of love and devotion. These people, it struck me, would do anything for her.

'We have two new members with us today,' she said. 'Richard and Rick. They will be joining us on our journey. I want you to make them both feel welcome.'

I heard many voices say, 'Welcome,' and a number of hands touched my back and shoulders, stroking and patting. I nodded at Lisa. Across the room, Rick received similar treatment. He looked as uncomfortable as I felt.

'Over the last few days,' Lisa announced, 'I've been communicating intensively with the Chorus. It's been exhausting—' A murmur of sympathy '—but *so* invigorating.' She beamed at us and everyone beamed back.

'I've spoken to our other embassies, who have also been communicating on the same level. We're each receiving the same message.' She paused dramatically. 'The message is that *contact is imminent.*'

All around me the Loved Ones whooped and clapped, embracing one another, their faces sparkling with excitement.

Lisa went on. 'There's been unprecedented UFO activity all over the country, all over the *world.* Sightings are coming in all the time.' Her tone darkened. 'Still, the world's governments choose to pretend they don't know what is going on. They continue to propagate lies, to cloud the minds of our fellow citizens.' The crowd hissed and gasped like kids at a pantomime.

'However, this doesn't mean they are not watching us. We must be extra-vigilant. We cannot let anyone try to stop us now.' She paused dramatically. 'It is time to break contact with the outside world.'

She waited for the murmurs to die down.

'I don't want anyone to stray beyond the beach from tonight on. You have eight hours to call and say goodbye to relatives and friends, if that is what you wish to do. But do not make it explicit that you are saying goodbye. That might make them try to stop us. Anyone who tries that will be dealt with in the harshest way possible. I want you all to stop using your social media accounts. Do not put anything on them that gives any hint of what is happening. Anyone who does not comply with my request will not be included when we make contact. You will be cast out. Is that understood?'

There were nods and grunts of affirmation. The words *cast out* had sent a shiver of fear through the room.

'So, if you choose to contact outsiders today, keep it casual. Don't say goodbye. And I want you all in a state of alert now. Contact could be made at any time. It could come with very little warning. I want you to stay pure. No drugs, no alcohol. Again, you have eight hours. Sex is allowed, but don't exhaust yourselves. If you can abstain, then that would be better. Remember, there will be greater pleasures to discover after contact is made.'

Lisa paused and looked around. 'So is everything clear? Very soon, that which we have waited for all our lives will occur. The truth will be known.' She raised her arms to the heavens. 'The stars will be our home.'

As everyone left the room, they buzzed with excitement. *At last, at last,* I could hear them say. It didn't matter to them if they had to give up some earthly pleasures, or that they would never see their friends or families again. That was trivial. None of them was in any doubt that the time was nigh. Deliverance was imminent.

I turned to Zara, to ask her something, but heard someone say, 'Zara, Richard, can I talk to you?'

I turned and found myself facing Lisa. She knocked the breath out of my lungs. It wasn't just the way she looked: she burned with charisma and power, like heat from a star. But there was something dark about her. Intimidating.

Zara hugged her, and they kissed.

'I'm so happy to have you here, Richard,' Lisa said, touching my arm. 'It's always a great pleasure when non-Americans join us. And I'm pleased you and Zara are getting along so well. Zara has needed friendship since her husband died.'

My shock must have been evident, as Lisa said, 'You haven't told him, Zara?'

Zara shook her head.

191

'Oh.' She addressed me. 'Zara was married to a great guy called Ben. A writer. Very talented.'

'Oh God, I'm sorry,' I said. 'What happened?'

'A motorcycle accident,' Zara whispered.'

Lisa said to me, 'She's over it now.'

I didn't believe her. Zara looked like she was about to start crying. Lisa touched her hand gently and Zara seemed to improve instantly. Her eyes dried and she gathered herself, shook off her grief like a dog shaking off water.

Lisa said, 'Did you bring the files? The flash drives?'

Zara's face fell. 'Oh hell . . .'

'Oh, Zara! Don't tell me you left them at the house? We *need* them.' Her eyes flashed with anger.

'I'm so sorry! I'll drive back and get them. I'll go now.'

Lisa sighed. 'Bring them straight to me when you get back. Great to meet you, Richard.' She turned and walked away.

'Why do you let her boss you around?' I said to Zara, when Lisa was out of earshot.

'Because I love her,' she replied, as if I were stupid. 'She guides us. And she always knows best. Dammit . . . I'd better go straight away, before the curfew starts.'

'Do you want me to come with you?'

She shook her head. 'No, you'd better stay here. Why don't you try to get to know the others better? The closer we all are, the better it will be when contact happens.'

After Zara had gone, I found Lisa outside, looking out to sea, smoking a cigarette. When she saw me, she quickly flicked the cigarette away, then turned and gave me a broad smile.

'Hey, Richard.'

'Hi. I just wanted to say thank you. For letting me join you.'

'You're very welcome.' She looked over my shoulder as she spoke, like she was dismissing me.

I hesitated but decided it couldn't do any harm. Zara would probably tell her anyway. 'Do you know someone called Marie Walker?'

She looked blank.

'Andrew Jade?'

She shook her head. 'Sorry, no.'

But her eyes had flickered as she'd said this. I didn't want to arouse her suspicions so I left it. But as I went back inside, I felt more convinced than ever. Somebody here must know something.

I drifted around the house, joining in conversations, slipping in questions about Marie and Andrew. No one knew anything – or they were all lying.

After an hour or so of this I sensed that, as a group, people were starting to get suspicious, noticing what I was doing, so I decided to leave it for a while. I went up to my room and lay down. I still felt hung over, so I closed my eyes . . .

When I woke up it was pouring with rain. It pummelled the window and made me feel thirsty. I splashed some cold water on my face then went downstairs to the kitchen. As I was pouring some orange juice into a glass, Carl came into the room.

'Hey,' he said. 'I guess you must be pretty stoked.'

'Erm . . . yes.' I wasn't sure what he was talking about. The forthcoming contact, I assumed.

'Looks like your friend will be the last to join us. He made it just in time, before the curfew kicks in.'

'Sorry? Friend?'

'Oh. Hasn't Lisa told you yet? Zara just called from her house. Apparently there was a guy hanging around there, looking for you.' My heart plummeted into my stomach. 'He said he'd come to join us. Zara said she could tell he was right for us so she's bringing him here. His name's Gary.'

I almost dropped the glass of juice.

'Gary,' I repeated.

Carl grinned. 'Yeah, that's right. Cool. Were you expecting him? Why didn't you . . . Hey, are you OK, Richard?'

My mind raced. Gary must have got the address of Lisa's house from Freya. Either she had betrayed me or he had coerced her. Beaten it out of her. I had an image of him torturing her, extracting the information with a pair of pliers. I felt sick. Probably she had given up the address easily. But whatever had happened, he was here.

He would expose me, blow my final chances of getting anyone to talk about Marie.

And when he found out Cherry wasn't here, I dreaded to think what he would do. But I had no doubt it would involve violence. He had told Simon he would kill me.

There was only one thing I could do.

'I need to talk to Lisa,' I said, grabbing hold of Carl.

'Hey, dude, chill . . .'

'Now!'

20

Carl came back into the kitchen with Lisa. He started to speak but she held up a hand and he was immediately silenced.

She said, 'Tell me everything, Richard.'

I took a deep breath. I stuttered the first few words. I hadn't stuttered since I was fifteen. I closed my eyes, took deep breaths.

'His name's Gary Kennedy – and he wants to destroy everything you've created here. He lied to Zara. He's not my friend. He's not a believer. Worse than that, he thinks our belief is obscene.'

I paced the room as I spoke.

'But Gary's girlfriend *was* a believer. She left him because she couldn't persuade him that visitors do exist – ran away without telling him where she was going.' It was an easy story to tell. 'And he went crazy. He hates people like us. Blames us for his girlfriend leaving him. He wants to hurt the movement, to bring it down. He goes to meetings of believers in England and disrupts them. He spreads propaganda against us, sets the police onto us, tries to frame us for things we haven't done. He's made my life – and the life of dozens of other believers in England – a misery. That's one of the reasons I came to America, to escape him. But he's followed me.'

It was easy, too, to look panicked, scared.

'Why you?' Lisa asked coolly. I could tell Carl believed every word, but Lisa was sceptical. 'Why follow you in particular?

'Because . . . because I helped his girlfriend escape him. I arranged a haven for her. I helped cover the trail. He knows this, although he can't prove it. That's why he follows me, because he thinks I'll lead him to her. And he doesn't even really love her. He only wants to control her, can't bear the fact that she got one over on him. He wants to punish her. He's violent. He used to beat her when they were together. He's evil, Lisa, truly evil.'

I was shaking by the time I finished. But I still couldn't tell if she believed me.

'If he comes into the Embassy,' I said, 'he'll ruin all you've got here. If he arrives here after travelling all this way and discovers that his girlfriend isn't here he'll go mad. He might get violent. He might have a gun. And if you turn him away he won't hesitate in going back to the authorities and telling them lies about you. He'll tell them there's a suicide cult here, that you're dealing drugs to local kids, whatever. The police will come and arrest everyone and then when the visitors come we won't be here.'

I was talking fast, almost babbling, my panic authentic. Lisa and Carl looked at each other.

'We're so close now, Lisa,' Carl said quietly. 'We can't let anything jeopardise contact. We can't afford the slightest risk.'

Lisa hesitated for a long, agonizing moment. Then, finally, she nodded decisively. 'Go get Jake, Denny, Steven and Frank.'

He ran from the room.

Lisa turned to me. 'I'm not happy about this, Richard. You have brought danger to our door. And I know you're not telling me everything.'

'But it's true,' I said, my voice rising an octave. 'You've got to stop Gary.'

'Oh, I believe that part. But there's something that doesn't ring true about you.'

I opened my mouth to protest but she narrowed her eyes at me and the words were choked in my throat.

'Go to your room,' she said, as if I were a bad child.

Head down, I obeyed. As I walked towards the stairs I passed Carl, who was emerging from the open room with Jake and Denny and two men I hadn't met before, although I had seen them at that morning's 'Trance' session. They were big men, strong and muscular. They looked like security guards, and I wondered if that was exactly what they were. Lisa wasn't stupid. She had prepared for everything.

The men looked at me with cold eyes. Behind them I could see Rick, eyeing the group with interest. I slunk past and went to my room.

From my window I had a view of the beach. I wiped the condensation from the windowpane with a trembling hand and looked out. It was still raining. The air was thick and drenched. The sky was shaded grey and black.

Below me, the front door opened. The five men Lisa had summoned stood by the door, waiting.

They didn't have to wait long. Zara's Mazda pulled up slowly, its tyres fighting for traction on the slippery ground. She opened her door and stepped out. She was smiling and waved to the group in the doorway. To me, behind my window, everything happened in silence, all sounds smothered by the relentless drumming of the rain.

The passenger door opened and Gary stepped out.

He came around the side of the car. He was scowling, squinting through the rain. Zara's expression changed from relaxed to concerned. I watched as the five men stepped from the doorway into the rain and walked purposefully towards Gary, who was staring at the house. Maybe he could see me, a dark figure at the upstairs window.

Carl went up to Zara and took her hand, leading her to one side. Her mouth was moving, he was shaking his head, pointing back to the house. Jake, Denny, Frank and Steven walked up to Gary, who smiled flickeringly, until Denny tried to grab him and Gary backed away. Now, he looked scared.

He reached inside his jacket and the four men jumped him.

Jake grabbed the arm that had been inside the jacket. Frank grabbed the other arm. Gary struggled and brought out a gun. I guessed he had contacts here, someone who could get a gun to him. Steven kicked it from his grasp and it fell onto the wet sand.

Beneath me, other Loved Ones came out to watch. They lined the front of the Embassy, staring impassively. I couldn't see Lisa.

Jake punched Gary in the face, hard. Blood spilled from Gary's broken lip but was immediately washed away by the rain. As Frank and Steven held Gary's arms, Jake punched him in the face again, then again. Gary's head drooped. He spat out a tooth. He tried to kick out, but Denny moved in and gracelessly kicked him in the balls. Gary doubled up, but the two men holding him pulled him up straight.

I pressed my face against the glass.

Steven and Frank turned Gary around and started to drag him down the beach. He kicked and struggled. Jake moved in front of him and punched him in the stomach. This seemed to weaken Gary considerably. He went limp. Jake and Denny grabbed his legs and pulled him up, so the four of them were carrying him. They looked like they were going to give him the bumps for his birthday.

The crowd edged forward. The four men carried Gary towards the sea.

With a sickening lurch in my stomach, I realised what they were going to do. I wanted them to scare him off, that was all. Oh Jesus . . . I had to stop this.

I ran to the door of my bedroom and yanked. It wouldn't open. The door had been locked from the outside. I thumped it a few times. I looked around for a key. Nothing.

I ran back to the window. The rain continued to beat down on the sand. They had taken Gary to the edge of the sea. The tide was in. I watched in horror as they carried him into the shallow waves. The churning foam covered their feet, then ankles, then shins. Soon they were knee deep in the water.

Gary realised what was happening. He thrashed and bucked but they were too strong for him. The men carried him deeper, until the ocean was around their thighs, and then they pushed him face down into the water. He disappeared from sight. They squatted and held him down. Denny put his foot on Gary's back. I saw an arm come up. Gary was wearing a black watch. The arm went back down.

They held him under the water.

I screamed and banged the window with both fists.

After he had drowned they lifted him out of the sea and carried his body up the beach. Jake stopped and picked up Gary's fallen gun, tucking it into his jeans. The other Loved Ones filed back into the house. I heard the front door slam, then open again. Lisa appeared outside. She held a black umbrella above her head and was carrying a spade. Zara ran up to her and Lisa stroked her face. Zara's face went blank and she disappeared inside the house.

Lisa went up to the four men who were holding Gary's corpse. She handed the spade to Jake and gestured towards the rear of the Embassy. I watched as they carried him behind the fence.

Lisa looked up at my window. I ducked down. When I looked again she was still standing beneath the black umbrella, staring at the sea, the rain filling the air around her. She stood like that for a long time.

21

I was locked in my room, hungry and thirsty and terrified I would be next. I kept imagining the sound of heavy male footsteps, Jake and Denny and the others coming for me, preparing to carry me out to sea, to push my face beneath the surface of the water. I pictured myself sucking up salt water, the air in my lungs filling with ocean and vomit. My last thought as I died would be that I had failed, that I would never see Marie again. I would end up in an unmarked grave beside another man whose death I was responsible for, another man who had hunted his missing girlfriend across the globe. And I still had no idea where Marie and Cherry were.

I paced the room, trying not to panic.

The beach outside my window was empty now. Lisa had come inside. I could hear people moving about downstairs, and doors opening and closing along the corridor. What were they doing? Probably they were just carrying on, as if nothing had happened.

I lay on the bed and chewed my nails. I had just about mutilated each of my fingers when I heard a key turn in the door. I tensed with fear.

Zara came in.

'Oh, thank God it's you . . .' I began.

She put a finger to her lips and I fell silent.

'I've been asked to see if there's anything you need,' she said.

'I want to go. I saw what they did to Gary. They murdered him, Zara. You have to let me get out of here.'

She shook her head. She looked so sad, her unhappiness tinged with disappointment. 'That's not possible.'

'Please, Zara.' I crossed the room, tried to put my hands on her arms but she backed away.

'They're having a meeting, trying to decide what to do with you,' she said.

'Oh my God.' I was going to be sick. 'Zara, they're going to kill me.'

She didn't speak.

'Zara—' I began, but she interrupted me.

'I can't believe I brought him here. I believed he was your friend.' She turned her face towards me. '*Was* he your friend? Lisa says you're a liar. But she doesn't know what you're lying about.'

'I'm not . . .' But I had run out of energy. Was sick of hearing myself lie.

'It's my fault that he's dead,' Zara said. She stood up. 'I'd better get back to Lisa. Are you sure you don't want anything?'

I shook my head.

Five minutes after leaving the room, she came back. 'Lisa wants to talk to you. She's in the watch room. Follow me.'

She turned around and walked out stiffly, like a soldier leading a prisoner of war to the interrogation room. I felt like that POW, fear clawing at my bowels as I was led towards the white light, the ways of making one talk. I could try to run but there were too many people around. I would never make it out. And if I got outside, where would I go?

Zara led me along the corridor to a door set in the far wall. She produced a key and unlocked the door, then led me up some steps.

This, I realised, was the spire that overlooked the beach. Lisa's office, the place where she meditated and received the messages from the aliens that she passed on to her troops. At the top of the stairs was another door. Zara pushed it open and led me into the room.

Lisa was sitting behind a long desk, flanked by Carl and Jake.

They leaned forward on their elbows and looked at me, scowling.

'Sit down,' Lisa said to me. Addressing Zara, she said, 'You may leave us now.'

Zara paused for a moment, then left the room. I sat down. It's hard to describe how I felt at that moment. Exhausted. Accepting of my fate, which felt like it was out of my hands. I felt curiously light, as if surrendering had lifted the burden of my search from my shoulders, had freed my chained soul.

A clap of thunder made me turn instinctively to the window. The view was captivating: the Pacific stretching to the point where it met the vast grey sky, where sailors might once have imagined the edge of the world to be. Above the ocean, the storm roared and sparked. Forked lightning crackled above the horizon, spidery, jagged lines lighting up the crashing waves, thunder booming and making the Embassy tremble. The clouds continued to chuck out cold, sharp rain.

For a moment the four of us watched the storm, forgetting why we were together in that room. Then Lisa said, 'Richard. I think you know why we've asked you to come up here.'

I nodded. Behind her, a computer screen blinked with the light of UFOs – her screen saver. All over the walls were pictures of Greys and UFOs, star charts and snapshots. It reminded me of Marie's tiny bedsit, the place where I had first kissed her. The hole at my centre – the space that Marie had left in me – ached. And then I saw it:

On the wall behind Lisa's head was a picture of a woman having sex with an alien. The woman was Laura, Denny's girlfriend.

It was almost identical to one of the photos I had found under my bed. The Photoshopped alien entered Laura from behind. I looked around frantically, but there were no more pictures. There were filing cabinets to my right. They could be full of similar pictures.

'Richard, are you listening to me?'

'Yes. Yes, I am.' Suddenly, anger flooded through me, brought on by the sight of the photo. I stood up. 'What the hell gives you the right to lock me in my room? I want to leave now!'

The three of them looked so shocked I almost laughed. But I was just warming up. I needed to lie my way out of this. I put on my most haughty British accent.

'I have a good mind to leave here right now, to go back to England and tell everyone who'll listen that the Loved Ones are nothing more than a sham, a bunch of pretenders who can't see the truth when it's right in front of them. I really believed in you. I really wanted to be one of you, to be part of all this. And this is how you treat me! Why don't you ask Zara? She knows I'm genuine.'

The two men turned to Lisa. She stood up and came around the desk, standing directly before me.

'You're a liar,' she said. 'The *vox celeste* told me. Though I am sure you think I am talking nonsense – because you're not a believer, are you?'

'I am—'

She cut me off. 'Why are you really here? Are you a government agent?'

I laughed.

The corner of her mouth lifted. 'No. You're too incompetent.' She leaned closer until I could smell her breath. Alcohol. She had broken her own rule. 'Nobody is going to stop contact from happening, especially not you.'

'Why don't you let me loosen his tongue?' Jake said, standing up and flexing his muscles.

Lisa studied me. 'Is that necessary, Richard?'

'We should remove him, like we did the other guy,' Carl said. Carl, who had been so friendly before.

'I'm starting to think that might be our only option,' Lisa said.

Without warning, she slapped my face, hard. She was wearing a ring and it caught my cheek. I was so shocked I couldn't move for a second, but when I raised my hand to my face I saw blood on my fingers.

'Tell us!' she screamed.

The two men got up and stepped towards me. Jake was, I realised with horror, holding a hunting knife. The gun he had taken from Gary was tucked into the waistband of his jeans.

'I'm going to slit your throat and bury you on the beach, next to your friend.'

'Please.'

Lisa slapped me again.

'Why are you here?' she yelled in my face, spraying me with spittle.

I didn't reply.

'OK,' she said, nodding to Jake. 'Kill him.'

He came towards me with the knife, a cold grin on his face.

'No!' I shouted. 'I'll tell you.'

He paused.

'I came here looking for my girlfriend. Marie Walker, the one I asked you about, Lisa. That's all. I've already told Zara this. The only thing I haven't told you is that . . . is that I don't believe in aliens or UFOs.' I gulped down air. 'I just thought someone here might know something about Marie. That's all, that's the truth.'

Jake looked at Lisa, who gestured for him to lower the knife.

'Why did you ask me about Andrew Jade?' she asked.

I panted. 'He was Marie's best friend, her business partner. Did you know him? Did you know Andrew?'

She ignored me.

'What do you think?' she asked the two men. 'Is he telling the truth?'

'Sounds like a crock of shit to me,' said Jake.

'I don't know,' said Carl.

Lisa stared at me. She didn't look so beautiful any more.

'Take him back to his room, shut him in.'

'Lisa, I think—' Jake began.

'I need to consult the *vox celeste*.'

That shut him up. Jake pulled me roughly to my feet and pushed my arm up behind my back.

'Ah, Jesus, that hurts.'

'Shut the fuck up.'

Jake shoved me into my room and pointed a meaty finger at me. 'You'd better pray the Chorus are feeling merciful. Where's your passport?'

I hesitated.

He pointed the knife at me. 'In my bag.'

He turned my suitcase over, shaking all the contents out and snatching up my passport. He opened it, checking I wasn't using a fake name. Then he stuck it in his pocket. 'I'm taking this to Lisa.'

He slammed the door.

———◡———

I sat on the floor, rubbing my shoulder, waiting for my pulse to return to normal.

I tried to work out what Lisa was doing. She couldn't *really* believe that the aliens were going to tell her what to do with me, though I didn't doubt that Carl and Jake believed it. I figured she was buying time to decide. And if she did decide to murder me, the others would put it down to the Chorus's will – conveniently ridding them of any guilt. Following orders.

My story, though true, sounded so weak. I was convinced that at any moment the door would open and Jake would be standing there with his hunting knife or the gun he had taken from Gary.

As I thought this, I heard a key in the lock. I sprang to my feet, looked around frantically. Could I smash the window and jump? Was there a weapon I could use? I tried to catch my breath. I was dead. They were going to kill me . . .

Zara came into the room.

'I thought you were Jake, coming to kill me,' I said.

She walked over to me. 'Is it really the only reason you came here?' she asked. 'To find Marie?'

'Yes. I swear. I'm sorry I—'

She cut me off. 'And you didn't tell Gary to come here?'

'No, of course not. He followed me . . .'

'You don't work for the government? Or the New World Order?'

'Zara, do I look like a government agent?'

She laughed softly. 'I guess not. But you're not a believer.'

'No. No, I'm not.'

A look of great sadness and disappointment came over her.

'Zara,' I said, placing my hands on her shoulders. 'You have to let me out of here. Lisa and Jake want to kill me. I'm not an agent, I'm not out to harm you in any way. All I wanted to do was find my girlfriend. If you let me out, I promise I'll go straight back to England. You'll never hear from me again. You can drive me to the airport if you want, watch me get on the plane.'

'I can't do that.'

I tried to look into her eyes but she wouldn't meet my gaze. 'I'm so sorry I lied to you. I really like you, Zara. I didn't like deceiving you. But I haven't done anything that means I deserve to die.' The last few words came out strangled.

Zara broke away from me and crossed to the window.

Any moment, Jake could arrive and take me away to be exe-cuted. I racked my brain for something that would convince Zara to let me out. Or maybe I could try to overpower her. She had the key in her pocket. It shouldn't be too hard. I didn't want to do that, but if I had no choice . . .

She turned from the window and interrupted my garbled thoughts. I drew in a deep breath.

'I don't want anyone else to get hurt,' she said.

I exhaled.

'You promise you'll go straight back to the UK? That you won't do anything to try to stop Contact?'

'I promise.'

She chewed her lower lip. 'I can't just let you out. There are people all over the place. You won't make it out of the house. We'll have to do it tonight.'

'But Lisa won't wait till then.'

'I'll talk to her.'

'But—'

'You'll have to trust me, Richard.'

There was nothing else I could do. She was right. There was no way I'd be able to get out of the house without being stopped. It was already eight p.m. so I wouldn't have to wait too long.

'OK,' I said.

She left the room, locking the door from the outside.

Hours passed. By the time the house grew quiet, I had worked myself into a frenzy of dread. I didn't really know if I could trust Zara. What if she and Lisa were up in the office now, laughing, imagining my torment as they planned to kill me in the dead of night?

Finally, at around one a.m., I heard the key scratching in the lock. I braced myself yet again.

It was Zara.

She came into the room, her finger on her lips. Checking that the coast was still clear, she gestured for me to follow her.

It was quiet in the hallway, though the overhead lights blazed. Zara padded quickly towards the stairs and I followed her. We went down the stairs and she paused to look around. Someone came out of the kitchen and Zara gestured for me to stay back. Whoever it was went into the front room and Zara tiptoed across to open the front door. She waved me for me to come, and within seconds I felt the welcoming kiss of fresh air.

Zara's Mazda was parked right there. We climbed in.

'My passport,' I said, suddenly remembering. 'Jake took it when—'

'Relax. I've got it. He left it on Lisa's desk.'

'Oh, thank God.'

'It should be me you're thanking, Richard,' she said with a little smile.

'I know. I'm so—'

'Oh shit.'

Jake had appeared from nowhere and was standing in front of the car, gesturing angrily. Zara pressed a button to lock the car doors. Jake began to yell and two or three other people came out of the house.

'We need to go,' I urged.

Zara hesitated.

'Please!'

'I can't run him down.'

There were people behind the car now too. And more were streaming out of the house, surrounding us. It was like a scene from a zombie film, where the undead crowd around the car, trying to get in.

'Oh, fuck!' Zara exclaimed, revving the engine and jerking forward, stopping an inch from Jake's thighs. His face was contorted with fury. I looked across and saw Lisa standing by the side of the car.

Then I heard someone shouting.

'Hey, hey – they're here. The Chorus! They've landed!'

Everyone standing around the car turned their heads to look. I leaned over Zara, craning my neck to see. It was Rick. He was standing down by the beach, waving and gesturing towards the sea.

'They're here!' he called again.

Everyone apart from Lisa and Jake broke into a run towards Rick. He was trying to save us. I had no idea what he would say when they reached the beach and there was no spaceship there, but at that moment I didn't care.

Then I realised Zara was staring at Rick too, and her hand moved towards the door. This was what she, too, had been waiting for. I reached across and took hold of her wrist.

'He's lying,' I whispered. 'He's doing it so we get away.'

'How do you know?'

'Because he's a journalist.'

'What?' she hissed.

'I'll explain when we get out of here. If that fucker ever gets out of the way.'

Still in front of the car, Jake looked at us, then at the beach.

Lisa shouted, 'He's lying. Jake—'

But nothing could stop him from checking it out. He joined the others, running towards Rick. Now only Lisa remained. She screamed with anger and tried to get in front of the car, but she was too slow. Zara shifted into drive and put her foot down.

I watched Lisa in the rearview mirror, gesticulating like a madwoman.

22

Zara's phone rang on and off all the way to the airport in Portland, until she eventually switched it off.

'Do you think they'll follow us?' I asked.

'I doubt it. But I won't ever be able to go back there now.'

Her words hung in the air between us.

'I'm so sorry,' I said.

She stared at the road ahead. 'It was my life.'

'They were murderers, Zara. They were going to murder me too.'

She didn't respond.

After a long silence, she said, 'I can't believe Rick is a journalist. What's he doing? Writing a story about us? And you've known all along?'

'He told me on the way out here. Again, I'm sorry. But I couldn't let you find out I didn't really believe.'

The city lights shone on the horizon. I wondered what story Rick had made up. I was worried about him. I hoped he'd made a run for it, managed to get away.

There was something I needed to ask Zara, that had been playing on my mind.

'I saw a picture on the wall in Lisa's office: Laura, having sex with an alien. Marie appeared in photos like that. So did Gary's girlfriend, Cherry, the one he was hunting.'

Zara's cheeks had gone pink.

'Is that how you fund what you do?'

She didn't look at me. 'When we started, we badly needed money to buy this place and to maintain it. The erotica was one way of bringing in a steady income. I think we were the first to do it. You know I told you about Jay, who runs the Embassy on the East Coast? It was his idea. He's a graphic designer, and he devised the first pictures. Lisa was the first woman to ever pose in such pictures.'

'Did you do it too?' I asked.

'I did, a long time ago. But Ben, my husband, found out, and . . . well, in the end I begged Lisa not to use the pictures and she agreed. By then we had Laura and a few other women, and men, who were happy to do it, though they wouldn't admit it now. It all stopped ages ago. We don't need the money anymore.'

'So why is there a picture on Lisa's wall?'

Zara shrugged. 'I don't know. Maybe as a reminder of what we've left behind?'

She didn't sound too convinced.

'I guess you don't need the money now because you persuade everyone who joins to sign over their property and all their possessions.'

'They do that voluntarily.'

I held up my hands. 'I'm not attacking or accusing you. Not *you*, anyway. But it seems to me that that's what the whole thing is about. Lisa doesn't really believe. It's about money and power. These things always are.'

'No,' she said. 'We believe. We all believe.' A long pause. I was pretty sure there were tears in her eyes. 'Guess you must think

I'm a joke, what with my so-called psychic powers and all. They didn't work very well with you, did they? You've made me look like a fool.'

'Zara. You're one of the nicest people I've ever met. I . . .'

She held up a hand to silence me. 'Shut up. Do you know why I helped you? Why I didn't just let Lisa do what she wanted with you? Why I've given up everything for you? It's because I know what it's like to lose someone you love. When my husband died I thought it was the end for me.' She paused, sniffed. 'Lisa saved me from my despair by giving me something new to devote myself to. And now that's gone too.'

I searched for something to say. I felt guilty. But I also felt like I'd saved her in some way, even if she didn't realise it yet.

'Why don't you come with me?'

She shook her head. 'That isn't possible.'

'I know you won't believe me right now but you don't belong with them, Zara. Something bad's going to happen at the Embassy. I can feel it. They're murderers. And how do you think they're going to react when contact doesn't actually happen? Lisa would probably have made up some excuse and had you posing for porn shots again. You need to go out into the world – the *real* world – and find somebody new to love you. That's what you deserve.'

We stopped at a light and she turned to me. 'Can you imagine how I'll feel if the Chorus come and I'm left behind?'

'But Zara, you don't really believe that's going to happen, do you?'

'Maybe not now . . . But it will. Some day.'

'And in the meantime, you need to live your life. Enjoy it. Don't waste it waiting.'

I hoped I had got through to her. But it was impossible to tell. I was just glad that she wouldn't be able to go back. I really was convinced something awful was going to happen there.

At the airport, we got out of the car. I hugged her and kissed her cheek. I could taste the salt of her tears.

'Goodbye, Richard. I hope you find Marie. I really hope it all works out.'

'I still have no idea where she is.'

'Then maybe you should take your own advice. Don't waste your life waiting.'

———

The next flight to London, via Minneapolis, was at six a.m. and, to my great relief, there were seats available. I was able to transfer my ticket and went into a Starbucks to load up on caffeine. After that, I decided I *really* needed a cigarette so bought some and went outside to smoke.

I stood in the cold night air filling my lungs and wondering if Zara was right, if I really should follow my own advice. How long was I going to go on searching? Perhaps I should give up, get on with my life, accept that Marie didn't want to be found. But it wouldn't be easy, even if I wanted to give up. I couldn't think about anything else. I couldn't stop scratching the itch.

I stubbed out my cigarette and was about to go back inside when a young guy came out through the doors of the airport, a stuffed rucksack on his back. He stopped to look around, probably trying to find a taxi. And as he looked up I realised, with a jolt that almost floored me, that I knew him.

It was Pete.

———

From his red forehead and nose, he looked like he'd spent a day lying on a beach with no sunblock on, and his hair was shorter. But it was definitely him. The Jinx. He began walking away.

'Pete!' I called.

He turned and squinted at me, taking a step closer.

'Do you remember me?' I asked.

With a grimace, he removed his rucksack and dropped it to the floor. 'Shit, that's better.' He rubbed his shoulder. 'Hey, you're that photographer dude from Hastings. I met you on the hill that night with Andrew and Marie. You were with that fat reporter.'

'That's me.'

He laughed. 'Fuck, what are you doing in Portland, dude?'

'I'm looking for Marie,' I said. 'I . . . I need to find her. After that night on the hill we became . . . well, she was my girlfriend. But then after Andrew died, she disappeared. She . . .'

He interrupted me. 'What did you say?'

'She disappeared.'

'No, before that. You said something about Andrew being dead.'

'Yes, and . . .'

'Andrew Jade?'

'Yes. Of course Andrew Jade.' I wanted to get on with my story.

Pete looked at me with a mixture of amusement and astonishment. 'Andrew Jade is the most healthy-looking dead man I've ever met,' he said. 'At least he was when I left him yesterday.'

It was like being punched in the face.

'Andrew's alive?' I whispered.

'Of course he's alive. And Marie's in pretty good shape too.'

PART THREE
VOX HUMANA

23

All the way to Minneapolis I was talked at by the middle-aged man who sat next to me. The British royal family, the cost of mountain rescue, the best barbecue equipment, the cheapest restaurants in Orlando and who was going to win the World Series. When he said, 'And what about those alien abductions in Texas, huh?' I thought I was going to scream. But I was trapped. There was no escape.

It was only on the second flight that I got some peace. I lay back, but I couldn't sleep. My head was buzzing too much, the clamour of anticipation loud in my skull. Soon. soon, soon . . .

After Pete had told me that Andrew was still alive and that Marie was with him, I couldn't speak for about thirty seconds. It seemed too unreal. I couldn't absorb it.

Pete quickly realised how shocked I was by his news and, worried that he'd said something he shouldn't, picked up his rucksack and took a stride towards the taxi rank. 'Well, see you around, dude.'

I stepped in front of him. 'Let's get a coffee,' I said.

'I don't—'

'Come on, Pete. I've come all this way.'

He grinned lopsidedly. 'I guess I could use a latte.'

Back at Starbucks I bought him a venti latte and a muffin.

'Tell me,' I said. 'Everything.'

He hesitated for another second, but the urge to impart this obviously shocking tale overcame any fears he had.

'I stopped by to see them on my way back from Greece. Man, Greece is so—'

I tapped the table impatiently. 'Are you here to join the Loved Ones?'

'You know about them?'

'That's where I've been for the past few days. I know them very well.'

He relaxed.

'I thought Marie might be there. But you need to tell me – how can Andrew be alive? He was killed in a car crash. Marie went to the funeral.'

Pete raised a bushy eyebrow. 'Man, this is fucked up.'

'So where are they? What are they doing? I need to know, Pete.'

'OK, OK. I need to explain . . .' He slurped his coffee. 'Andrew's group used to be affiliated with the Loved Ones here, but a year ago, something like that, he emailed Lisa to tell her that his group had discovered "a deeper truth" and that they were going to form their own cell. Lisa was, like, whatever, dude. Andrew Jade's always been an awkward fucker, since we first got involved with him years ago. And his cell's, like, tiny. There are only thirteen of them.'

He stared at an attractive Asian girl who slinked past our table.

'Pete . . .'

'Yeah, sorry. Lisa asked me to check up on them again on the way back, see what they were up to. She knew where they were staying. That's also what I was doing the first time you met me – I mean, of course I was stoked by the sighting in Hastings but the real reason I was there was to make sure they weren't up to anything . . . what's that word you Brits use? Dodgy.'

He swigged the last of his coffee.

'They didn't exactly lay out the freaking welcome mats this time. The moment I got there Andrew said I wasn't welcome, that I was going to, like, disturb their aura. But I did persuade them to let me come in for a minute, to use the bathroom. They were sat around this big oak table – it was like some kind of ye olde worlde farmhouse kitchen, y'know? Andrew told me that he had been visited that very day, and that there were only a few days to go until the Big One.'

He looked up at me over his cup.

'Marie was there, plus that writer chick, Samantha O'Connell, and a bunch of others. Mostly girls actually, plus two or three guys. There was a scrawny little dude called Kevin, who seemed kind of in awe of all these women. Because they were *hot*, all of them. It was like some kind of fucking *harem*.'

Kevin? Could it be the same Kevin who had shown me his alien porn collection? If so, what the hell was he doing there? Then I remembered – I had seen him coming out of the bookshop where Samantha had been doing her book signing. My God. It was a fucking conspiracy.

'Andrew threw me out after about five minutes. None of the others spoke to me at all. They just stared, like they were on tranquilizers or some shit. It was creepy. You ever see that ancient movie, *Village of the Damned*? So anyway, I left and came straight back here.'

'Did you send Andrew a flyer, inviting him here?'

He shook his head. 'Uh-uh. I've been in Europe since the summer. But maybe he's still on the mailing list. Lisa and Zara aren't too hot at keeping that shit up to date.'

My heart was beating hard. 'I need the address of where they're staying.'

'Sure.' He produced his phone and flicked at the screen, cramming muffin into his mouth with the other hand. 'Here we go. So, what, you gonna head down there, give them a big surprise?'

'Something like that.'

He grinned, his mouth full of muffin, crumbs on his lips.

'Say hi from me, won'tcha?'

It was light when I left Minneapolis, and light too when I landed at Gatwick. I hadn't slept at all on the plane, and I yawned as my feet touched *terra firma*.

After a stroll through customs I tried to call Simon on his mobile. To my surprise, Susan answered.

'Oh, hi, Sue. I don't suppose Simon's there?'

'Richard!' She actually sounded pleased to hear from me. 'No, he's at work. Idiot forgot to take his phone with him.'

'But he's living there with you?'

'Yeah. I gave in to his begging.'

'That's fantastic. I'm really pleased.' I paused. 'So who's feeding Calico?'

'He's in a cattery. It's costing you seven pounds a day. The details are on your fridge.'

'OK. Cool. Well, look, I'm so happy to hear about you and Simon. I'll come round and see you as soon as I can.' I paused and added, 'I'll bring Marie,' then hung up.

I found my car in the car park. England was freezing; winter had arrived while I was away, and it reached through the concrete walls of the car park and made me shiver. I sat in my car and turned the engine and heating on.

Pete had given me the address where Andrew and Marie were based. It was just outside Eastbourne.

'It's a big old farmhouse in the middle of nowhere,' he said. 'They seem to be totally isolated and self-sufficient. They've even got chickens.'

I eased my car out into the open air. The sky was frosted blue, the colour of Marie's eyes.

England seemed so strange and flat after Oregon. Where America had mountains, we had hills; where they had huge pine trees, we had hedgerows and shrubs. But this was my country, the place where I belonged. As I drove away from Gatwick, America receded into the distance, a fading memory, already yellowing at the edges like an old newspaper.

The A23 seemed to go on forever. I felt like I'd entered some kind of time loop, where you find yourself passing the same piece of scenery over and over. I could have sworn I passed the same pub half a dozen times. My hands were slippery on the wheel.

Unwanted thoughts strafed my brain. Was Marie sleeping with Andrew? That was what cult leaders did, wasn't it, screw their disciples? Look at David Koresh, Charles Manson, the Bhagwan Shree Rajneesh, who claimed to have slept with more women than any other man on the planet.

I could picture Andrew, with his little glasses all steamed up, his forehead gleaming sweatily as he leaned over Cherry and Samantha and Marie – my Marie – and pawed them. It made my flesh creep. And another grotesque thought: what if she had been sleeping with him all the time she was with me? I remembered the way she had laughed that night on the way home from the nightclub, when I had asked her if Andrew was her boyfriend. I tried to recall the sound of the laugh, to work out if it was a false one.

I wished Andrew really was dead.

The needle on the fuel gauge was worryingly low. At the first opportunity I pulled into a petrol station and filled up. I bought a cup of coffee and a bag of crisps. The man behind the counter sniggered at my Loved Ones outfit. I sat in my car and drank my coffee, ate the crisps and studied my road map.

When Pete had given me the address of Andrew's group, or cell, he added, 'It's not easy to find. I hitched a ride out there, but I was wandering round for hours before I finally found it. It's not exactly well signposted.'

'I can't believe,' I said, 'that I came all this way – to the far side of America – and Marie was only twenty miles away all the time.'

Pete shrugged. 'Like I said, it's not well signposted.'

Then he said, 'Hey, don't take this the wrong way, dude, but don't you think if Marie had wanted you to find her she would have let you know where she was? Doesn't the way that she's hidden away from you tell you something?'

I shook my head. 'No! She doesn't know what she wants. She's been brainwashed by Andrew. She's probably being kept a prisoner.'

'She didn't look like a prisoner to me.'

Now, I turned off the A23 just north of Brighton and headed towards Lewes. I passed Falmer and the universities – where all this had started, years before, when Andrew met Samantha – and soon I was driving across the South Downs.

I suppressed a yawn as I passed the Long Man of Wilmington, a huge chalk figure in the face of the Downs. No doubt some conspiracy theorist somewhere believed that the Long Man of Wilmington had been carved into the hill as a message to extraterrestrials, or that aliens had created him themselves, making him a distant cousin of the Easter Island sculptures.

I was so sick of it all. Aliens, UFOs, conspiracy theories, the fucking Chorus, the word 'contact'. Sick, sick, sick. After I had saved Marie and taken her home I was going to make my house an alien-free zone. The *X-Files* box sets would be chucked out; all of the books Marie had about abductions would be thrown on a bonfire. It would all be for her own good . . .

Fuck. What the hell was I thinking? I was as bad as Andrew or Lisa, trying to control people's beliefs.

When I found her, I was going to talk to her. Set out my case. Try to persuade her that we should be together. If she didn't want that, if she would prefer to stay with Andrew, then I would have to accept it. I would be heartbroken, but I would learn to live with it.

I just needed to hear it from her mouth.

I just needed to *know*.

I turned off the A-road and crossed the Downs, heading towards the sea. Apparently, Andrew and company were based quite close to a village called East Dean. I slowed the car.

A thick mist had drifted in from the sea, enveloping the southern part of the Downs. It was like driving through a cloud that had fallen to earth. The mist crept into the car, making goose bumps rise on my flesh. There was no other traffic around. I felt like I'd driven into some other world, a Twilight Zone, and I could almost hear that creepy music all around me.

I pulled over to the side of the road beside a large wooden gate. I got out of the car. I had a feeling I was close.

'It's down a little lane between two farms,' Pete had said.

Beyond the wooden gate I could see a herd of Friesian cows. I could hear sheep bleating in the next field along. Separating the fields was a narrow country lane. It fitted Pete's description.

I rifled through the boot of my car and found a screwed-up kagoule. I put it on and walked down the lane. Small trees had been planted in rows on one side and they stood like sentries in the mist, dark figures silhouetted against the white fog. To my right were neat, clipped hedgerows. The birds sang loudly but tunelessly in the trees above me.

I hugged myself against the chill. The mist clung damply to my clothes and hair. The path beneath my feet was wet. Spider webs glistened on the hedgerow.

The country lane branched off in two directions. I peered through the mist. One branch led towards an open field. The other path turned a corner. I decided to try the second and there, at the end of the lane, was a gate set between two hedges. I pushed the gate open and stepped into a farmyard.

The house was large and very old. The roof was thatched, the chimney crooked, the white paint cracked and flaky. Ivy crept up to the first floor where damp had pushed through the paintwork. Could this really be the right place? A farmer would probably appear at any moment to tell me I was trespassing on his land.

All around my feet, chickens pecked at the ground. A pair of hens scattered as I walked towards the house, emitting loud, unhappy squawks. There was a knot in my stomach like a fist. I tried to look through the windows but the curtains were drawn. There were no sounds coming from within. I stepped back and looked up at the first floor windows. I thought I saw somebody step away from one window. Had they seen me? I was almost paralysed with trepidation. I was acutely aware that right here, right now, everything could go wrong. All my searching could prove to have been in vain.

I walked around the side of the building, where a large white van was parked. It had no markings, just a few muddy smears across its flanks. I looked through the window. There was nothing to see.

I took a deep breath, strode up to the front door and knocked.

There was no reply. I knocked harder. Behind me the chickens clucked and scratched. I rang the doorbell. Exasperated, I walked around the other side of the house. As I turned the corner I saw a face at the window, looking out at me, shock displayed on pale female features. The face pulled away the instant I turned, leaving smudges of breath on the glass.

It had been Marie.

⌣

I ran up to the glass and thumped it.

'Marie! It's me! It's Richard!' I banged the glass harder. I pressed my face to the window and looked into an empty kitchen. I saw a door open inside and a woman looked straight at me.

Samantha O'Connell. I banged the glass again. I shouted Marie's name, over and over.

Driven by desperation, I stooped, picked up a stone and threw it with all my strength at the window.

As the glass smashed, shards flying, the front door flew open and two men ran out. One of them was Kevin. The other one was holding a shotgun, which he pointed at my chest. I put my hands up to shoulder level and stepped backwards, stopping a few feet in front of the gate.

Kevin looked me up and down. 'So you found us after all.'

He seemed nervous, probably remembering the first time we had met, when I had almost strangled him on the floor of his flat.

'Andrew said you would. I thought you were too stupid, myself.'

'I just want to see Marie,' I said, as calmly as I could. My voice didn't sound natural. It was too high, cracked with nerves.

'That's not going to happen,' said Kevin.

'Shall I shoot him now?' The man holding the shotgun lifted the barrel in my direction, reminding me of Jake in Portland. I was tempted to tell him he had a spiritual twin across the ocean.

'No,' said a voice from behind them, and Andrew stepped into view.

I almost ran at him but was deterred by the shotgun barrels that were pointing at my face. I clenched and unclenched my fists. I tried to breathe slowly, calmly.

Andrew was dressed head to toe in black. His hair was slicked back. His glasses were different, with thicker, darker frames. He looked very confident, powerful, arrogant. Bile rose in my throat. When Andrew smiled the rage inside me roared. I looked at the shotgun. I was helpless, and now I was this close to Marie I wasn't going to take any risks.

'Reports of your death were exaggerated,' I said.

Andrew smiled thinly.

'How did you do it? Fake your death.'

He snorted through his nose. 'It wasn't hard. You believed what you wanted to believe, Richard.'

I had no time for this.

'I want to see Marie,' I said. 'I know she's here.'

Andrew interlaced his fingers. 'She doesn't want to see you.'

'Let her tell me that herself.'

He laughed softly. 'It's pretty obvious, isn't it? Why do you think she left you in the first place? She hates you, Richard. You're one of them. A non-believer. She knows that you would try to keep her tied to the Earth. Only here, with me, will she meet her true destiny.'

'What, to be taken away into outer space? It's not going to fucking happen. The Chorus,' I spat. 'What a fucking joke. You don't even believe it yourself. You're just here because you like having all these people worshipping you like you're some kind of prophet, when you're actually a liar and a fucking pornographer. It's all crap. Evil crap.'

Andrew shook his head sadly. He smirked.

'Oh, Richard, Richard . . . Can't you see? This is why Marie couldn't stay with you. You're such a cynic. You don't believe in anything, do you? Not a thing.'

Quietly, I said, 'I believe in Marie and me. I know that I love her.'

Kevin sniggered.

Andrew came closer. 'It's not really love that you feel for Marie. Lust, yes, and who can blame you? She's very attractive. As a lot of people have seen.' He looked at Kevin, who blushed. 'And maybe you think you love her, but you could never love her as much as I do, as much as the Chorus do. And if you really did love her, you'd be happy to let her go.'

'If you love somebody set them free?' I said with a sneer.

'Exactly.'

'Crap. If you love somebody you want them near you. You don't want to let them go. You want them beside you, to share everything with you. That's how I feel about Marie. You're the one who's keeping her prisoner. Why don't you let her come outside and talk to me? Because you know she'll want to come home with me.'

'She's happy here,' Kevin interjected. 'She loves it here. She loves us all.'

'You're her family, I suppose.'

'That's right.'

We were silent for a few moments. I could see faces at the windows, but I couldn't make out Marie among them. I had found her at last, but I couldn't talk to her, couldn't see her. Anger and frustration eddied inside me.

'I'm not leaving until I can talk to her,' I said.

'No,' Andrew replied. 'That isn't possible.'

'How would you feel,' I threatened, 'if all this were to appear in next week's *Herald*? "Alien cult members hide out near Eastbourne. Internet porn circle smashed by police".'

Andrew laughed. 'I couldn't care less what you put in your pathetic newspaper.'

'I don't believe you.'

Andrew raised an eyebrow. 'Look at me, Richard. I'm hardly trembling, am I?'

I stepped towards him, looking at the shotgun from the corner of my eye.

'You ought to be afraid,' I said. As I spoke, a young woman came to the doorway. I recognised her immediately. Cherry Nova.

Andrew looked over his shoulder and shooed Cherry back inside.

He turned back to me. 'Who am I supposed to be afraid of? Gary Kennedy?' Though as he said this, there was a flicker of fear in his eyes that betrayed his true feelings.

'He's dead,' I said.

Andrew raised both eyebrows and smiled broadly. 'What good news. How did that happen?'

I explained: 'He followed me to America, looking for Cherry. The Loved Ones murdered him.'

'Well, well. Good for them. And you've been to Oregon? Goodness, Richard, I'm mildly impressed. How did you get on with Lisa? A little darling, isn't she? I trust you were faithful to Marie while you were out there.'

My face betrayed me. Of course, I hadn't actually been unfaithful to Marie, but I had come so close.

'Oh! So you weren't so in love with Marie that you could keep your hands to yourself? Tut. How disappointing. Don't tell me you screwed Lisa? That *would* be impressive.'

'No. No, I—'

'And I expect it was Pete who told you where to find us. I knew we should never have let him leave here.'

I opened my mouth to speak but Andrew said, 'I'm getting bored now. I'm going to go back indoors. I've got a lot to sort out.'

He walked back to the door of the farmhouse. Before going inside he said, 'This is goodbye, Richard. We won't meet again. Kevin and Philip will escort you from the yard.'

He went inside.

Philip lifted the shotgun again and said, 'You heard him.'

'Marie!' I yelled, peering desperately at the house.

'Come on. It's time to fuck off.' Philip jabbed the gun towards me.

I had no choice. I turned around and walked as slowly as I could out of the farmyard, past the chickens and through the rusted gate. Halfway up the path I turned around to look at Kevin and his shotgun-toting companion, but they had been swallowed up by the mist.

———⌣———

There was only one thing I could do: go home and get reinforcements. I would talk to Simon, buy a baseball bat, a knife and a torch, and go back under the cover of darkness. I had to get into that house, find Marie and take her home. And if all else failed I would go to the police. I would tell them that Andrew was holding Marie against her will. I knew that they still wanted to talk to me about Simon's beating, which would lead to all sorts of awkward questions about Gary . . . I needed to report his murder anyway, should have done it before I left America. But I had been too worried about being detained, and I was still scared that it would be my word against thirty Loved Ones.

I would have to risk it, though. I would go to the police – I had no choice – but I was still concerned they would slow me down, ask loads of questions, stop me getting to Marie. I was scared Andrew was going to do something to her. I had to get back to that farmhouse as quickly as possible.

I got in my car and headed back towards Hastings. It sickened me to think I had been so close to Marie and yet was going home without her. Only a pane of glass had separated us, and she had looked so beautiful, a ghost at the window. There were hot and cold currents of air blowing through my chest, a dryness in my mouth. Driving was difficult, but I made it home before dark.

I opened my front door and kicked aside the small pile of post. I sat down on the sofa. I had been awake for over twenty-four hours, and with my emotions up and down and all over the place, I was shattered. My mind was still fizzing and zipping around, but my body had given up. It didn't want to do anything except sleep.

'No,' I said aloud, as a yawn tried to surface. I would get out of this ridiculous outfit, drink more coffee and then go and get Simon. He would help me. After everything – all the animosity there used to be between us – he had turned out to be a good friend.

I went upstairs to get changed. Dusk had fallen and the street-lights were beginning to come on. In the half-light I undressed. I was too weary to stand. I sat on the bed and pulled my socks off. I could feel sleep clawing at me, trying to pull me under. I closed my heavy eyelids, forced them open. But I couldn't do it. I felt myself slipping into sleep, my body betraying me.

I was gone.

24

I watched the spaceship descend. It broke through the underbelly of the clouds in a haze of colour: red and green and violet and white. The colours flickered in random patterns around the base of the ship, which was black and shone like the armour of some great beetle. I was rooted where I stood, my car parked out of reach, beyond the next field. There was nobody else around. I was alone.

There was no sound from the ship. It descended in silence, an eerie quiet that made me clasp my hands over my ears. The circular base of the spaceship came closer, and in a smooth, fluid motion, four huge legs unfolded themselves from the undercarriage, as if this was an organic structure, a living being, and a few seconds later the legs touched the Earth. The ground shook a little, barely enough to register on the Richter scale, but enough to make me lose my footing and fall down.

I lay on my back, sick with terror, looking up.

They had landed. It was all true.

For a long time nothing happened. I was frozen, unable to lift my body from the ground. Along with the terror was a sense of wonder, and one of privilege: they had chosen me. I would be the first to make contact. Perhaps they would ask me to be their spokesman upon Earth, to spread their message of peace.

If it *was* peace.

Because what if it was war that they wanted? What weapons did they have? I pictured tripods and death machines, death rays demolishing the streets, cities falling, mankind massacred. We would be their slaves. Or food. All these movie images of acid blood and evil eyes, of malevolent intelligence – these images paralysed me.

And so when the hatch swung open and a bright light appeared in the belly of the ship, I tried to scream.

It caught in my throat and I swallowed it.

Shadows were cast in the doorway; dark figures that peered at the landscape. Had they been here before? Was this their first visit? And would I be the first human they had come across? An instinctive fear told me to run, and with an unprecedented act of willpower, I rose to my feet, just as two of the visitors began to descend from the ship. They floated down without the aid of steps or other visible means. As soon as they touched the soil I uprooted my legs and ran.

I hurdled barbed wire. It caught on my trousers and made me fall, my hands ripping on the wire. I cried out in pain then examined my palms. Blood poured from open wounds like stigmata. I clenched my fists and ran on, across the field, the sky turning purple above me, a cold wind pressing against me, trying to force me backwards. I knew the aliens were behind me, but I didn't dare turn round.

Shortness of breath pricked my lungs, but soon I would be at my car. Just over the crest of the hill . . .

Across another barbed wire fence, more carefully this time though; the wounds on my palms had healed. There was no trace of blood, no scars.

I looked up from my examination of my hands and saw them:

A dozen or so humanoid figures walked in a line towards me, blocking my escape. They wore cloaks and hoods. A small figure near the centre of the line stretched out an arm.

'Come with us,' it said.

I jumped up from the bed and checked my watch. It was still set to Pacific time. I turned to the alarm clock. It was half-eight. I had slept for more than twelve hours, and my head still felt heavy with jet lag. And Jesus, the dream . . . It had seemed so real.

I peeked out through the curtains, just to make sure no spaceship had landed during the night. Then I thought: *Marie.* I had to get moving. I needed to get back to the farmhouse. On the way I would buy weapons, whatever I could find. I needed a gun, but I had no idea where to get hold of one. Or maybe I should go straight to the police after all. I couldn't think straight. I decided I would phone Simon. He would know what to do.

But first I had to get ready. I ran around the house in a disorganised flap, washing the stale sweat from my skin, getting dressed, shoving biscuits into my face. I pinched the bridge of my nose and squeezed my eyes shut. I visualised what I wanted to happen. I wanted Marie to walk out of that house and choose to come with me, to walk past Andrew and his gun-toting friend and wave goodbye to them. We would link arms and I would walk her to my car. Then I would bring her home.

I sat on the sofa with the intention of calling Simon. I noticed that I had a new voicemail. I pressed play.

A female voice said, 'Check your email,' then hung up.

I ran across the room to the PC. It had been Marie's voice. Unmistakably her. The voicemail had been left at two o'clock that morning, while I was unconscious upstairs, deep in REM sleep, deaf to the sound of the telephone. Fuck! My stupid body, letting me down when I needed to be awake and alert.

I switched on the PC and went into my email account. The internet was infuriatingly slow. I banged the monitor, shouted, 'Come on, come *on.*'

There it was. At the very top of my inbox, a new message from her. From Marie.

25

Dear Richard

It's been such a long time, I really don't know where to start. Perhaps with sorry, though I don't think that word could ever be enough. How can five letters make up for the way I've made you feel? I just hope the words I'm going to write go some way to make you see why I did what I did. Why I had no choice. Maybe then, I hope, you'll be able to accept it, and forgive me. I hope.

A few hours ago I watched from the window as Andrew and the others forced you to leave. I could see the anguish on your face. It hurt me, Richard. Right here in my heart. I wanted to run down into the yard, to put my arms around you, hold you for one last time. But I knew that if I did you wouldn't let me go. You would ask me to go with you, to leave Andrew and the others.

"Come home with me," you would say. And I might not be able to resist.

That was my fear.

Because I do love you. I know that must be hard for you to believe. Would I believe you if it were the other way round? I don't know. I really don't know. But leaving you was the hardest thing I've ever had to do in my life.

Those hot, summer months we spent together ... They were sublime. Beautiful times.

I remember so much. That night we first met. I thought you were gorgeous, and when I spotted you later in the club I made my friends hang around outside for ages, waiting for you to come out. I didn't want to approach you in that horrible meat market. But I wanted you to walk me home. I could almost have invited you in that first night, but well, you know! A girl doesn't like to appear easy :)

Do you remember when I was late for our first date? I really did plan to be on time but then I bumped into Andrew in town. You remember we were arguing? I told you it was about what time we were going to go to the convention. That was my first lie to you. Really, we were arguing about you. Andrew said it was too dangerous for me to have a boyfriend. He said it would get in the way, present difficulties later. He was right. But at the time I was angry with him. I thought it was jealousy (yes, Andrew and I were lovers, once), and his opposition made me more determined to go ahead. It was the first and only time I have acted against Andrew's wishes.

Richard, if I had known the pain we would go through later, I would have stood you up that first day. But I couldn't help myself. I went ahead. I fell in love with you. And that nearly fucked everything up.

No doubt you are fixating on my statement that Andrew and I were once together. I know what men are like. But it was a long time ago, when we first met, and I swear to you, there is nothing sexual in our relationship now. He is my best friend, my teacher, my guide. Yes, I love him. But it is not a physical relationship now. I know that's the kind of thing you would worry about, so I hope this puts your mind at rest, on that point at least.

But you must have loads of questions. I would love to be able to sit down and talk to you, face to face, but like I said, it's impossible. Too dangerous. You might try to persuade me. But I will try to explain things as best I can. I'll start at the beginning:

I met Andrew when I was sixteen. I was still at school, but already I had come to believe firmly in the existence of extraterrestrials. I didn't have any real friends at school – they thought I was weird – plus my dad had left and my mum had withdrawn into a spiky shell.

I'm not even sure what got me interested in the visitors. A TV show, a library book? But I do remember reading something online about the vox celeste. And when I concentrated I discovered I had the gift. I could hear it! The voice, the singing, the abstract music. It made me feel special, when nothing else did.

I was a member of several forums and groups online, where experiencers and believers could chat. After I'd been on one these forums a while, I got a PM from Andrew, asking if we could meet in the flesh.

We met in a café in Eastbourne. He was older than me, yes, but I liked that. He was a real man, so unlike the little boys at school. I guess, if you want to analyse it, he reminded me of my dad, or was filling a 'father figure' void in my life. The reason he wanted to meet, he said, was because I'd mentioned hearing the vox celeste.

"You're the first person I've met who can hear it too," he said. He told me there were people in America who could also hear it, but he thought he was the only one in Britain. He said the fact that we lived just a few miles apart showed it must be fate. We were meant to find each other. I believed him.

My mum didn't approve of Andrew. She said he was too old for me. I told her we were just friends, but she didn't believe me. She turned out to be right. Andrew said that to cement our bond, to strengthen our aural capacities, we should become lovers. He said the voice had suggested it. I thought I had heard something too, although being a young stupid schoolgirl I had resisted it. Sex was the unknown. It frightened me. But Andrew was so gentle, so caring. And when we made love it did make the voices grow louder. They were amplified tenfold. It was almost deafening.

I stopped reading for a moment, realising that my fists were clenched with anger. I felt overcome with sickness. Andrew had 'seduced' her when she was a sixteen-year-old schoolgirl, exploited her beliefs, just as I had suspected. I wanted to kill him.

I read on.

I left school and home at 16 and moved into Andrew's flat.

Through our online activities, we came into contact with the Loved Ones, and Andrew flew out to Oregon to meet Lisa and Jay. He came back inspired. He spoke of setting up our own branch of the Loved

Ones, in preparation for contact. Samantha – Andrew's ex-girlfriend – was always popping round, discussing things with Andrew for her books. And there were others too: Philip, Jacqui and Melissa. The girls were both around my age – they're with us here now, in fact.

After the disaster of my family, it felt so good to be part of something. For the first time in my life I felt like I belonged.

A few months after his return from Oregon, Andrew said we needed to make money. "The Loved Ones have discovered a clever way of making cash," he said, and he explained about the erotica.

At first I was really opposed to the idea. It was pandering to sickos, the kind of people who gave us a bad name. But we were desperate for money to buy a house where we could live undisturbed, and although we earned some money from the consultancy, and Samantha made a fair amount from her books, we needed more. So I agreed.

Kevin told me you found the pictures. I'm not proud of them. I agreed to it for the greater good, and the pictures and the videos, which featured some of the other girls, did bring in some money. Andrew came up with the name Candy for me, and it could have been the start of a whole career. But after a few months I said I wouldn't do it anymore. I felt a deep sense of shame, of self-disgust. I was terrified that my mum would find out. So I refused. I felt like the photos had stolen some of my soul. I developed a phobia of having my photo taken at all.

It wasn't long afterwards that Andrew found an easier way of making money through alien erotica. He started working for Gary Kennedy. We were all out one night in Brighton – myself, Andrew and a girl called Charlotte – or Cherry, as they called her – who is actually asleep in the room next to mine right now. Andrew sent Charlotte home with Gary, and soon afterwards he started taking photographs for Planet Flesh.

Andrew took photos and shot videos for Gary. Charlotte was the most popular model, though there were a few others who would come round to the flat, whose names I couldn't remember. Charlotte became my best girlfriend. But then one day I came home and found her and Andrew having sex in our bed. This was when Andrew was still my boyfriend.

I was so angry I almost left the group. They had betrayed me. I stormed out, and Andrew chased after me. He found me sitting on the beach. He persuaded me that he had done nothing wrong. The vox celeste had told him that by making love to Charlotte he could make her hear too. It was fated that she would be one of us. She had been chosen. He said he still loved me, but he loved Charlotte as well.

"When we join the Chorus we will need to learn to share. There will be no possessiveness, no selfish jealousy," Andrew said, and I saw that he was right. However, I decided to move out, to give him and Charlotte space. Andrew reluctantly agreed and I moved back into the bedsit with Calico. Then Gary complicated things by falling in love with Charlotte as well, but Andrew said it was OK for her to see both of them. It suited him for a while.

We spent the next couple of years recruiting. It's not easy. Everyone has to be vetted very carefully.

Only a certain type of person could be allowed to join the group. They had to be 100% committed, prepared to sacrifice everything.

For a brief while I hoped that I might be able to show you that Andrew and I were right, that alien abduction is real. I wanted to make you believe, so you could join us. I clung to the hope that you would change your mind for ages.

We recruited nine people to join the group alongside myself, Andrew, Charlotte/Cherry and Samantha. The last of them was Kevin, who found us just a week ago, when we were already in the house. He didn't know about us when you met him – but you did him a favour. You set him on our trail.

When I met you, we were almost ready. There had been an incredible increase in UFO activity. Crop circles were springing up all over the place, for the first time in years; animal mutilations had started to happen all across Sussex and Kent; there were so many sightings and reports of abductions that we had a hard time keeping up with it all. And the vox celeste was growing louder. Andrew and I knew something was going to happen soon. We started to prepare.

I must be blunt: meeting you almost wrecked everything. You were in the way. You worked for a newspaper and could therefore have made things very difficult for us. A lot of the girls in the group are very young. Jenny is sixteen, Alison only fifteen. Their parents have no idea where they are. We could have had all sorts of problems.

Andrew was furious when I moved in with you. I still hoped that we could convert you, and that's why we brought Sally round your house. We hoped that after hearing her experience – when she was abducted and her baby removed – you would see the truth. But it backfired. You were horrified, and when I ran off that night it was partly because I panicked. I spoke to Andrew the next day and together we decided what we had to do.

We needed to be in the house by the end of October, so we would have time to get ready for contact. I knew that you would never let me go. You would disturb us, cause trouble . . . It would be impossible. I knew that if I just disappeared you would guess that I had gone off with Andrew somewhere. You would be out there asking questions, trying to track us down.

That's when we came up with the idea of faking Andrew's death. If you thought Andrew was dead it would mislead you, muddy the waters. Better still, it gave me a motive for having disappeared: after Andrew's death I would be so grief-stricken I would lose it and run away somewhere. It would set you on the wrong track, and delay you enough for us to fulfil our destinies before you found us. And faking Andrew's death also helped us break our ties with Gary and allowed Andrew and Charlotte to be together. Andrew had become more and more worried about her. Gary was violent towards her but was obsessed with her. We knew he would never let her go, especially if he thought she was leaving him to be with Andrew.

We also knew it would help us shake off Fraser, who had become increasingly obsessed with Andrew.

To put it bluntly, we only needed to fool three people: you, Gary and Fraser.

The cremation never took place. The ashes we scattered that night were those of a pig Andrew bought from a butcher and burned. Melissa and Katie, who are here now, were in on the act.

There was only one negative repercussion of this scheme: Fraser Howard's death. We had needed to shake off Fraser because the vox celeste told Andrew that Fraser was not chosen after all. Fraser couldn't handle it and I understand from reading the news that he came looking for me after I went.

That was unfortunate.

To be honest, I never realised you would pursue me as hard as you have. You've surprised me. Kevin told me about how you attacked him, and I was afraid I had driven you over the edge. And I never thought you'd go to Oregon. If I had known, we would have warned Pete, spun him a lie that made him wary of you, so he wouldn't have told you where we were. That was our one mistake: we underestimated your persistence.

Oh Richard, maybe if I'd known that you felt that strongly about me I would have made a different choice. I might have stayed with you longer. Tried harder to persuade you to share my beliefs. But although I knew you loved me, I didn't know how much. Who ever does? How can you measure love? I thought you would recover quickly. I thought you would try to find me for a while and then give up. I thought you would heal. But your persistence has taught me a lesson – never underestimate what love can do.

It is a lesson I will carry forward with me, but not one I can use to alter the past.

I paused again. I was furious with Andrew, my loathing for him at a fever pitch. But I also felt angry with Marie. For going along with it, the deceit, the way she called Fraser's death 'unfortunate' and the fact they were harbouring teenage runaways, one of them only fifteen. I could imagine the hair-tearing panic their parents must be feeling. I wanted to reach into the email, through the computer, and shake Marie, ask her if she knew what she was doing.

I squeezed my eyes shut. A great sense of disillusionment hit me. Had I been wrong about Marie all this time? If she'd known how much I had been fearful and worried about her . . .

What she had done to me was cruel. It was not the way you treated someone you supposedly loved.

It would be easy to put all the blame on Andrew, to believe that he coerced or brainwashed her. But it didn't sound like it. It sounded like she had been fully aware of what she was doing. Her belief in the Chorus and this ridiculous idea of a coming rapturous day had made her feel she had licence to do whatever she liked. To hurt people.

I stood up and threw my coffee cup across the room, watching it shatter against the wall, coffee splattering the wallpaper.

I sunk back into my seat, heart beating hard, and returned to the final part of the email.

I'm running out of time here, Richard. I'm afraid that someone's going to hear my fingers on the keyboard and come and find out what I'm doing. And I need sleep. Tomorrow is the big day. In just a few hours' time we will make contact.

There's no way I will be able to sleep.

This is what I've waited for all my life. Since my dad left and I discovered the truth. I've waited and watched and listened since I was fourteen. I've given my life to the pursuit of the truth: that we are not alone in the universe; that there is a great intelligence that wants us, the chosen few, to join it. All across the world, different groups are preparing, each of them waiting to be taken to the Chorus, to be part of it. Andrew believes that only our group are the true chosen ones. Soon, we will see.

I'm shaking. I feel so nervous. But also excited, happy. This is like everything you've ever wished for rolled into one – every Christmas, every birthday, every love affair, every present, every exam pass, every job; like losing your virginity, like meeting your true love, like getting your dream job, having beautiful, healthy children, enjoying the perfect night beneath the stars, surrounded by perfect friends. All those things, collected together and multiplied infinitely. Because this is all I've ever wanted. And we are the first in human history. The very first.

That, Richard, is why I could not stay with you. Why I had to deceive you and hurt you and leave you. Why I lied and hid and made you cry. One night I almost gave in, and I phoned you, but I chickened out before you could answer. I wept that night, wondered if I was doing the right thing, almost had a crisis of faith. Were we wrong? Have we been fooling ourselves all this time? I lay awake all night, and then I talked to Charlotte, told her my fears. Charlotte went to Andrew, and we talked, and it was just like when we had first met. We talked and talked, and he helped me renew my faith.

I know we're right, Richard. I know it's going to happen.

And maybe one day you and I will meet again. Who knows, I may return to Earth to spread the message. Otherwise, I will wait until the Chorus embraces

Earth as a whole, welcomes the entire planet, and you will be there among the newcomers. You will see that I was right all along. And I will be waiting.

Until that day, goodbye my love. Please don't be unhappy. Go on with your life. Be successful, fall in love again, have babies. And watch the stars. That's where I'll be.

Love Marie xxxx

I stared at the screen.

Despite my anger and disillusionment, I still cared about her. I couldn't help it.

And I had a horrible, sickening feeling in my gut . . .

I ran out of the house to my car, then realised I had forgotten my key. I ran back indoors again. I stood in the middle of the living room for a moment and forgot what I was supposed to be doing. I held my face in my hands until the world stopped spinning and grabbed the key from the table.

In the car, I turned on the radio.

The last few bars of a song I didn't recognise faded into the news. I pulled out behind a bus and headed down the hill.

The first story on the news made me hit the brake, swerve to the side of the road and almost lose my life. I missed the bus by inches.

'Police in Eastbourne, East Sussex, have confirmed that approximately a dozen people committed suicide today by apparently throwing themselves over the clifftop at Beachy Head in the early hours of this morning. The people who killed themselves are believed to have been part of an alien abduction cult that was based in a village near Eastbourne. The police report that they have one witness to the event, but are unable to confirm at present either the number of people who died or their names. The event is similar to—'

I switched the radio off.

I sat and stared.

It took me ten minutes to get to Simon's. I sat in the car and leaned on my hooter until he appeared. As soon as he saw it was me he looked anxious and uncomfortable.

'You've heard the news?' he said, opening the passenger door.

I nodded.

'It might not be her,' he said. 'It might . . .'

I looked at him and he shut up.

The road to Beachy Head was crowded with ghouls and journalists. Luckily I had one of the latter in the car with me. Simon flashed his press pass, said, 'Local press,' and we were allowed through by the roadblock. I had never seen so many people in this one spot before. They came from all over the surrounding area – Eastbourne, Pevensey, Bexhill, as far away as Lewes – to take a look. The words *alien, cult* and *suicide* had combined to whip up a feverish interest. Of course, anyone who lived near Beachy Head was accustomed to suicide – as the huge Samaritans billboard testified – but *mass* suicides were unknown here.

The edge of the cliff had been cordoned off, and police kept out undesirables while the emergency services set about trying to recover the dead. Below us, the authorities went about the awful task of recovering the broken bodies from the rocks.

I couldn't speak. Simon went over and talked to one of the policemen, asked him if they had a list of names yet. The policeman shook his head.

A middle-aged couple stood nearby, both ashen-faced, the woman weeping on her husband's shoulder. Simon approached them.

'Do you know somebody who . . . might have jumped?' he asked.

The woman let out a shrill cry. The man said, 'Our daughter.'

'What was her name?' Simon asked softly.

'Emily,' the man replied, turning away. He looked over at the cliff. Wind ruffled the grass; the sky was so low it almost touched our hair. The clouds were dark grey, pregnant and threatening.

'Was one of them called Emily?' Simon asked me. I shook my head. I didn't know.

I managed to speak: 'I want to go to the farmhouse.'

With Simon behind the wheel, we made it back past the ever-growing number of voyeurs, who had been joined by reporters from national newspapers. A BBC news crew were trying to get their van through the crowds.

I gave Simon instructions and we headed to East Dean. I pointed out the gate where I had parked the day before and we pulled up, then walked down the lane into the farmyard. All the chickens had gone, as had the white van. It was silent.

The front door stood open. We went inside.

We wandered from room to room, not bothering to call out any names. There were no farewell notes, no clues as to what had happened. The fridge was half-full; the TV had been left on standby. The washing up had been left in the sink. Upstairs were half a dozen bedrooms. The largest room, with the best view, contained a double bed that had been made neatly that morning.

Down the hall was a small bedroom containing a single bed and a laptop. Marie's room. I knew this immediately. The room smelled of her. There were pale red hairs on the pillow. This was where she had slept while I chased around, following her trail. I flipped the laptop open, ran a finger over the keys, where her teardrops had fallen.

'Come on, mate.' Simon put his hand on my shoulder. 'This place gives me the creeps.'

We walked outside. Rain had started to fall. I turned my face to the clouds and closed my eyes, felt the cleansing kiss of rain on my eyelids and mouth and nose. I opened my eyes. I wanted to see into space, but the clouds were in the way.

———

Andrew had sent out a press release via his website that morning, tweeting a link to it shortly before the mass suicide.

This morning, contact was made between ourselves, the Vox Humana, and an extraterrestrial intelligence known as the Chorus. The Chorus is an interplanetary council made up of various species from across the universe. They have been in contact with Earth for over 70 years now, although successive governments have consistently denied this. Today the Chorus bypassed government and made contact directly with The People.

A craft will land at Beachy Head today to transport us from this solar system. We will step onto the craft from the cliff edge. When we return, it will be to welcome all of humankind to the Chorus.

Until then – farewell.

Vox Humana

It was headline news. And by the following morning, the police and the coastguard had recovered and identified all of the bodies. The names were all over the web, along with the video testimony of the only eyewitness, a man called Gerald Potter, who had been walking his dogs at six a.m., as he did every morning.

In the video, Potter stood on the clifftop, squinting into the winter sun. He read from a piece of paper, making his statement sound stilted and unemotional.

'I was just heading home when I saw this white van. It pulled up about fifteen yards from the edge of the cliff, maybe a bit further – just over there.' He pointed. 'I thought it was a bit odd, a white van at that time of the morning. I thought maybe someone was going to chuck rubbish off the cliff. If so, I was going to have words with them.' He coughed.

'The back of the van opened and a number of people climbed out. They were mostly young women, plus a few chaps. They were all dressed in white robes with hoods, except for one chap, who was wearing black. The one in black gathered the others around him and started talking to them. At this point I thought I'd stumbled upon a coven of Devil worshippers, and that he was their high priest or something. I wasn't sure what to do. Then they stood in a line holding hands, the chap in black at the centre of the row. I counted them. There were thirteen of them. I know that for certain because I remember thinking it tied in with my idea that they were Satanists. Then they started to walk slowly towards the edge of the cliff, and I realised what was going on. I was too far away to stop them . . .'

Mr Potter was asked by a reporter if there were definitely thirteen people.

'I'm absolutely certain,' he replied. 'My eyesight's as sharp as when I was a boy.'

I stared at the list of names. Of those who had jumped.

Samantha O'Connell. Charlotte Myers. Philip Warner.

Kevin Stiller. Melissa Bourne. Jacqui Etheridge.

Kelly Smith. Katie Johnstone. Alison Bradfield.

Jenny Taylor-Reeves. Maggie Sherman.

I scanned the list from top to bottom, then from bottom to top. I closed my eyes, refocused, then read it again, counting to eleven.

There were two names missing.

Epilogue

I tread the crooked path to the top of the hill.

The first colours of spring are breaking through, and the world smells fresh, new. Reborn. The sun is sinking and the sky turns cobalt. Soon the stars will come out. And I will watch.

I will watch the sky.

⌣

The bodies of Marie Walker and Andrew Jade were never found. I phoned around the news agencies that first day – or rather, I got Simon to do it – to check that it wasn't a mistake, that they hadn't just omitted two names from the list.

'That's the funny thing,' one news editor told Simon. 'That guy who saw the whole thing swears blind there were thirteen people who walked over the cliff, but they only found eleven bodies. I guess they must have been swept out to sea – or the old guy miscounted. Easily done, isn't it?'

I watched the news for weeks afterwards, expecting them to say that two bodies had been washed up on the beach, but it never happened.

The story was big news for about a week. The police quickly located the farmhouse, and pictures of the empty rooms appeared in all the papers. The media made a big fuss over the fact that there were some very young girls involved. When they found the alien porn sites on the internet they almost exploded with excitement. The government promised to look into it. Samantha O'Connell's books temporarily went to the top of the bestseller lists. Everyone who had ever had any contact with Andrew was interviewed and his university past was dredged up.

There was great debate over the missing bodies. The coastguard explained that it was possible they had been carried away to sea, but very unlikely. Many people thought Andrew and Marie must have planned their escape, fooling their fellow pact members. A lovers' tryst, they called it. The witness was old, had been busy operating his new mobile phone when the group jumped. Had Andrew and Marie broken free of the line and saved their own skins? Most people thought so.

A lovers' tryst. Could that be true? Had Andrew chosen Marie over Cherry?

Had Marie chosen him over me?

Meanwhile, the ufology community had its own ideas about what had happened.

Contact had been made. Andrew and Marie were the only true chosen ones, and they were, at this moment, among the Chorus, the first humans to join an extraterrestrial culture.

The mystery had been taken away from me. It was no longer mine to solve alone.

By Christmas, the fuss had died down. The story had been replaced by some other tragedy. I hear there's going to be a BBC documentary screened soon. Simon said I should talk to them, give my side of the story, tell them what I know. But I don't want to. I don't want to be dragged into it.

The Vox Humana story tied in with stories from across the world. Government agencies in Japan, Italy and the USA planted undercover operatives in a number of known alien abduction cults. Each of the cults was raided on the very same day that Andrew's thirteen walked towards the edge of Beachy Head.

In Oregon, an undercover FBI agent called Rick Delaney gave evidence against a cult known as the Loved Ones. The cult's leader, Lisa Mendelsohn, and five men were arrested for fraud, deception, harbouring known criminals – and the murder of a British citizen, Gary Kennedy.

I couldn't believe it – Rick, an FBI agent! He had fooled us all. And part of the evidence included the flash drives Zara had fetched from her house, which contained details of everyone who had ever been part of the Loved Ones, of the money and possessions they had signed over and the enormous shopping spree it had funded – cars, diamonds, houses, cocaine, and so on – to bring criminal prosecutions against Lisa.

I scoured the reports, in print and on the Net, but there was no mention of Zara.

Maybe she never went back after dropping me at the airport, although it seemed unlikely. Some dark nights, at four a.m., when my soul howled with loneliness and I imagined Marie and Andrew together, I thought about going back to America and finding her.

There had been a connection there. We had both lost people we loved. I should go out there, find her, start again. But then morning would come and I'd change my mind.

Because I'm getting on with my life. I'm healing.

Healing.

Bob Milner asked me to go back and work for the *Herald*. I said no. I've found a much better job. The *Sunday Telegram* wants me to work as a features photographer on their magazine. It looks like my ambitions might be fulfilled after all. Marie would be proud. It should be exciting: a new life, a new start. A new me.

A week or so after the suicide, I went to visit Marie's mum. She was back home and had good news: her cancer was in remission.

'Waiting for the all-clear from the oncologist,' she said, attempting a smile.

She made us a cup of tea and we sat out in the porch, on wicker chairs, looking out at the birds hopping about in the bright winter sunshine. She thanked me for searching for her daughter, and I said sorry that I was unable to bring her home.

'I think she's still out there,' she said. She stared at me, an imploring look that made me uncomfortable. 'I'd be able to feel it, wouldn't I, if she was dead? And they would have found the body.'

I began to say 'Not necessarily,' but she talked over me. She looked exhausted, puffy bags drooping beneath her eyes. 'She's either out there somewhere,' she said, gesturing at the garden and beyond, 'or she's out *there*.'

She looked up at the sky.

And that's the end of my story. Later tonight I'll go home and feed Calico, who seems to have settled since Marie's final disappearance. He doesn't stand on the windowsill any more. He seems content. Maybe he knows something I don't.

Or maybe he's just a cat, with a short memory.

I will never forget Marie. She was the sun at the heart of my system; she was the fire in my personal hell. She changed me. She showed me the summits and the depths, the zenith and nadir of

love. I am scarred and scared – it will be a while before I am able
to open myself up again, expose myself to hurt. But I know I will.
I know how sweet love can be, and I couldn't go the rest of my life
without tasting that sweetness again.

I will only ask one thing of any future lover: that they don't
believe in aliens.

Except . . . I don't mean that. It's my attempt to make a joke
out of what I've been through (although, to be honest, it's one of
the things that stops me going out to find Zara). I've spent a lot of
time trying to make sense of it all, to squeeze some meaning, some
lesson, from my experience. To think about what Marie did in a
rational, unemotional way.

Andrew accused me of not believing in anything, an accusa-
tion I had already aimed at myself. What makes me different from
people like Marie and people who go to church, or join cults, or
become protestors or jihadists or risk their lives for a cause? I have
no religion, no great political passion, no creed that governs my life.
I don't belong to any organization. I vote, but I have never marched.

Marie's mum told me that, from when she could first talk,
Marie was 'always asking questions. She'd want to know everything.
Why did God allow people to suffer, did animals go to Heaven,
why do we have wars? All the usual stuff kids ask. There were a few
Muslim kids in her class, and Hindus. They talked about going to
the mosque or the temple. And Marie wanted to know why we
didn't go to church, started pestering her dad and me. So I took
her – her dad moaning about what a waste of time it all was – and
she loved it. Loved singing the hymns, reading all the Bible stories,
talking about Jesus like he was a pop star or something. It was sweet.
But then her dad stopped her going, told her it was all a load of
crap, that he didn't want his daughter to be a "Bible basher".

'After he left us, I thought maybe she'd start going again. But
she wasn't interested any more. She wasn't interested in anything,

I thought. Until the aliens. It started with a book she got from the library about these people who said they'd had experiences . . . you know, all the stuff she went on about. And that was it. It was like there was a hole inside her, a *space*, that needed filling. Marie had a need to believe in something different, something *better*.' She paused before making a final declaration. 'I blame her dad.'

It's easy to think that anyone who becomes a born-again Christian or gives up their life to become an animal rights protestor, or who joins a cult like the Loved Ones, is searching to fill the hole that Marie's mum talked about. That they do it because they have something missing in their lives.

And perhaps there's an element of truth in that – but what about the rest of us? Are we content, fulfilled, happy with our lot? What about me? Before I met Marie I was drifting, going through the motions, getting by day to day, like most people. My basic needs – food, shelter, water – were met. But the closest I got to spiritual ecstasy was watching my football team win the league, or buying a cool new phone. Why didn't I join a church or take up a cause?

Where was the meaning in my life?

Here is what I've concluded. That just because I don't believe in anything doesn't mean I believe in nothing. I am not a nihilist. I have rules, guidelines, morals, ethics, a code by which I live my life. I have dreams and desires. I want what most people want: a decent job, enough money to stop me worrying about getting into debt, someone to love, someone to love me back. I want kids some day. I want a family, friends, people to care for and who care about me. I want to look back on my life and feel I tried hard, that I took opportunities when they came, that I was a good person, that I didn't waste my years on this planet.

I do believe in something. I believe in people. I don't care if it sounds sappy, but I believe in love, in its redemptive and transformative powers. And I believe in myself. Or, at least, I know myself – far better now than before I met Marie.

Maybe that was the difference between Marie and me. She didn't believe in herself. She felt she needed rescuing, but for reasons of nurture or nature or both, she never built the self-belief that would give her the strength to save herself. Instead, Andrew became the person she saw as her saviour. That was her tragedy. Because I believe the only person who could save Marie was Marie herself. All I could have done was help, and my failure to do so will haunt me until I die.

Having said all that, maybe I'm wrong. Maybe Marie *was* saved. Maybe she found the fulfilment, the peace, she sought. Perhaps she's out there now, happy, all her dreams come true.

I may never know, but I hope that she found what she was looking for, even if it was in her final moment on Earth.

⌣

I lie on my back on the cold, damp grass. I close my eyes. I can hear the sea below me, and the seagulls swooping over the rocks.

The world becomes dark and I open my eyes. As always, the brightness of the stars surprises me. But now I know the names of the constellations; names that Marie taught me. That we invented. My eyes roam from star to star, and I try to imagine where she might be. Is she up there somewhere, looking down? There is still a large part of me that says no, that favours other, more rational explanations. But when I concentrate – when I really listen hard – I can hear the singing, the choir, the Chorus.

And somewhere among the choir, I hear a human voice.

Author's Note

Thanks for reading *What You Wish For*. I hope you enjoyed it. If you did and can spare a few minutes to leave a review on Amazon or Goodreads, I'd be very grateful. I love hearing from readers and you can contact me by email (mredwards@me.com), via Twitter (@mredwards) or on Facebook (facebook.com/markedwardsbooks). I promise to respond.

This book has had a long journey to publication. I started writing it way back in the 1990s, when I still had a good head of hair and was first pursuing my dreams of being a writer. At the time, *The X-Files* was massive, crop circles were always in the news and Babylon Zoo were at the top of the charts with their *Spaceman* song. Aliens were big, and that influenced me when it came to writing this book.

When I returned to the book recently, I tore the whole thing up and started again, rewriting it from scratch. But I decided to keep Marie's obsession with aliens – even though I could have changed it to something more fashionable.

Because *What You Wish For* needn't have been about alien abduction cults. This novel is about belief, and Marie could have belonged to any number of belief systems: religious, political, spiritual. For the record, my views are more like Richard's than Marie's. I am a rationalist. I want to see the hard evidence before I believe in something. It seems unlikely – impossible, even – that the Earth can be the only planet to harbour life. But I don't believe that grey, large-headed aliens regularly visit us and abduct people.

(Though at the same time, I hope they don't have Kindles on other planets. That some intelligent otherworldly being won't read this book and decide to pay me a visit . . .)

I have deliberately left the ending of *What You Wish For* open. What do you think happened to Marie and Andrew? The truth is out there, as somebody once said . . . And I'd love to know what you think.

For those of you who read *The Magpies* and are still wondering what happened to Lucy, she has a small part in *Because She Loves Me*, published September 2014. *Because She Loves Me* is similar to *The Magpies* in theme and tone, although this time the terror is even closer to home. I can't wait for everyone to read it.

Until then, thanks again for reading this book.

Mark Edwards

Acknowledgements

Thanks to:

My wife, Sara, for being a wise and honest reader and for everything you do to allow me to pursue my dreams.

Louise Voss for excellent suggestions and insight as always.

Jennifer Vince for yet another striking cover. (If you're looking to hire an excellent book cover designer, Jennifer can be contacted via www.jennifervince.com.)

Isabella Tan for the cover image and Sarah Ann Loreth.

Julia Gibbs for proofreading the manuscript. Julia can be found on Twitter @ProofreadJulia.

Sam Copeland, my fantastic agent.

Emilie Marneur and everyone at Amazon Publishing.

Andrea Walker for helping me come up with the title.

Sue Vaughan for the 'Fifty Shades of Greys' joke!

And everyone on the Voss & Edwards Facebook page (facebook.com /vossandedwards) for your constant support, help, enthusiasm and all-round awesomeness.

About the Author

Mark Earthy

Mark writes psychological thrillers. He loves stories in which scary things happen to ordinary people and is inspired by writers such as Stephen King, Ira Levin, Ruth Rendell, Ian McEwan, Val McDermid and Donna Tartt.

Mark is now a full-time writer. Before that, he once picked broad beans, answered complaint calls for a rail company, taught English in Japan, and worked as a marketing director.

Mark co-published a series of crime novels with Louise Voss. *The Magpies*, his first solo, topped the UK Kindle charts for three months when it first released. Since its success, the novel has been re-edited and published by Thomas & Mercer. Mark is now writing his next spine-tingling thriller, to be published in late 2014.

He lives in England with his wife, their three children, and a ginger cat.

He can be contacted on:
Twitter: @mredwards
Facebook: www.facebook.com/markedwardsbooks

Made in the USA
San Bernardino, CA
25 January 2020